T0067890

JAKE'S STORY PART 1

PAUL JONES

Order this book online at www.trafford.com
or email orders@trafford.com

Most Trafford titles are also available at major online book retailers.

Print information available on the last page.

ISBN: 978-1-6987-1254-3 (sc)
ISBN: 978-1-6987-1253-6 (e)

Trafford rev. 09/02/2022

www.trafford.com

North America & international
toll-free: 844-688-6899 (USA & Canada)
fax: 812 355 4082

The great William Shakespeare said, "All the world's a stage, and all the men and women merely players: they have their exits and their entrances; and one man in his time plays many parts, his acts being seven ages."

We try to take matters into our own hands. The scientist and psychiatrists say that it's all in our genes or our surroundings. They try to rule out that in this life we all have a purpose.

From the birth of Jake to his dreams, Jake's journey was not any different from others—the struggle to find his purpose and life's true meaning. Jake goes from being happy and in love to confused and frustrated, back to being happy and in love again. Follow Jake as he takes this journey and the many parts that he plays not only in his life but others as well.

Contents

The Birth of Jake

(It was about 4:00 am when the old wooden floor made a loud squeaking sound.)

JACOB. Maw is that you?
MAW. Yeah, it's me. I gots up to fix you's some breakfast and lunch.
JACOB. I gots to be leavin' pretty soon. You knows that boss don't take kindly of those who be gettin' to work late. He says that if I works hard enough, I coulds buy this here house from him. I knows the flo' squeaks, the roof leaks, and the wind blows through the walls, but this coulds be ours.
MAW. Jacob, I thoughts we be free, but you still works like a slave. And for what, this old shack! We's gots only one bedroom, and it right smack in the middle of the house.

(Jacob folded his hands together and looked down at the floor. Maw got quiet. She looked down as if she knew that she had just cut her man with a knife.)

MAW. Jacob, I is sorry, but I gots somethin' to tells you. I is late. Jacob. What you means late?
MAW. I is late! We is going to haves us a baby, and we is gonna need some mo' room.
JACOB. A baby? How? What? When? Who?
MAW. Yeah, a baby, and I knows you knows how, and you probably knows when and I knows you better knows who!
JACOB. When the little scatter bug coming? Boy or girl?
MAW. Calms down, not for a while now. And only the good Lords knows for sho if it be a boy or girl. But I reckon it bes' a boy. Jacob you's better be going. You knows that that old saw mill ain't gonna run right withouts you pulling that old horn.

(After Jacob calmed down, he thought about what Maw was saying.)

JACOB. Maw, is you gonna be okay? I hates to leave you, honey! I guess I coulds ask boss if he gots a bigger place, or if I coulds use some old lumber to adds on.

MAW. Jacob, if you's don't be gettin' outta here, we ain't gonna haves the money to take care of this here young'un.

(Jacob hurried and finished his breakfast, grabbed his lunch, and headed out the door. Jacob made it to work just in time to sound the horn. Whoa, whoop, whoa! *The horn sounded, and all of the men started hard at it. That old saw mill was just huffing and puffing. It seemed as if they had just gotten started when Jacob sounded the lunch horn.* Whoa, whoa! *Jacob knew that this would be the perfect time to talk to his boss.)*

JACOB. Boss, you's got a minute, suh?

BOSS. What you wants, boy?

JACOB. Suh, me and the missus is gonna have us a little one, and I is wondering if you's got a bigger house that we's can use.

BOSS. Hell, boy, looks like you can't keep that thang in your pants! How many do that make?

JACOB. That would be my only one, suh.

BOSS. Just one, huh? Boy, what is your name, Jacob, ain't it? Well, lookit here, boy. I is gonna do you's and that fine missus you got a favor. I is gonna take that old house off your hands.

JACOB. Boss, I didn't means to complain.

BOSS. Boy, just shut up and waits till I is finished. I gots this new buck, and he ain't gots nobody so I is gonna take your old house and gives it to him. I gots this other house off the plantation, and it needs some work, but a strong healthy bulk like you can fix it up in no time. You just come sees me after work, and we will works out the details. But for now, blow that horn, boy. Blow that horn!

(Jacob ran over to the pull cord and blew the horn like it had never been blown before. Whoa Whoop Whoa! *It sounded all over that ole mill. That evening after work, Jacob met with the boss.)*

BOSS. Jacob, my boy, I's got a pretty good deal for you. You sees I's got this ole house at the end of my farm. It's got two bedrooms an old living room and a pretty nice kitchen for the missus.

(Jacob was so excited that he couldn't wait to hear the rest from his boss.)

JACOB. I's take it!

BOSS. Hold on, lets me finish. It needs a little fixin' up—the roof, the front porch, and so' more little thangs.

JACOB. I's take it!

BOSS. Hold up. As long as you works for me, you and the missus and that new little one gots somewhere to live, I's take five mo' dollars a week out of your check and it's be like you is buying it from me.

JACOB. I's take it!

(Jacob shook the old boss's hand and started to leave.)

BOSS. Jacob, ain't you gonna ask me when can you move in and where it's at?

(The boss began to tell Jacob how to find it and told him that he could move in immediately. Jacob took off running as fast as he could. He stop by Mr. Eli's to ask if he could come by and help them move tomorrow, because he knew that the news would make his wife very happy, and besides, they didn't have much to get together. Jacob sprinted home from Mr. Eli's.)

JACOB. Maw, Maw, Maw! Where you at?

MAW. Jacob, what is you all fired up about?

JACOB. Maw, you's never guess what's happen to us today! We's done gots us a new house. We's done gots a new house!

MAW. Jacob, what in the tar nations is you talking 'bout?

JACOB. I was tellin' boss how's you done got yourself in a fix and that we's needed mo' room. He tells me that he gots this house and that we's can move in right now!

MAW. Yeah, I done did this all by myself. He just up and gave it to you?

JACOB. He says some'um 'bout five mo' dollars a week, but I's figure that I's can makes up that on the weekend doing odd jobs.

(Jacob, in all his excitement, didn't hear the boss mention that as long as he worked for him he could stay there. Being that it was the weekend and Jacob being so excited about moving, he was ready to move the very next day.)

JACOB. Maw, we's get all our stuff together tonight so we's can leave this old place in da morning!

MAW. If you says so. We is taking my good cook stove? How is we gonna move?

JACOB. You knows you gots to cooks me that hot water cornbread. I done asked Mr. Eli to comes over with his truck in da morning to help us!

(That night, Jacob and Maw gathered their stuff. Jacob knew that Mr. Eli would be there early the next morning. Morning would seem to take forever. Jacob was so ready to get out of that too small house, but there was one thing—he didn't exactly know how the other house looked, but he thought, It gots to be better than what we's in. *If only he knew. The next morning finally arrived.)*

JACOB. Maw, is you up?

MAW. I's been up and is ready to go.

(At the crack of dawn, Jacob heard a vehicle pull up in front of his house.)

JACOB. That must be Mr. Eli.

MR. ELI. Jacob, you's and da missus ready to go?

JACOB. We's ready, Mr. Eli.

MR. ELI. Wells, come on. I's got a heap of others to help out today!

(They didn't have much, but what they did have they were able to load onto the back of that old truck and trailer. After loading all their stuff on Mr. Eli's truck and trailer, Maw and Jacob walked to the truck, looking back one last time.)

MR. ELI. Jacob, you's means ta tell me that boss just lets you move out of this house into another one?

JACOB. Yeah, he tolds me that if I was to pays him five mo' dollars a week, I would be able to live there.

MR. ELI. Yeah, he done told ole Slim the same thang, but he also says that Slim had to always work fors him. If not, he's can put him out.

JACOB. Comes to thank 'bout it, I thank he did says somethang likes that.

(Maw, sitting in between the two, would say nothing, because she knew that it would be very rude to question her husband's decision in front of another man. After driving about fifteen miles deep into the Delta, they made it to the old shotgun house. It was a shotgun house true enough, but it was much larger than the one they had just left. And Jacob knew that they were going to need the room for his newborn. Mr. Eli pulled in front of the shotgun house, and they all just looked. The house was dark lumbered, the roof was tin, the porch was sagging, and while looking in the front door, you saw right out the back at the same time.)

MAW. We's here.
JACOB. Well, we is here!
MR. ELI. You's here all right.

(Jacob jumped out the old single cab truck, grabbed some of their stuff, and headed toward the old sagging porch. He placed the stuff on the old sagging porch and heard a loud squeak. He then turned around to get some more, and by this time, a maw was standing behind him, and once again, she just looked. Jacob, looking at the ground, walked past her and started unloading the rest of their stuff. It only took Jacob a few trips to the truck. With the help of Maw and Mr. Eli, the truck and trailer were quickly emptied. Months seemed to pass like days, with Jacob working two and sometimes three jobs, plus doing his best to fix up the old broken-down shotgun house. He worked very hard, because he wanted things to be right for his new baby.)

MAW. Jacob, go and gets Ms. Esther!
JACOB. Fors what?
MAW. GO AND GETS MS. ESTHER!

Jacob. My god! It's time, ain't it? Its time! I's gone!

(Jacob left out so fast that he almost took the front door with him. He ran to the old dirt road.)

JACOB. MS. ESTHER, MS. ESTHER!

(Jacob didn't have to say much more because Ms. Esther was very experience in these types of situations.)

MS. ESTHER. Jacob, now you just calms yourself. I's a coming.
JACOB. Hurry, Ms. Esther, hurry!

(As they were leaving, Jacob took off running, leaving Ms. Esther behind. Ms. Esther was also used to being left behind as well. When Jacob made it back home, he ran into the house, shouting at the top of his voice.)

JACOB. Maw, is you okay?
MAW. Jacob, what is you shouting for? I's having a baby. I's ain't deaf. I's in here in the bed. Where is Ms. Esther?
JACOB. She is right, Ms. Esther. Ms. Esther, I must have gone off and left her. I's go back.
MAW. That will be okay. I's thank she knows how to gets here.

(Ms. Esther arrived and walked into the old house, straight behind the curtains into the bedroom.)

MS. ESTHER. Maw is you okay? 'Bout how much times do we got?
MAW. I reckon I's can hold up another hour or so before this little one makes up its mind to come on out.

(From the moment Ms. Esther walked into the bedroom she knew that something wasn't right.)

MS. ESTHER. Jacob, what is you looking at? Go in there and boils me some hot water, and makes sure we gots plenty of towels. Maw, now that he is out of here, how much time?
MAW. It's a coming!
MS. ESTHER. That's what I thought. Now I's gonna needs you to push. Come on, Maw, push! I's going to needs you to push and don't stops. I's got its feet, but his head is stills in there, and if we's don't gets him on out, he just might not make it out breathing. NOW PUSH!

(*Maw pushed as hard as she could. She pushed until she nearly passed out.*)

MAW. I's can't do no mo'.

Ms. ESTHER. Maw, don't you gives up now. We done just about gots him!

MAW. Him? Mom pushed harder.

(*All of a sudden, Jacob heard a slap and a loud cry. He dropped everything he had in his hands and ran toward the room. But Ms. Esther stopped him from going behind the curtains.*)

MS. ESTHER. Jacob, holds up a minute. Maw had a hard time bringing this one in the world. It probably ain't gonna be another one. But you gots a boy and a big'un too! I ain't never seens a baby this big in all my dab burn life!

JACOB. A boy! I knew it, I knew it! Catsackit, I knew it. A boy! Cans I go in? I wants to see him, and Maw too.

MS. ESTHER. I reckon so it's your house, but try to be a little quiet. Remember, Maw had a hard time bringing him in this world.

JACOB. Maw, is you all right? It's a boy! It's a boy!

MS. ESTHER. Jacob, mind your voice, not too loud.

JACOB. It's a boy. Maw, what is we gonna name him? Maw?

(*Maw couldn't say anything because she passed out. Jacob didn't know how hard of a time Maw really had. He didn't know that, because the baby was breached, he almost didn't make it. She had such a rough time that she would never be able to have another baby.*)

MS. ESTHER. Jacob, you cans go now. Go and spread the news that Jacob Martin done gone and had himself a big healthy baby boy.

(*Ms. Esther needed to get Jacob out of the house so that she could doctor on Maw. She was hurting and still bleeding, but Ms. Esther knew exactly what to do. She was very experienced. Jacob did just that. He ran as fast as he could and told every person he came in contact with.*)

Jacob. I's got me a boy, a biggin too. I gots me a boy. He is bigger than any baby around these parts!

(Because of the hard time Maw had having the baby, it took her months to fully recover. But Jacob was patient. He waited for Maw to recover before he asked her again what they were going to name him.)

JACOB. Maw, what is we gonna name my son?

MAW. I thoughts we would names him after his paw.

JACOB. No, not Jacob. This name was given to me by my mom's master, and I is not gonna give it to my boy.

MAW. How's about Jake?

JACOB. Jake? Hmm, I's like that Jake. A real manly name Jake, Jake Martin! I's like it! My boy Jake Martin. You is gonna grow up and be educated.

(From that moment on, Jacob knew that he had to work extra hard, extra long, and just plain extra to make sure that he provided for Maw and little Jake. Yes, he knew that he had to work extra hard, but he also knew that he had to make time for his family. In everyone's eyes, Jacob was a very good man, and he loved his wife and son very much, but we all have our little secrets. Time seemed to fly by. Before they knew it, Jake was three. He was walking better and was much larger than all the kids his age, and he talked some.)

JAKE. Maw, where Jucob?

MAW. No, not Jucob, but Jacob. But you's had better be callin' him daddy.

JAKE. Maw, how comes you calls him Jucob?

MAW. Well, because that's his name.

JAKE. Thens how come I's can't calls him Jucob?

MAW. 'Cause he's your daddy, and it ain't right for you to calls him by his name.

JAKE. Cans I's calls him Pappy?

MAW. I don't thinks that he would be too happy with that either.

JAKE. So I's just calls him Dad?

MAW. Yes, Jake, you just calls him Dad.

JAKE. Why?

MAW. 'Cause I is gonna tan your hide if I ever hears you call him anything else.

JAKE. Maw, where is Dad?

MAW. He is working.

JAKE. Maw, how comes Dad works all the time?

MAW. I know, Jake, I know.

(Maw knew exactly why Jacob worked all the time. He had to make the payments and make repairs on their new house, plus he had to provide for his family. Jacob was a really good man. He provided for his family, and he always wanted Jake to have and do more than he ever accomplished. He wanted Jake to have the best things in life and wanted Jake to get an education. Whenever Jacob was at home, he was very loving. He would hold Jake and tell him different stories. He would tell Jake about his grandparents, about how they were slaves and what it truly meant to be free, and the importance of an education. Jacob not only took time out for Jake, he also loved on Maw. They would sit out together and look at the sunset.)

MAW. Jacob, I's glad you done made it home. Jake was just ta askin' me whys you be gone so much. I's didn't wants ta tells him it so we cans eat.
JACOB. Maw, I's just wants my son to have mo' than we's got. I wants him to have the best and to gets an edumacation.

(Jacob reached over and grabbed Maw and started kissing her.)

MAW. Come on now, not in fronts of Jake.
JAKE. Dad, why you always holding on to Maw? Why you and Maw always putting your faces together?
JACOB. 'Cause I loves her very much! I loves you too. Come here, boy!
JAKE. You ain't gonna put your face to mines.

(Jacob grabbed Jake hugged him and wrestled with him. A couple more years went by, and Jake was five now, and his dad, Jacob, was still working day and night. One day Jacob got up after about an hour of sleep and headed toward the ole saw mill. About nine o'clock, Maw heard a knock at the door.)

MAW. I's a coming.

(It was Mr. Eli. He stood at the front door with his hat in his hand. He didn't have to say a word Maw already knew.)

MAW. How's did it happen?

MR. ELI. He was at the saw mill, and I's guess he falls asleep. He falls into the saw, and it cuts him plum into before anybody could cuts it off.

(*Maw slowly turned and falls, to her knees she began to pray.*)

MAW. Lord, you knows Jacob was a good man. He didn't go to church much, but he had a good heart. He was baptized when he was a young'un, and, Lord, I's knows that Jacob took a drank every now and then, but he always said that it was for his health, but I's thank that we both knew better. I guess what I's trying to ask is that when my man Jacob comes a knockin' on those pearly gates, you will have mercy and let him in. Amen.

MR. ELI. Maw, is you gonna be all right?

MAW. Me and Jake is gonna be just fine. I reckon the Lord was getting us prepared for this by keepin' my Jacob away so much.

(*As years passed, Maw kept busy and made a living by washing other people's clothes. Over time, the old boss at the saw mill died and his son, Lenny, who was older than Jake, took over.*)

MAW. Jake, here is the money for the house. Takes it over to Mr. Lenny.

JAKE. Maw, how much longer does we got on this old house?

MAW. I don't rightly know. Just takes this money and gives it to Mr.

LENNY. He the boss now.

(*Jake was about eleven now and had started some school, but he would miss more days than he attended. But on his way to pay Mr. Lenny, he would have to pass right by the school house. He tried to walk on the far side of the dirt road, wishing that an old truck or buggy would pass so that Mrs. Jackson wouldn't see him. He had no such luck.*)

MRS. JACKSON. Jake, Jake Martin, you coming to school?

JAKE. I's got ta take this house money for my maw.

MRS. JACKSON. Jake Martin, you will try anything to not come to class. What would your mother say if I was to tell her that you haven't been to class all week?

JAKE. I's coming, but you can't make me learn.

(By this time, Jake was really bigger than most kids his age. He was naturally built. He had muscles on top of muscles. The other children would have made fun of him, but they were too afraid. He would try to sit in the desks, but they were too small, so he just sat at the table and pretended to pay attention. Jake was eleven, but according to his teacher, he was only on the third-grade level. He wasn't a dumb child; he just thought he had better things to do.)

MRS. JACKSON. Jake Martin, what are you doing?

JAKE. Huh?

MRS. JACKSON. Jake, how are you planning to go to college if you don't pay attention and do your work? Don't you know that you are already behind most of your classmates?

JAKE. I don't care.

(Jake got up from the table and left the school house. He continued on his way to see Mr. Lenny so that he could give him the house money.)

JAKE. Mr. Lenny, did you goes to school?

LENNY. Naw.

JAKE. Why do they makes such a big deal out of it anyhow?

LENNY. I's don't know.

JAKE. You is makin' it okay, and you ain't had no schoolin'. Oh, here is the money for our house.

LENNY. The money is fine. Yeah, I's doing okay, but my dad done leave me and maw a lot of money. Did your dad leaves you and your maw a lot of money?

JAKE. Naw, we ain't got no money. Maw washes clothes for other folk so that we's can pay for our house.

LENNY. Oh. Jake, I's got to go. I's got to make sure these lazy boys work. Saw mill ain't gonna run by itself. We can talk some mo' later.

(Later that evening, while Jake and his mother were sitting on the front porch, Mrs. Jackson walked up.)

MAW. While howdy, Mrs. Jackson. What cans I do for ya? Can I gets you some fresh lemonade? How's 'bout a tea cake?

MRS. JACKSON. Hello, Maw. No thank you. Maw, did you know that Jake has missed more days of school than he has attended?

He cares little about doing his work, and he just walked out of class today while I was speaking with him.

MAW. What? Jake, you means to tells me that you ain't been goin' to class? Po' old Jacob must be turnin' over in his grave. Mrs. Jackson, I sho' is glad you's stop by. I's take care of this.

(As Mrs. Jackson was walking off, Mr. Lenny walked up.)

LENNY. Howdy, Maw, how is you been?

MAW. I's been doing purty good.

LENNY. Maw, I's got something to tells you. The money Jake gave me this morning I's come to gives it back.

MAW. Huh? Gives it back? Ain't it no good?

LENNY. Maw, you and Jake done been livin' here for enough years, and you done gave me enough money. You ain't got to gives me no more money. The house is yours, and here is the money back that Jake done gave me this morning.

MAW. Praise God. Thank ya, Jesus!

(Maw stood there with tears running down her cheeks. She knew then that everything was going to be all right. Maw offered Mr. Lenny some tea cakes and some fresh lemonade.)

LENNY. No, thank ya, Maw, but I's got to be runnin', I's do got a business to run.

(That evening, Maw almost forgot about Jake not going to school, but Jake wouldn't have any such luck.)

MAW. Jake, gets in here!

JAKE. Yes, Maw.

MAW. Jake, you know why your daddy was never here, why he worked all the time? When you were born, he made a promise that you's would not have ta work in that ole saw mill. He says that he wanted you to go to school and gets the edumacation that he never did. And now here you is not even trying. You means to tells me that my po' Jacob did all that hard work for nothing?

(Jake stood there with tears in his eyes because he knew that his maw was telling the truth, that he wasn't even trying to go to school. And to be honest, until this point, he didn't care about school.)

JAKE. Maw, I promise that I's gonna get my edumacation no matter how long it take. I's gonna get it.

(Later that night, Jake started thinking about how he was going to make his daddy proud. The next morning, Jake went to school, and he became the student that his maw thought he could be. He made decent grades, but he was still no rocket scientist. Years went by for Jake and his maw. She still did other people's laundry, and Jake did odd jobs for people just to make ends meet. By this time, it was time for Jake's graduation.)

MAW. Jake, I's so proud of you. I's knowed you could do it. I's know Jacob is proud also.

JAKE. Momma nows that I's about to graduate from high school, what next?

The Dream

(Jake had just decided it was time to do something with his life; after all, he had just turned twenty-two and was fresh out of high school. He had no job and not really any skills, but he really wanted to do what was right. He turned to his mother, and you know mothers; she gave him the best advice that she knew to give.)

MAW. Son, you needs to go to college to make it in this old world. You needs more edumacation.

(All was fine, but Maw, not having any education at all, didn't have any idea on telling her son how to get into college.)

JAKE. That is it! I is going to college. Thank you, but I's gots one question … What's I must do first?

(Jake knew exactly what to do. That night, Jake got his old notebook, pen, and pencil together and decided he was going to college the next day. That night, Jake was so tired that he fell into a deep sleep, thinking of nothing but college. The next morning seemed to have come so quickly; it was as if he didn't get any sleep at all. It didn't matter because Jake was so anxious to go to college, he damn near choked on the wood-like sausage his mother had prepared for breakfast.)

JAKE. Maw, I is off to college. I wonders what type of class they is gonna put me in, and who will my teachers be?

(Jake went to the community college. He had to walk, but it was only about twenty miles. Once he had made it into town, all the different sights overtook him. The town was so big; it had a population of 2010. Jake thought, "I is here I finally made it." Once Jake went in and he saw all the paperwork involved in going to college and with the administrators talking over his head, he slowly began to think that college was not for him. Jake turned around and ran as fast as his feet could take him. Jake not wanting to disappoint his mother didn't know what to do next. He walked around thinking, "I did not know that getting into college would be so hard." Jake didn't want to face that college crowd again, but he did remember hearing about this man. He was a black man, a rich black man, Mr. Eli! Jake saw this older woman, and he asked her if she knew Mr. Eli. She tore into him; she told him that he should stay away from that ole no-good snake. The reply he got wasn't too nice, but he didn't care about what the old woman was talking about, so he continued looking for Mr. Eli. Jake saw a sharp-dressed black man; he had on a lime-green leisure suit, a lime-green gangster hat with a long feather sticking out of it, and a pair of shoes that would make a circus midget six feet tall.)

JAKE. That gots to be him. That gots to be him, Mr. Eli! Sharp-dressed man. Mr. Eli? Boy, who you call me?

JAKE. It gots to be you. Your clothes ... you is the sharpest-dressed man around here!

SHARP-DRESSED MAN. If I is this Eli fella, what in Sam's Hill you want with him?

JAKE. Well, you see, I wants to do somethin' with my life to makes my momma proud of me.

SHARP-DRESSED MAN. I guess you wants to go to college. You see, there ain't nothing wrong with that, but it takes money. Do you gots any money?

JAKE. Naw, I ain't gots no money, and if you ain't Mr. Eli, you can't helps me no how.

SHARP-DRESSED MAN. Well, boy, you is lookin' at the one and only Mr. Eli.

JAKE. Mr. Eli, I knew it. I knew it! Mr. Eli did you goes to college?

MR. ELI. Naw, I ain't went to no college, and look at me!

JAKE. Well, how did you gets to be so rich?

MR. ELI. Boy, I could tells you, but you won't learns, but I could learns you if you wants to learns.

JAKE. Learn me, Mr. Eli, Learn me!

MR. ELI. Boy, do you really wants to learn?

JAKE. Yeah, I wants to learn. I wants you to learn me, so I cans be like you, I wants to be just like you!

MR. ELI. Okay, boy, I's gonna tell you what. You meets me here damorrow morning, at seven o'clock, and don't be late.

(Jake was very excited about having met the infamous Mr. Eli. He was so excited that he had forgotten all about going to college. It was getting kind of late, and he did have a pretty good distance to cover before he would make it home, so he decided that he better get started. When Jake finally made it home, his mother was on the front porch, waiting for him.)

MAW. How was your first day of college?

JAKE. It was a heap mo' than I thought it to be.

MAW. I bakes us a cake to celebrate.

JAKE. Momma, you ought not done that.

MAW. Boy, you just hush and eat so we can enjoy this here cake.

(That night, Jake was so excited that he could not get any sleep, so he just sat in bed, thinking of all the money he was going to make. He did not think about how he was supposed to make this money; all he knew was he was going to make a lot of money. With morning finally arriving, Jake was so anxious that he could not eat any breakfast. He decided to skip breakfast altogether so he could hurry down to meet with Mr. Eli. Once Jake made it into town, he went about two or three blocks before he saw this tall image of a man he thought he wanted to be like.)

MR. ELI. Boy, you is late.

JAKE. But you tells me to meets you here at seven o'clock, and it just 7:05 now.

MR. ELI. Listens, boy, when I's says 7:00, I means 6:55. You gots that? Don't lets it happen again, or you be back at home, sucking on your momma … Well, just don't let it happen again.

(Mr. Eli saw that he was being just a little too hard on the poor old country boy, plus Jake was a mountain of a man someone Mr. Eli didn't want to make mad, so he decided to cut him a little slack, just a little.)

JAKE. What I does first?

MR. ELI. First of all, you shuts your mouth and pays close attention. This is what I wants you to do. Do you sees that brown paper bag?

(Jake picked up the paper bag.)

MR. ELI. Put it down, stupid! What you doing, boy? Boy, I's don't knows if I should waste my time with you. Just wait until I tell you to pick it up. You can picks it up now.

JAKE. Picks it up now?

MR. ELI. Yeah, picks it up. If you is every picked up, never ever mentions my name. Gots that?

JAKE. Picked up? Picked up by who?

(Mr. Eli went on to explain the business to Jake, who was not as sure as he was before that this was what he still wanted to do. Mr. Eli saw that he was losing Jake, so he pulled out a hundred- dollar bill and gave it to the young man. Mr. Eli knew that he had to do something to get Jake back on the same level of excitement as before. Jake's eyes bulked, and he had a smile on his face as wide as the Mississippi itself. Mr. Eli knew that a young man like Jake could be very valuable to him. Mr. Eli knew that he had to give Jake something very simple to do for his first assignment. He decided not to send him with the paper bag. He decided to send Jake on a little lookout job.)

MR. ELI. Go to the next corner and tells me when you sees somebody a-coming—you know, any strange persons.

(Mr. Eli didn't want to come out and tell Jake to look out for the police, but that was what he really wanted. He was sure that an old country boy like Jake was always taught to respect the police, and he didn't want to put any doubt in his mind again. Jake, not sure about what to do, walked to the corner and just stood there. Jake must have stood there for hours before he saw his first car approaching. Jake, not knowing what to do, looked over his shoulder. He looked for Mr. Eli, but he was not there. The car pulled beside him and came to a screeching stop. A big, fat, sweaty, smelly, doughnut-eating, pale-color hog of a man, with a badge on his chest and a gun on his hip, wiggled his way out of the car.)

OFFICER. Ay, boy, what the hell is you doing on my corna?

JAKE. I is jut, jut, just standing here, sur.

(That big potbellied pig grabbed Jake by the back of his neck and slammed his face into the hood of that car. He slammed him so hard that he must have left an imprint of Jake's face on the hood.)

OFFICER. Boy, I knows you ain't up to no good, and if I sees you on my corna or any of my cornas again, I is gonna bust your ass. You gots that, boy?

(That big redneck pig somehow got back into that sardine can of a car and drove off, as if he was in a hurry. Jake, about to wet his pants, waited until he was out of sight before he took off running. He did not know where he was running to, but he just knew that he had to get away. Just as soon as Jake turned the corner, there stood Mr. Eli.)

MR. ELI. Boy, you did real good.

JAKE. You means to tell me that you saw that big, fat stankin', redneck put his hands on me?

MR. ELI. Sure I did, and you's did reals good by not talking too much.

(Mr. Eli knew that Jake's idea about the police had just changed, and that was what he was counting on. He knew that he had to develop his own opinion of the police. He went on to give him some advice for the next time he might encounter a run-in with the police. By the time, Mr. Eli was finished teaching, it was getting late.)

JAKE. It seems to be gettin late, ain't it?

MR. ELI. Yeah, you ought to be rushin' home afore you momma gets worried. One day you be able to stay out late.

(He knew that he would soon need Jake for more important things, but he had to first get him from under his mother's skirt. Jake had to hurry. He knew his mother would be up waiting for him.)

MAW. Jake, where is you been? You knows I don't want you hangin' on no cornas after school.

JAKE. I ain't been on no corna. I is been lookin' for a job.

(Jake went to his hole-filled room after eating dinner and rested. He lay on a mattress that had more lumps in it than badly cooked grits. Jake began thinking, "I really wants to do good. I's wants to make my momma proud of me.")

MAW. Jake, it's time you got those bones out of bed.

(Jake thought, "So soon?" Jake finally got out of bed, thinking he might stay home today, but he knew that if he stayed home, Mr. Eli would be very upset. He hurried his breakfast down and kissed his mother, and then he rushed to the door. Just before he went out the door, he noticed some new things in the hole-filled house.)

JAKE. Momma, did we find some money?
MAW. Boy, don't you be talking silly. You done told me to fix up this old place and with the money you gives me.

(Jake, scratching his head, seemed very confused. He knew that Mr. Eli had given him that hundred, but even he knew that a hundred dollars could not buy all the things his mother had brought. On his way to see Mr. Eli, Jake saw what he thought to be the most beautiful girl in the world. He was looking at her so hard that he ran into a light pole. He quickly looked up and around to see if anyone was looking at him. He saw her cutting her eyes and smiling. He was more embarrassed than hurt. He picked up his pride, dusted himself off, and continued on his way to see Mr. Eli.)

JAKE. Mr. Eli, I just seen the most beautifulest girl in the whole world. She was 'bout tall as that old scarecrow, as pretty as a newborn pup, and her body … it was just too much!

(Jake saw her and pointed her out to Mr. Eli.)

MR. ELI. Where? Oh, shut, boy. I thought you wuz talking 'bout somebody. That trash. She done been round mo' times than a Ferris wheel.
JAKE. What you mean, done been around?
MR. ELI. Boy, is you that green? Never mind. You just find it your business to stay away from her. She ain't nothing but bad news.

(Jake heard him, but it was too late. Jake knew that he had to get to know that woman. It was something about the way she made him feel. It was a feeling like a pig in a fresh bucket of warm slob.)

JAKE. Mr. Eli, could you please help me? She just do something to me. Every time I sees her, she make my … my … you know!

MR. ELI. Naw, I doesn't knows she make your what do what?

JAKE. Well, she makes my pants swell!

MR. ELI. Your pants swell. Boy, what in the hell is you talking about? Oh, I gets it. You means to tells that you ain't never been with no woman before? You means to tell me that my boy here is a virgin? Boy, how old is you?

JAKE. I is twenty-two.

MR. ELI. Hell, boy, I guess I is got to get you laid!

JAKE. What is so funny? I done seen plenty of women, and I even kissed this gal on the lips too.

(Mr. Eli was getting tired of this small talk.)

MR. ELI. Boy, that is enough of this talk. We gots thangs to do and money to make. Jake, takes this bag down the street and give it to Slim. You will know him. He looks just like his name, and 'member, don't stop and talk to nobody!

(Jake knew that if he went down the street, he would see the girl of his dreams, so he decided that if she was out, he would say something to her. Jake didn't get three blocks away before he could smell her perfume, and just as soon as he turned the corner, there she stood. Jake stopped and took a breath.)

JAKE. Hi, what's your name? My name is Jake, and I seen you standing here a couple of hours ago.

(She told him her name as if it really hurt her in doing so.)

YOUNG LADY. Faydra!

FAYDRA. My friends call me Faye, but seeing that we ain't friends, you can calls me Faydra!

JAKE. I would like to become your friend. You looks so good to me, and I ain't never saw no woman made up like you. How 'bout it? Can I be your friend?

FAYE. That depends on what you got in that bag.

JAKE. What you mean? What in the bag? What do that gots to do with anythang?

FAYE. You knows, you is cute, and those muscles, I could do a lot with all that.

(Jake, an old country boy, might have been dumb, but he was a mountain of a man, and he wasn't bad-looking at that. Now we get to Faye. Faye, how can I say this, without getting ugly? Faye had a body that would put a coke bottle to shame. From what I heard about her, she also knew how to use that body, and often did she use it.)

JAKE. I gots to be leavin'. if Mr. Eli…

FAYE. Mr. Eli, is you workin' for that no-good son of a…

JAKE. Don't you badmouth Mr. Eli! I's gots to be goin'. Can I sees you later?

FAYE (*under her breath*). Oh, he is working for that snake in the grass. This is gonna be mo' fun than I ever dreamed. Sure you can see me later.

(Faye, keeping her distance, followed Jake to see just where he was taking that paper bag. Jake, not looking to be followed, didn't see Faye behind him. He delivered the package to Slim (Lenny). Lenny was one of the poorest excuses for a dope dealer, even less of a human being.)

JAKE. Here the package, Lenny.

LENNY. Boy, what da hell takes you so long?

JAKE. I knows that I's a little late, but…

LENNY. But nothin'. Just waits till Mr. Eli gets wind of this.

JAKE. Lenny, you's just gots to help me!

LENNY. Help you with what, fool? Is you in trouble?

JAKE. Naw, I ain't in no trouble, but this girl…

LENNY. Gal … I thought yo says that you ain't in no type of trouble. Well, tells me about her.

JAKE. She is the most beautifulest creature I done ever saw.

LENNY. Yeah, yeah, tells me 'bout the body.

JAKE. The body is like a picture-book girl. She gots mo' curves than that old Coon Creek Road.

LENNY. Daaamn, boy, do this gal gots a name?

JAKE. She sho' do. Her name is Faydra.

LENNY. Faydra, I's don't thank I's knows hur at all.

JAKE. Well, she saids that all hur friends call hur Faye.

LENNY. Holy Moses, booy, you's talkin 'bout ha ha ha ha, whoa ... You's talking 'bout nas nice FAYE. Yeah, she sho' is a fine one all right.

(Jake, being confused, didn't know what to think. He knew it was getting late, and he had to finish his business and get home to his mother before it got too late.)

MR. ELI. Boy, what done took you so long, and where is my money? I know you gots to go! Boy, but you is forgettin' two thangs—one is my money, and two I tells you when you gots to go!

JAKE. Mr. Eli, here is yo money. I's thought that I's was finish for the day. My momma will worry if I's...

MR. ELI. Looks here, boy, I's 'bout to let you's go.

(Around the corner peeping in on Mr. Eli and Jake was Faye, and she had a scheme of her own. Mr. Eli told Jake that he could go. Jake started home, but Faye had other plans for this young virgin. Jake was about halfway home when he ran into Faye.)

JAKE. Faye, what is you doin' here?

FAYE. Well, I's was thankin' 'bout you, and I's wants to know some mo' 'bout you.

JAKE. Well, I's on my ways home now.

FAYE. Do you gots to be there now, or do you gots a little time?

JAKE. Well, I's guess I's gots some time yet.

(Faye knew then that she had him right where she wanted him. She asked him to go for a walk in the woods with her.)

JAKE. What fur?

FAYE. I thank that the woods is so romantic this time of evening!

JAKE. Yeah, romantic, what you mean?

FAYE. Ha, ha, ha, you means to tells me that you is that, well, let's just says green. Well, I's guess I's just gonna have to teach you.

(Faye began doing things to Jake that he never dreamed of. Jake's eyes were crossing, his toes were popping, he felt lightheaded, and he felt as if his heart had moved down into his pants. Jake let out a scream so loud that it could have awakened the dead. Faye didn't know what to think. Then she realized what had just happened.)

FAYE. This was your first one!

(Several minutes passed. In the back of Jake's mind, he knew that he had to get home.)

JAKE. Cans I sees you later?

(Faye didn't answer.)

MAW. Jake, where is you been? Look at your britches. They is so dirty? You knows what time it is? Did you has to works late? Well, yo supper is kept. Boy, you knows you better not sat at my table with those dirty britches!
JAKE. Momma, you don't knows how hungry I is!
MAW. You must have had a hard day of work.
JAKE. If you only knew how hard!

(All night, Jake tossed and turned. He could not sleep for thinking about Faye. The next morning, he could not wait to go tell Lenny what had happened. Before he could reach Lenny, he ran into Faye. Like a schoolboy after his first kiss, Jake smiled and kicked the ground, but to his surprise, Faye acted as if she didn't see him at all. Jake ran and stopped in front of her, making sure that she saw him.)

FAYE. Excuse me, but you can gets out of my face.
JAKE. But, Faye, it me Jake!
FAYE. And so what that 'pose to mean?
JAKE. Don't cha want ta see me?
FAYE. Looks here, Jake, until you is done messing with that low-down snake in the grass Mr. Eli, I ain't gots nothing to say to ya.

JAKE. Now, Faye, you knows I can't stop messin' with him 'cause he pays me. He pays real good!

FAYE. Well, Jake, I guess we ain't gots nothing else to say, and you can just go for walks in the woods with him, bye!

(Jake was torn up on the inside. He had not felt this bad, not since he had to kill his pet pig for food. Jake still felt as if he had to find Lenny. He wanted to tell him about the day before and ask him how he could keep Faye and continue to keep working for Mr. Eli.)

JAKE. Lenny, guess what done happen to me on my way home yesterday?

LENNY. Let me guess. You gots wet.

JAKE. Naw, it don't rain yesteda, but I was on da way home when all da sudden … Faye was right…

LENNY. Hold on, boy, you says Faye was there? You mean she was waiting for ya? She was where?

JAKE. I was 'bout half da way home when there she was in da front of me.

LENNY. You aims to tell that gal just happen to be in da same neck of the woods as you?

JAKE. What is you trying to say? Anyhow, on my way here today, I runs into her, and she tolds me that if I wanted to see her some mo' I's gots to quit my job.

LENNY. Boy, I is trying to tells you that no-good stankin' B ain't up to no good! I is gonna tells Mr. Eli as soons as I sees him. He gonna be one mad boss!

JAKE. Lenny, you cain't tells him, you just cain't!

LENNY. Listen, boy, I is just trying to help you.

(Jake, fearing what Mr. Eli might do to him and most of all to Faye, knew that he had to do something to get Lenny's mind off what they had just spoke of. Jake panicked; he picked up an old tire iron off the ground and started hitting Lenny in the head. He must have hit him nine or ten times before he came back to his senses. Blood was gushing out. It was all over Jake. It was everywhere. There Lenny lay in the cold, dark, bloodstained alley, with a stone cold killer standing over him, thinking about how good it felt to have such power—the power to take another's life. Jake knew he had to get cleaned up before he saw Mr. Eli, but there was one problem. He didn't know where to go. Faye was

the only person that would come to mind, but how was he to find her? He was covered with blood, so he couldn't just began asking people. Jake spotted her, but she was on the other side of the street. He ducked and dodged and made his way over to her, but seeing the blood on him, she was afraid to approach him.)

FAYE. Jake! What in the name of … ?

JAKE. Faye! Just hush up and listen. You member Lenny…

FAYE. That stooge?

JAKE. Yeah, you know he be Mr. Eli's number-one man. Well, I done, done away with him. You see, he was talking sumin' bad 'bout cha!

FAYE. Jake, you fool! Boy, you ain't got the sense God gives a mule. We is gots to get cleaned up.

(Jake and Faye made their way to her one-bedroom apartment, which Jake thought was the best thing ever. Faye began cleaning Jake. He could not help that he still had feelings for her—after all, he had just killed for her. He began touching, rubbing, and kissing her as she finished cleaning him. At first, Faye was fighting her feelings. She was trying not to get caught up in the heat of the moment, but she knew she wanted him as much as he wanted her, if not more.)

JAKE. Don't fight it, Faye. You know that I loves you.

FAYE. Noooo, Jake, it's over with. I told you that we could not do this no more, not until…

JAKE. Faye, you feels so good to me. You is so wet. YEAH!

FAYE. Oh Jake, Jake, Jake! You gots to go now. You gots to go! I don't want to gets caught up with no killer.

JAKE. You means to tells me you is gonna put me out?

FAYE. You gots to go. Leave!

(Jake left, not looking back. If only he had looked back, he would have seen Faye begging him to stay, not with her voice but with her eyes. Jake left. He went to the only place he knew he would be welcomed. He went home, went to his mother, but when he made it to the front porch, it was something missing, something missing indeed. There were no smells—no smell of cornbread cooking in the oven, and no smell of beans on the stove. Jake knew that something was not right.)

JAKE. Momma!

(There was no answer. Jake ran into the old broken-down house only to find his old mother lying on the kitchen floor. Jake fell to his knees with tears in his eyes. He knew that his mother was no longer with him. Several days passed, but with Jake's mother passing, he had such an empty feeling he couldn't explain it, but he just knew he couldn't stay in that old house any longer. It had been several weeks after his mother's funeral. Jake finally decided to go into town. Who was the first person he would run into?)

MR. ELI. Hello, Jake, my boy. I hates to hear 'bout your momma, but you might have heard that I's had a loss myself. Yeah, somebody up and took a tire iron to po' old Lenny's head, and just beat him to death. Po', po' Lenny.

JAKE. Yeah! That is too bad 'bout po' old Lenny.

(Jake, feeling guilty about the deaths of Lenny and his mother, knew that he had to get away. Jake left. Where he was going, he did not know. All Jake knew was that he had to get away. It didn't matter how far Jake ran, he would find himself in the same place. He finally decided he would run no more, so he went to the only place he thought he could go.)

FAYE. What is you doing back here?

JAKE. Faye, I's knows that you don't wants me here, but I's gots nowhere else to go.

FAYE. I's ain't trying to be mean, but what 'bout home?

JAKE. No!

FAYE. Whys not, it's all yours, ain't it?

JAKE. I's just can't go back to that old broken-down shack.

(Faye was very upset, but at the same time, she felt sorry for Jake. She felt even sorrier than he could ever imagine. Faye knew that if she were to tell him her secret, it would just ruin his life, what little life he had left. She decided to tell him that she was pregnant.)

FAYE. Jake, I's understanding the pain you is in, but I gots to tell you this. Jake, I is pregnant, and it ain't yours. It ain't your baby! It's Lenny's.

(Jake was without words. He was so upset that he felt the steam rise from his feet to his head. He knew that if he didn't leave, he would probably do

something that he was taught never to do. That was to hit a woman. Once again, Jake didn't know where he was going, but he knew that he had to get out of there. He took off running, and he ran as hard and as fast as he could for as long as he could. He ran until he couldn't run anymore. He ran until he just collapsed. Jake must have been out for at least an hour. He suddenly felt the warm gentle touch of what he thought to be his mother's hand. Jake slowly opened his eyes, and to his disbelief, it was his mother, and he was in his hole-filled room, with the sunlight coming in from the loose-fitting boards. For, you see, Jake was awakened from his dream.)

JAKE. Momma, what is you doing here?

MAW. Boy, what is you talking about? I's do lives here, don't I?

JAKE. Momma, woulds you be a whole lot mad if I's changed my mind about college?

MAW. Baby, your old momma just wants you to be happy, and I is always gonna love you no matter what.

(Jake got out of bed and went into the same old broken-down kitchen to wash his face. He sat down with his momma. He sat there with a huge smile on his face, thinking how good he had it. Jake knew his life was grand, yet there was something still missing. Two years had passed, and Jake was still home with his mother. He and his mother were still happy together, but one night, while they were sitting down at the dinner table, Jake knew that he had to talk to his mother about his feelings.)

JAKE. Momma, I is gots to talk to you.

MAW. What you wants to talk 'bout, baby?

JAKE. Momma, I knows that I loves you a whole lots, but I feels like I needs more. I feels like I is missing something.

MOMMA. Jake, baby, I knows that this time was a coming, and I knows the reasons why you feels this way.

JAKE. Momma, if you knows, then tell me so I can know.

MOMMA. Jake, you sees you's a man now, baby, and you needs to get out and finds what is in this old world for you. I knows that you still loves me, but, baby, it is a lots mo' that your momma can't gives you.

JAKE. Momma, what is you trying to say? You done been here all my life. You done give me everythang I needs.

MOMMA. Jake, boy, don't be so dumb. Boy, you needs a woman! Jake, baby, you's 'member when you was tellin' me 'bout that dream you had and that gal Tray was in it?

JAKE. You mean, Faye?

MOMMA. That let me knows that it was time for you to go.

JAKE. Momma, I's gots to go to haves a woman.

MOMMA. Jake, boy, does you see anymo' womens around here besides the ones that done growed up here, and they gots two or three babys? Jake, I is gonna let you make your own mind up on what you must do.

(That night, Jake studied long and hard. He knew that his mother was right, because every night for the past month or so, he was not able to sleep. It was hard. It was really hard. Jake was having all types of dreams with all of ending the same way, with him having to get up in the middle of the night to clean himself. Morning came. Jake knew that he had to make up his mind. Oh, his mind was made up. He was going to leave. He just didn't know when and where he was going to go. He thought about it long and hard, until...)

MOMMA. Jake, boy, I guess you's be heading out and lookin' for that Faye gal?

(While Jake wasn't too sure about when he was leaving, it had just become clear to him which direction he was going to head. Jake knew that he had to leave, but he didn't want to leave his mother behind.)

MOMMA. Jake, boy, don't you go and worry 'bout me. I's gonna be all right. Now you gets up from my table so I can clean my kitchen.

(Jake slowly got up from the table and went into his hole-filled room, and he looked around as if it would be his last time in that room. He only had a bundle of clothes to get, so he grabbed his bundle and turned to leave, but before leaving, he turned, with tears in his eyes, to get one last look at his room.)

JAKE. Momma, I's guess I is ready to go.
MOMMA. Jake, baby, you's just don't forget where you's come from. I loves you. Now gets gone before I does something.

(Mother turned with tears in her eyes, knowing that indeed this would be the last time she would see her son. It was only two weeks after Jake had left that his mother's illness finally became too much for her to handle. One day, while she was cleaning, she just collapsed, never to rise again.)

Jake

(Jake had gone to this wonderful city that he had dreamed about. When he arrived, he found that things were not as much different from what they were in his dreams. Instead of seeing one Mr. Eli, he saw dozens of what he thought to be sharp-dressed men and women. He felt somewhat ashamed because his shirt did not come over the front of his pants and his pants were too short. Jake had been in town about three weeks, and not yet had he heard about his mother's passing, nor did he take the time out to write her. You see, as soon as he made it into town, he met a young what you might or might not call a lady. She was the type you wouldn't write home to mother about. She even made Faye appear to be a saint.)

JAKE. Nikki, I's thank I's need to be writin' home to sees 'bout Momma.

NIKKI. Jake, you ain't gots to do nothing but what I tells you to do!

JAKE. But, Nikki, I's needs to…

NIKKI. What I's tell you, fool? You says you wants to have money and you's wants your momma to be proud of you. You gots to do whats I says! Besides, you knows I is the only one that loves you.

(Nikki knew exactly how to get Jake. She took his hand and placed it upon her mountainous breast while she gently massaged his inner thigh area with her other hand until he could not take it. Nikki had yet to sleep with Jake because they never got passed the rubbing without Jake wetting his pants.)

JAKE. Nikki, stop. You knows what you does to me. You knows that I has to make these runs for us some money, and I's can't does that all sticky.

(Nikki knew exactly what she was doing. She had control of the most powerful mind Jake had, and she used it to the fullest.)

NIKKI. Yeah, you right. Run on and make us some money, baby.

(What Jake didn't know was as soon as he left the house, Clyde came in. Clyde was one of several of Nikki's so-called used to be lovers.)

CLYDE. Nikki, where you done sent that po' old dumb country boy?
NIKKI: Listen here, Clyde. Don't you go talking 'bout Jake that way.
CLYDE. You listen. Don't you be getting sweet in that dumb…
NIKKI. I ain't gettin sweet on nobody, it just…
CLYDE. Just what?
NIKKI. Just that he knows how to makes me feels good.
CLYDE. You's trying to say I don't knows what I's doin'?

(Nikki failed to answer him fast enough. Clyde slapped Nikki to the floor. He then ripped her blouse off and jumped on top of her.)

NIKKI. No, no, no, don't stop, don't, stop.
CLYDE. Does that po' old dumb country boy makes you feel like that?
NIKKI. No, baby, no.

(Clyde would have killed Nikki if he only knew what she was really thinking. Nikki wanted to kill Clyde, but this was one man that she could not control. Jake was walking in the rain, trying to make his delivery when he saw this beautiful young lady that reminded him of his mother. You see, Jake's mother was a beautiful dark-skinned woman. She was so dark that she made Hershey's chocolate look pale. This woman had beautiful short jet-black hair and big bright shining brown eyes. She had a set of lips that looked as soft and smooth as a newborn baby's bottom. Her skin was about as black as her hair, but it was ravishing black, not too dry, nor too oily, and a body that would take first place in any contest. Jake wanted to meet her. He wanted to meet her in the worst way. He wanted to meet her so badly that he had a fancy for her right there on the spot. But poor old Jake was afraid to say anything to her, because he

thought, "What a beautiful lady like that wanted with the like of me?" Then Jake remembered that he had Nikki back at the house, waiting on him. At that moment, something happened. She turned and started walking toward him. She was walking fast, trying to get out of the rain. In her hurry, she bumped into Jake's shoulder.)

JAKE. Pardon me.
YOUNG LADY. No, excuse me. I bumped you.
JAKE. That is all right. You coulds bump me anytime.
YOUNG LADY. You are so sweet.
JAKE. If you pardon me for saying, you is the most beautifulest lady I every set my eyes to, besides my momma. Can I ask your name?
YOUNG LADY. Well, yes, you may ask my name. It's Cleo Jones. My friends call me Cleo, so I guess you may call me Cleo. Your name is?
JAKE. My n-n-name huh, uh, my name is Jake!
CLEO. Well, Jake, do you have a last name?
JAKE. I was just figuring if maybe you's be walkin' the same way I is, we can walk with each other. My last name is Martin.
CLEO. Well, Jake Martin, I am going the same direction as you are, and yes, you may walk with me.
JAKE. You sho' does talk funny.
CLEO. Well, Jake, I guess I would sound funny to you, but I think that I'm speaking correct English. I may slip every once in a while, but I try.
JAKE. You thank you's can learn me this correct English?
CLEO. Jake, it may take some long hard hours on your behalf, but yes, if you are willing to learn, I'm willing to try. Jake, is there a way that I can get in touch with you?

(What Jake didn't know was that Cleo was also looking at him and that she actually bumped him on purpose to get to know him.)

JAKE. I's can meets you right here.
CLEO. Oh, I see. Is there a Mrs. Martin?
JAKE. Naw, it ain't no Mrs. Martin. I stays with this friend, but she ain't my girl or nothing.
CLEO. She's not your girl? Does she know that? Never mind. I'm getting too deep into your business. Well, I guess it'll be okay

if I give you my phone number. You seem harmless enough. Of course, I don't want to get you into any trouble.

JAKE. I ain't gonna get in no trouble.

CLEO. Well, I'm here. I guess I'll see you later. That's if you can get out. Oh, and here is my phone number.

(Cleo smiled and walked right into the high-rise building. Jake knew then that she was the one for him, but he hadn't forgotten about Nikki. He knew that getting rid of her was not gonna be easy. However, for the moment, as he walked home, he could do nothing but think about Cleo.)

NIKKI. What took you so long? You was late with the package, and what you done been doing?

JAKE. I's ain't been doin' nothing!

NIKKI. Who you raising your voice at?

JAKE. It ain't but two of us in this room, and I ain't talking to myself!

(Nikki had never seen Jake like this. She knew that she had better not push him too far. You need to remember that Jake was a carved mountain of a young man. He was built like Zeus himself. Nikki tried to get close to Jake to calm him, but…)

JAKE. What you doin'? Stop! What done happen to your face? Look like somebody done slapped you silly.

NIKKI. Ain't anybody done slap me. You know I don't plays for no man to put his hand on me.

JAKE. I ain't say nothing 'bout no man! It even smells funny in here.

(Nikki tried once more to get close to Jake to calm him and take his mind off the surroundings.)

JAKE. Woman, I done told you to gets off me and let me be!

NIKKI. Where you done been, and who you done been with? You ain't the same Jake that left here this morning.

(The next morning, Jake could do nothing but think about Cleo. He thought about her smooth black skin, her short but ever so neat hair, and her elegant speech. Jake was so deep into his thoughts that he didn't notice that Nikki had entered the room.)

NIKKI. Jake, what is you doin'? Jake, Jake, Jake! This be the second time I's done called you and you's not paid me no mind. What or who is you gots on your mind?

JAKE. You says some'um? I's got to go!

(Jake could wait no longer; he had to see Cleo, if only to just catch a glimpse of her. Jake knew where she was working, so he started toward her office building, but before he could reach the building, he saw her walking up the street.)

CLEO. Hi, how are you this morning? Did you sleep well? I just parked my car down the street. As I was walking, I was wondering when did you want to start those lessons? Now I'm glad that I ran into you.

JAKE. Hay, naw, I didn't sleep too good. I tossed and turned all night long.

CLEO. You tossed and turned? Oh, I hate to hear that.

JAKE. It don't be a fault of yours. Cleo, I's been thanking, when you gonna take some time up with me? That is to learn me!

CLEO. Didn't I just ask you that? Oh, Jake, let's see. I'm free this evening. Is that good for you? Well, I guess I've arrived once again. So I guess I will see you later this evening, about six? Just give me a call.

(Cleo didn't realize that she didn't give Jake much time to answer.)

JAKE. Six o'clock be okay!

(Cleo entered her office building with a big smile on her face. Jake watched her go into the building with a smile on his face. Jake went on with his daily activities, but for some reason, the day was not going by fast enough. Cleo also was wondering what was taking the day so long to end. "Five o'clock finally," Cleo thought. "I told Jake six o'clock. Wow, I didn't give myself much time to get to my place." Jake thought about it. Through all the excitement, he didn't get Cleo's address, but he did have her phone number. He saw a payphone. He could have broken his neck getting to the phone. Although impatient, Cleo fought back the feeling to answer on the first ring. This was before caller ID.)

CLEO. Hello.

JAKE. Cleo, it me, Jake.

CLEO. Jake, it's almost six o'clock. Are you still coming?
JAKE. Cleo, I's still coming, but…
CLEO. But what?
JAKE. But you forgots to give me your address.

(Cleo and Jake both had a good laugh. She gave Jake her address. He could hardly wait to get off the phone so that he could see her! He knew the address, and he knew that he was only about nine blocks away. He quickly made it to her front door; he rang the doorbell. Cleo answered the door. She just didn't answer the door; she had on a red silk gown and a pair of red pumps, with her finger and toenails matching her gown. She was so beautiful; she was everything that a man could hope for. She even had on the perfect perfume. Oh, yes, the night was perfect for Jake. He stood in the doorway in shock.)

JAKE. You is so beautiful!
CLEO. Not is so, but you are so. And thank you. I have this English book I want you to have and study. Oh, by the way, come on in.

(While Cleo was talking, Jake could not help but stare at her beauty. Jake knew that he had come there for a specific reason, but it was very hard to concentrate on the matter at hand.)

CLEO. Jake, are you okay?

(Cleo knew that her garments were not suitable for studying, so she went into her bedroom and put on a long housecoat. What she failed to realize was that she could have put on anything she wanted, and Jake's reaction would have been the same. He was not only looking at her outer beauty but her inner beauty as well. The hours seemed to fly by. They not only studied, but they laughed and talked and got to know each other better. It was getting rather late, and Cleo knew that she had to get up pretty early the next morning. She wanted so much for Jake to stay the night, but she knew that it was much too soon for that. Jake said with deep regret.)

JAKE. I must be going now.

(He and Cleo knew that it was time for him to go, but they continued holding conversation with each other for another thirty minutes or so. Meanwhile, across

town, Nikki was beginning to worry about Jake, someone she thought she cared nothing about.)

NIKKI. You done decided to come home, huh?
JAKE. Don't you be messing with me! I ain't in no mood for your foolishness. Leave me alone!

(Jake walked past Nikki as if she wasn't there. Nikki, being no complete fool, knew right then that it was another woman involved in Jake's life, plus she smelled the perfume. She felt like an old dog with a used bone. She didn't want him, but she didn't want anyone else to have him. Cleo, lying in her room on her bed, could do nothing but think about him. He's just a big old dumb country boy with little to no education. She thought, "As far as I know he's married." Jake was lying in his room, trying to think of a way to get out of his situation with Nikki. He found himself having strong feelings for Cleo, feelings so strong that knew he wanted to write to his mother about her. A couple of days later, he called Cleo and asked her if he could come over.)

CLEO. Well, I guess it will be okay.

(She didn't want to sound too anxious, but deep inside, her heart was racing up to her throat. It wasn't too long, Jake rang the doorbell.)

CLEO. Jake, dear, I am so happy to see you.

(Cleo, although not knowing Jake long, could tell by the expression on his face that something was wrong.)

Jake. Cleo, I done been here for some months, and I ain't done wrote my momma yet. I want to know if you could help me.

(Cleo, without saying a word, escorted Jake to her little home office, and she sat down at her typewriter.)

CLEO. Jake, I'm ready if you are.

(Jake knew what he wanted to say, but he didn't know how to say it. You see, it has been about six months since Jake left home. That is about six months he had not contacted his mother.)

CLEO. Jake, just tell me what you want to say, and I'll make sure that I will put it on paper the way it should be.

(Jake smiled.)

Dear Mom,

I am doing fine, and how are you? I hope that this letter finds you in the best of health. I am staying in what they call a two-bedroom apartment. I share the rent with a roommate. I really don't have a job yet, but I do run packages back and forth for my roommate's friend, and he pays well. Mom, what I really want to tell you is that I have met this intelligent, beautiful young lady that reminds me so much of you. She is all that I could ever ask for. Her name is Cleopatra, but she lets me call her Cleo. I'm in a somewhat bad predicament. You see, my roommate is a female named Nikki, and I think she kind of likes me, but I have feelings for Cleo. I have not told her yet, but I guess she knows now since she is the one typing this letter. Well, Momma, I guess that I'm going to end this letter, but never my love for you. I am sorry that it has taken so long for me to write.

Your loving son,
Jake

(Cleo sat at the typewriter with tears in her eyes, not knowing what to think or what to say. She pulled out the letter and read it over to Jake. Jake agreed with the letter. Cleo sealed it and told Jake she would mail it for him. He gave her the address. He asked her if he could use her address for a return address.)

CLEO. Yes, you may!

(The next day, Cleo sent the letter off. It would only take a few days to get a return to sender. When Cleo got the letter back, her first thought was he doesn't

remember his own mother's address. By this time, Jake and Cleo had a pretty good understanding, so he came right over without calling first.)

CLEO. Jake, your letter came back return to sender.
JAKE. What do you mean?
CLEO. It means either you gave me the wrong address or that the address is no longer any good.

(Jake checked the address.)

JAKE. This is the right address.
CLEO. Jake, maybe we should go down there. After all, it is only about an hour's ride. With it being Saturday and with us having nothing to do, I think the fresh air would be nice.

(All the way there, Jake was as quiet as a church mouse. When they arrived, Jake received a painful shock. The grass had overtaken the small shotgun house, the porch had fallen in, and a tree had fallen onto the roof and caved it in. Jake ran toward the house, screaming for his mother. Cleo could only fear the worse. Jake entered the pile of rubble that resembled a house only to find nothing.)

JAKE. Momma, Momma, Momma!

(Cleo went in behind him; she put her arms around him, trying to comfort him.)

CLEO. Jake, surely someone will be able to tell you what might have happened.
JAKE. You is right. I go check with old man Cyrus.

(They got back into the car. Jake, not knowing what to say or think, just pointed in a direction. Cleo understood where Jake wanted to go. Old man Cyrus lived about a mile from Jake's old home. When they arrived, they saw an old man looking like a scarecrow walking behind a plow pulled by a beat-up tired-looking old mule. Old man Cyrus looked up.)

CYRUS: Whoa, mule.

(Old man Cyrus slowly walked from his garden to where Jake and Cleo were standing. It seemed to take forever for him to make it to them.)

CYRUS: Jake, boy, how is you been, and where in tar nations have you been? We done been trying to get ya for the longest. You sees 'bout da week or two you done left, your momma took down mighty sick. She, not wantin' to bother nobody, lay up in that old house and died.

JAKE. She what? How come I just not to hear about this?

(Jake broke down; he knew it was his fault that his mother had died.)

JAKE. If I had just stayed here, she would be here!

CLEO. No, Jake, you can't blame yourself for your mother's death.

JAKE. You don't understand. If I had just stayed here, I could have took care of her.

(Cleo knew that this was not the time or place to correct him, nor was it the time to make him feel better. She knew he had to get the pain out. Jake took off running. Where was he going, no one knew, not even JAKE. Jake ran until he made it back to that old broken-down house. Once again he went inside.)

JAKE. Momma, I knows you hear me. Momma, why did you have to tell me to go?

(All of a sudden, Jake heard his mother's voice.)

VOICE. Jake, my baby, if I did not tell you to leave, you would still be here, and if you were still here, what could you have done for yourself or me?

JAKE. Momma, you could have told me. I make you this promise, I is gonna make. No, I am going to make something out of myself.

(Jake left that old broken-down house more determined than ever. When he made it back to Cleo and old man Cyrus, he had a different look in his face. It was the look of a man that had a direction and a purpose in life.)

JAKE. Cleo, let's go.

CLEO. Jake, are you okay?

JAKE. I'm just fine. We should be going. It's getting late.

(Cleo didn't notice the grammar, but she did notice the determined look on his face.)

JAKE. Cleo, I want you to teach me. I want you to teach me not only how to speak but how to present myself as well so that I might get a real job.

(They made it back into the city. Jake knew what he had to do.)

JAKE. Take me home.
CLEO. Are you sure?
JAKE. I said take me home, please.

(Cleo drove to Jake's house.)

JAKE. Wait for me.
CLEO. Are you sure?
JAKE. I said wait for me. And stop questioning me, please!

(Jake went inside. He left the door open. Nikki was waiting for him. She peeped out of the blinds.)

NIKKI. Who is that? That your bitch! She ain't got nothing. She ain't even got no hair. I's got long pretty hair, and look at her, she is black as night. My skin is pretty and bright!

(Jake stopped and looked.)

JAKE. You know what, Nikki? You are right. She is black as night, and her hair maybe as short as a toad's hair, but she has two things that you will never have.
NIKKI. What do she gots?
JAKE. She has class, and she has me!
NIKKI. That all right. Get your stuff and gets out. I didn't never wants you no ways!

(Jake politely walked past Nikki to his room. He gathered his things. Nikki, seeing he was actually leaving, fell to the floor and grabbed his leg, begging him not to go. Jake looked down at her, and without him saying a word, Nikki knew that she had better let go. After Jake and Cleo made it back to her house, Jake apologized.)

JAKE. Cleo, I am sorry that you had to take me over there and that you had to see all of that.

CLEO. Jake, it was not a problem, but where are you going now?

JAKE. Well, I guess I'm going to have to find somewhere to go, huh?

Jake The Man

(*Months had gone by, and Jake found him a real job making real money, and he had his own place. Jake and Cleo were still seeing each other. Cleo had invited Jake to spend the night because she knew that the next day was his birthday. She decided to get up before he did and cook him a wonderful breakfast. After all, the way to a man's heart is through his stomach; that's what they say. Cleo, knowing that Jake was a country boy and by now knowing the things he liked to eat, she cooked his favorite. But before she would carry it in to him, she decided to fix herself up a little so that she would be more attractive than the food. It didn't take much!*)

CLEO. Good morning, sleepy head. Come on, wake up! It's your birthday!

(*As Jake turned over, all he could see was a beautiful black goddess standing in front of him in a red transparent negligee revealing every curve. Jake swallowed as if he was going to swallow his Adam's apple.*)

CLEO. I thought I would give you something to eat while you were still in bed.

(*Jake's mouth was watering like Niagara Falls as it flew wide open. He was completely speechless; it took all he had just to swallow again.*)

JAKE. Wow! (*He said in a whisper.*)

(*Cleo put the breakfast tray down on the nightstand, then she straddled his midsection as if she was in the rodeo about to ride a bull, but before it went any farther, she jumped up and left the bedroom. Jake, feeling like Mount Saint Helen waiting to erupt, wondered what just happened. Why did she jump up all of a sudden? He called out to her.*)

JAKE. Cleo, Cleo, are you okay?

(*He got up to find out if anything was wrong with her. He found her sitting on the living room couch, crying.*)

JAKE. Is there anything wrong? Did I do something?
CLEO. No, there's nothing wrong. (*Sobbing.*) Are you going in to work? You need to eat and get dressed.
JAKE. Well, I was planning on it. Why?

(*Jake knew today was a work day and his birthday, but he had made other plans. He thought he would go see an old friend and do something for Cleo as well.*)

CLEO. I guess you had better start getting ready. Your suit is ready, and your shoes and tie are over there.

(*Jake, being a bit confused, didn't know what to think. He went into the bedroom and started to dress. Cleo shouted with a loud but sweet and sexy tone.*)

CLEO. Jake I love you, I love you so much!

(*Jake was stunned. He wondered where that came from.*)

JAKE. Wow, all of this because it's my birthday? I love you too.

(*What Jake didn't know was that Cleo also was from a small country town and that she had left home at an early age and had to fight for everything she had every gotten. She started thinking back.*)

★ ★ ★

CLEO. Momma, please don't leave me here. I wants to go with you!

MOMMA. Cleo Jones, you is thirteen years old. You is old enough to stay here on your own, and besides, Henry will be here in a few.

(Henry was the live-in boyfriend of Cleo's mother. He was an older guy that was smelly, and he walked around the house in his tight white underwear. His belly would always hang over the front, and his butt crack was always showing. He would always look at Cleo funny and always made her scratch his back, which reminded her of an old dog that had just been dipped for fleas. Cleo's mother decided to leave her there anyway, and it wasn't long before Henry came home.)

HENRY. Betty! Where you at, woman?

(You see, Betty was Cleo's mother. Betty was also a beautiful dark-skinned woman. She had skin as dark as a moonless night and long silk-like hair, and her body—wow, her body was a sight to see. There was only one thing negative about Cleo's mother—she liked men. And when I say she liked men, I really mean men! She only kept Henry around because he worked and he brought his money home.)

HENRY. Betty, is you home? Cleo, is you in there, girl?
CLEO. I is.
HENRY. Where is your mammy?
CLEO. I don't know. She didn't tell me nothing.
HENRY. Cleo, goes fix me some bath water, and I wants it hot!

(Even at the age of thirteen, Cleo's body was very mature, and she was dark just like her mother. Cleo went into the bathroom and started running Henry's bathwater. Henry was upset and getting more upset by the moment because he had a thought on where Betty might be and what she was doing. He knew that she didn't love him, and he knew that she was only using him, but he thought that if he stayed there long enough, she would come to love him. Henry got undressed as usual and walked through the house in his underwear as usual. His butt crack was out as usual, but something different happened. Once he got into the tub, he called Cleo.)

HENRY. Cleo, come wash my back!

(This was something that he never had done. He never had called Cleo into the bathroom while he was taking a bath.)

CLEO. What? You want me to do what?
HENRY. You heards me. I says I want you to comes wash my back.
CLEO. I can't do that!
HENRY. Girl, if you don't gets your little black ass in here, I gonna beat you, and when your mammy gets here, I gonna beat her as well.

(Cleo didn't know what to do, so she thought washing his back wouldn't be so bad. All I gots to do is to turn my head and scrub his old mangy back. But as Cleo walked into the bathroom, Henry looked at her curvy tender body, and he started to have improper thoughts. He wanted to touch her; he wanted to feel her tenderness. As Cleo started to wash his back, he grabbed her and pulled her into the water and started to rub his hands all over her and inside of her. He then ripped off the few clothes that she had on and penetrated her with his oversized man tool.)

CLEO. Stop! Please stop! You are hurting me! Stop please stop!

(The bath water ran red with blood. For Cleo it seemed to take hours, but in actuality, it only took seconds. It took seconds, not only to damage her physically but mentally as well. Once Henry had finished, he realized what he had done.)

HENRY. I'm so sorry I didn't mean it. You know that I love you and wouldn't hurt you. I got carried away. If you had not come in here rubbing my back, this wouldn't have happened. It's not my fault!

(Cleo was lying on the cold bathroom floor in the fetus position, crying and not knowing what to do. She was in a great deal of pain! She had all kind of thoughts going through her mind. "What can I do? Who can I tell? Will my momma believe me, or will she blame me?" After a while, Cleo picked herself off the floor.)

CLEO. Are you finished? I would like to clean up now.
HENRY. Aw, sure, I gets out of your way so you's can clean up. Everythang gonna be all right.

(Cleo slowly moved around, because she was still in a lot of pain. She let the bloodstained water out of the tub, cleaned the tub out, and ran some fresh bathwater. She ran the water as hot as she could stand it, plus some. All Cleo wanted to do was to wash the feel of Henry off her and the feeling of him being inside of her away! A couple of years passed, and Cleo was now fifteen. She finally decided to tell her momma what happened.)

CLEO. Momma, can we talk?

MOMMA. Talk about what? I really don't have time for this, but hurry and tells me what's on your mind!

CLEO. Momma, do you remember when I was thirteen and you came home late one night and I was sitting on the couch, and the TV had signed off, and I was still watching it?

MOMMA. Yeah, so? You needs to get to the point. I gots to go before that man Henry makes it home.

CLEO. Well, I was waiting up for you because Henry had raped me!

MOMMA. He what? What happened? Why didn't you tell me then? Are you sure it was rape?

Cleo. Yes! It was rape! Why did you ask me that?

MOMMA. I don't think Henry would do something like that, and if he did and it happened two years ago, ain't too much we can do about it now. I's got to go! I's ask him about it when I's make it home.

⋆ ⋆ ⋆

JAKE. Cleo, Cleo!

CLEO. Yes, what's wrong?

JAKE. Nothing, I have been calling you for a few minutes. I'm leaving now, I'm off to work.

(Jake wasn't really going to work, for you see, it was his birthday. Jake had been thinking a lot about Nikki, not because he had feelings for her but because something on the inside of him told him that he needed to check on her. So he decided to drive toward her place to see what was wrong, because he knew in his gut that something was wrong. But as he arrived, he saw several police cars, and there was yellow police tape everywhere. He recognized one of the neighbors and called out to her.)

JAKE. Paula, Paula, what's going on?

(Paula stood there with tears running down.)

PAULA. Oh, Jake, it's Nikki, she is dead!
JAKE. Dead? What do you mean *dead*? What happened? How did she die?
PAULA. Jake, I have to start from the beginning. You see, after you left, Nikki started talking to me. She told me that she never loved a man the way she loved you.
JAKE. Yeah right!
PAULA. No, really, she was just afraid to show it because she didn't know what Clyde would do to her or to you. But after you left, she told me that she didn't care what Clyde might do to her, that she was tired of feeling like his pin cushion. Every time he felt horny he would come over and expected her to open her legs and show feelings for him automatically. One day, she told him that she didn't want him and that she never wanted him, that she was always in love with you.
JAKE. Oh my.
PAULA. Clyde didn't take it too well. He began to stalk her. Nikki had requested for another apartment off the first floor because she had spotted Clyde peeping into her bedroom window.
JAKE. Why didn't she call the police?
PAULA. She did, but you know how it is. A domestic, they just figured that they were just upset with each other and they would work things out.
JAKE. Wow, I didn't know, I didn't know.

(As Jake turned and walked away, he then knew what he must do. He had to stop wasting time; life is too short. He knew that he had to show and tell Cleo exactly how he felt. After all, it was his birthday. Even though he was feeling sad about Nikki, he just knew what he had to do. Jake got back into his car and drove away, and as he drove off, he looked back for one last time. Knowing that he was not going to work, he started to do what he had set off to do. Although he was hurt, Jake knew that he would have left Nikki anyway. She was not for him, and he knew it. But he hated very much for her life to end the way it did. Jake went to this log cabin jewelry store that was the best in town. He picked out this beautiful 2-carat princess-cut white-gold diamond engagement ring. The diamond was so big and bright one would think that it would have blinded the sun. On the other end, Cleo had made reservations for this top-of-the-line steak

restaurant that Jake loved so well. You see, he was a meat and a potato man. Jake knew that Cleo had gone to work, so he stopped by the florist and ordered her some flowers and signed the card with a little poem.)

When I first saw your beautiful dark silk skin,
I immediately knew that I wanted to be more than friends.
When I first looked into those beautiful black pearls,
I knew right then that I wanted you to share my world.
And when I touched your heavenly soft lips,
My heart started to skip what am I trying to say.
And what I'm trying to tell you is that my love for you
is here to stay!
I love you Cleo.
Your man, Jake.

(Jake had the florist to deliver the yellow red-tipped roses to Cleo's office. He knew that her office was filled with female workers, and he knew that once she got those roses and read that poem in front of her coworkers, he would be able to finish what she had started that morning.)

DELIVERY PERSON. Cleo Jones, Cleo Jones, I have a package for Cleo Jones.

(As Cleo received the beautiful roses, she knew that they could have come from only one man. She thought to herself, "Jake, my Jake." All her coworkers gathered around.)

GLADIS. Girl, hm, what did you do to get those? You finally gave up the booty, huh? And it's about time. If that fine man was mine, I would have been satisfied him.

CLEO. We know, Gladis. No, I did not. As a matter of fact, it's his birthday.

GLADIS. His birthday? Why is he sending you roses on his birthday? Girl, if I were you, I have to check him because he has done something!

CLEO. Gladis, maybe if he was one of the guys you date. Jake is sweet like this. Sometime I feel like he cares more about me than he does himself.

SHARON. Cleo, you must not pay any attention to a word that Gladis is saying. We both know the type of men she dates and the type of slut she is! Did I see a card in there? What does it say?

CLEO. Come on, Sharon. I will read it to you.

CLEO (*reading*). When I first saw your beautiful dark silk skin, I immediately knew that I wanted to be more than friends...

(*As Cleo was reading, her voice started to get lower and lower, and tears started to roll down her cheeks. She could not finish reading aloud.*)

SHARON. What is it, girl?

(*Sharon took the card and started reading where Cleo had left off.*)

SHARON (*reading*). When I first looked into those beautiful black pearls, I knew right then that I wanted you to share my world. And when I touched your heavenly soft lips, my heart started to skip what am I trying to say. And what I'm trying tell you is that my love for you is here to stay! I love you, Cleo. Your man, Jake!

SHARON. Wow! Girl, does he have any brothers?

(*Sharon, wiping her eyes, started walking out when she bumped into their boss, Candice.*)

CANDICE. What's the matter with you two?

(*Cleo and Sharon didn't have to say anything; all they had to do was to hand over the card. And before you knew it, Candice was reaching for some tissues. Meanwhile, Jake was at the barber shop, getting his head freshly shaved and his mustache neatly trimmed. After he left, he went shopping. He wanted to be at his best, for he knew what he was about to do. While he was out, he ran into his coworker and friend, Dennis.*)

DENNIS. What's up, Jake? You took off today to go shopping?

JAKE. Dennis, you know today is my birthday. What are you tripping about?

DENNIS. Nothing, I thought you would be with that fine woman of yours? When are you going to marry her? Man, if she was my woman and I had the day off, we would be lying up right now, bumping ugly! I would never leave a fine woman like that. I would ask her to marry me in a heartbeat. She is…

JAKE. Okay! That's enough! And for you, it would be ugly!

(That was all Jake had to say. We must not forget that Jake was not your average-sized man, and he spoke and walked with authority.)

JAKE. You know, Dennis, I'm going to ask her to marry me.

DENNIS. Man, I wouldn't do that. Why buy the cow when you can get the milk free? And besides, she's not all of that.

JAKE. First of all, I don't know why I even talk to you, and you were just saying how fine she was and if you had her! Man, get out of my face before I do something to you. Step!

(Dennis did not say another word. He just looked down at the cold floor and slithered away. Time was passing, and Jake knew he had to hurry home and make things right. He knew that after dinner he was going to ask Cleo back to his place so he hurried home. Jake was a very neat man, so there was not much to do, but he knew he had to have things perfect for his lady. While he was home cleaning, his phone rang.)

JAKE. Hello.

CLEO. Jake, thanks so much, I love them!

JAKE. I was hoping instead of saying you love them you might have said you love me.

CLEO. Don't be silly, you big handsome country mountain of a man. Jake, you should know that I love you more than I can express.

JAKE Martin, I love you.

JAKE. Did you like the card?

CLEO. Jake, I can't tell you enough how much I liked the—no, I loved the card! Oh, Jake! I want you so bad. Oops, did I say that out loud?

JAKE. Excuse me? You really did.

CLEO. I'm sorry.

JAKE. Don't be. I want you too. I want to feel your silk skin pressed against my…

CLEO. Hold that thought, my big man. I must go. After all, I'm at work.

(What Jake didn't know was that if Cleo had continued to listen, she would have to leave work and change her underclothes. Cleo could hardly concentrate. She was thinking about the evening to come. She never had been one to watch the clock, but this day was different. She was not only watching the clock. She wanted to grab it and push the hands forward. Cleo had given no thought about what she would wear, but she knew her man, Jake. She knew that he would put on those jeans—the ones that fitted ever so perfect, you know not to tight but tight enough—he would grab one of his pullover three-button polo shirts that gripped every hard muscle, his sports jacket and Polo boots.)

CLEO (*thinking*). Yeah, that's my man, and I can't wait to show him. Oh, I forgot, what am I going to wear?

(Jake too was watching the clock. Although he had gone shopping earlier this day, he looked into his closet, and what he saw was his favorite pair of jeans, and hanging in formation were his polo shirts.)

JAKE. I should just grab my favorite pair of jeans and a polo shirt.

(After Jake had decided on what he would wear, he sat down and reached into the beautiful package and pulled out the ring box. He opened it and just started to wonder.) Wow, what a beautiful ring. Never in my wildest dreams would I have thought that I, Jake Martin, would be able to buy such a ring. I thank God and I thank you momma. For if you did not make me leave, I would not had left.

(As Jake sat there and a tear started to fall from his eye.)

JAKE. Lord, I wish my momma was here to see me now. I wish she was here to meet Cleo. I know she would love her. I wish she was here to hear me talk. I wish she was here so I could take her to my job and show her where I work. I wish she was here so I could take her for a ride in my car. Lord, I miss my momma so much, and I love her so much.

(Jake knew deep in his heart that his momma was proud of him, and that's all that mattered. Jake then put the ring in his nightstand next to his bed. He went into his bathroom and turned the shower on, getting the water as hot as he thought he could stand it. He took off his shirt, his pants, then his underwear,

and placed each in the dirty clothes basket. Jake got into the shower and began to let the water run down from the top of his head as if it was washing all his stress and worries away. Finally, five o'clock. Cleo was as excited as a six-year-old on Christmas morning. She quickly cleared her desk and gathered up her things because she knew that she was about to be with Jake and she was planning on giving him one hell of a birthday present, which included finishing up what she had started this morning. She had made up in her mind that she was going to do all that she could to put the past behind her. She rushed home, stripping off her clothes as she entered her door. But the phone would ring.)

CLEO. Who could this be? Hello! (*Remember, this was before caller ID.*)

JAKE. Hold on, baby. Sounds like you are about to cut someone's throat.

CLEO. Oh, Jake, it's you, baby. Now you know that I wouldn't dare dream about doing anything like that to you. It's just that I'm standing here naked because I was about to jump into the shower.

JAKE. Naked, huh? Wow! I will be right over!

CLEO. I bet you would, huh? No, seriously, honey, I need to jump into the shower so that we won't be late for dinner.

JAKE. I want to jump into something also, and it's not the shower.

CLEO. Just be here in about forty-five minutes to pick me up.

JAKE. Perfect, okay.

(Now it was Jake's turn to watch the clock. He had gotten dress so he thought that he would sit down and watch a little TV. But we all know that when you are trying to get time to pass, it seems to drag.)

JAKE (*thinking*). Did she say to be there in forty-five minutes or for me to leave in forty-five minutes? If she said for me to be there in forty-five minutes, I would have to leave in less than thirty minutes, but if she said for me to leave in forty-five minutes, I will have to wait for another thirty-seven minutes. Oh, what the hell, I'll just leave now and drive slow.

(Jake put his cologne on as he was about to walk out the door. He wanted it to be fresh but have enough time so it wouldn't be too strong. Jake got into his ride and put his eight-track in. It was Al Green's "Tired of Being Alone," and he started to sing to it.)

JAKE. I'm so tired of being alone, I'm so tired of on my own. Won't you help me girl as soon as you can…

(*While Jake was singing, it took all that he had to concentrate on the street. He visualized Cleo, and he slowly wondered what her answer would be and how she would react.*)

JAKE. What if she says no? What if she rejects me? Will we still be able to continue with our relationship? Will I want to continue? Will she want to continue? Wow, I never thought about it like this.

(*By this time he was pulling up in front of her apartment.*)

JAKE. Wow. Maybe I should have given this some more thought?

(*Jake got out of his car and walked up to Cleo's apartment and pushed the doorbell. It took a while, which seemed like an eternity to Jake, but Cleo finally came to the door. When Cleo opened the door, it was as if they were seeing each other for the first time. Jake stood there with his mouth opened as Cleo stood there in nothing but a towel.*)

CLEO. Well, are you coming in? I knew that you would be here early, but I'm glad!

(*Jake walked in and snatched Cleo off her feet, holding her as if it would be his last time.*)

JAKE. Am I early? I tried to wait, then I tried to drive slowly. I guess it didn't work, huh?

CLEO. No, it did not. But I'm very happy to see you. Now you will just have to wait for me to get ready, and I know how much you hate to wait.

JAKE. You just go and get dressed. I'm pretty sure that it will be well worth my wait! Oh, do you need some help?

CLEO. No, and besides, I want you to behave.

JAKE. Behave, don't I always?

CLEO. No! But I guess that's why I'm so in love with you.

(Jake sat down and turned on some music, and once again it was Al Green singing "Let's Stay Together." Jake sat through several songs before Cleo would come back into the room.)

CLEO. Jake, I'm ready. How do I look?
JAKE. Wow! You are so sexy. I mean beautiful. I mean both!
CLEO. I have to look good for my man. After all, it is your birthday! Aren't you going to kiss me, or are you just going to stand there with your mouth wide opened?

(Jake once again picked her off her feet while kissing her. We must not forget that Jake was not just an ordinary man. He had very good size and strength; others would say that he didn't know his own strength.)

CLEO. Jake, I thought I told you that I wanted you to behave. What's that bulge I feel pressing against me?
JAKE. You know what it is!
CLEO. It will just have to wait come on, or we will be late.

(Jake walked around the car to open the door for Cleo, and then he got into the car, started it up, and on the radio, Marvin Gaye was playing "Let's Get It On." Jake looked over at Cleo like a predator would look at its prey.)

CLEO. Drive, Jake, drive!
JAKE. Where to?
CLEO. Oh, that's right. I haven't told you where we are going. You know that new steak place? You know, where you can pick your own steak and they will even let you cook it yourself.
JAKE. Yeah, I know exactly where you are talking about. You know me so well. I know exactly what I'm going to order. But I refuse to go out and pay to cook my own food. If I wanted to cook, we could have stayed home. We could have really cooked!
CLEO. Jake, I'm surprised. Wow, is this my man talking like this? I guess you are still thinking about this morning?

(What Cleo didn't know was that in his mind he was still feeling her hot wet body touching his. Jake had to change his thoughts. But it would not be as easy as he thought.)

JAKE. So what are your plans after dinner? I was hoping that we could go back to my place.

CLEO. I was just thinking the same thing. I want to go back to your place also.

(*They continued their conversation, finally arriving at the restaurant.*)

JAKE. Yes, this I like!

CLEO. I figured you would.

CLEO. Yes, we have reservations for two under Jones, Cleo Jones.

WAITER. You two can follow me. Can I get you anything to drink?

JAKE. Cleo, what will you have? I'm going to have water.

CLEO. Water, really? You can get me a coke.

WAITER. Do you know what you want, or should I give you some more time?

(*Jake was looking at Cleo.*)

JAKE. I know exactly what I want!

(*Jake looked at Cleo as if she were a three-course meal.*)

CLEO. Food, Jake, food.

JAKE. Oh, yes, I will have … Cleo what do you want?

CLEO. I will have the smoked chicken.

JAKE. I will have the twenty-ounce big bubba T-bone medium, wellloaded baked potato, and baby carrots.

(*Jake and Cleo enjoyed each other during dinner. It was during that time Jake wanted to share with Cleo a little more about his past.*)

JAKE. Cleo, you know a lot about me that I came from an little ole country town deep in the Delta, but what you don't know is when I was five, my dad died and left me and my mom alone. My dad was a very good man. He would leave the house before sunup and come back right before sunset. My momma used to say that's what killed him. He worked himself to death. He worked like a dog, but we still didn't have much. But what I did have for the first five years of my life was my daddy's love. He loved me and my momma with all his heart. I remember seeing him and my momma sitting on the front porch, just holding each other, looking at the sunset. My momma used to tell me that my daddy always wanted the best for me. And I say that if he could see you now, he would say that I got all that he wanted me to have plus more. Why am I telling you this? Well, I thought it was something that you needed to know.

(By the time their food had come, they ate, and they both were ready to go. Jake got ready to pay, but Cleo wouldn't let him.)

CLEO. It's your birthday, remember? Uh, Jake, why did you feel like you had to tell me about your father?

JAKE. Cleo, I wanted you to know that I know how to be a good father, that I know how to be a good man, and that I know how to love.

CLEO. I see.

(They got back into the car, turned the radio on, but neither one was listening. They sat there like two teenagers on a hot date. Jake tried to drive slowly, but it was like the streets just cleared the way for him.)

JAKE. We are here, shall we go in?

Jake got out, walked around to her side, and opened the door for her. She looked and smelled so good that he wanted to pick her up and carry her in. But he thought that would be a bit too much.

CLEO. Jake, would you mind if I slipped into something a little softer?

(Cleo had only a small purse with her.)

JAKE. No! By all means, do so!

(But Jake wondered what she was going to slip into. She didn't bring anything in with her, nor had she left anything over to his place. Cleo left out and came back in with a little black teddy on, with little on beneath.

It was about mid-thigh, but to her surprise, when she entered back into the room, it was candle light, and rose petals were down for her to follow, and once she reached the end, there was Jake. He was on one knee, and in his hand, he held a diamond ring. The diamond appeared to be large enough to block the sun.)

JAKE. Cleo, from the moment I saw you, I knew you were the one for me. When I first looked into your beautiful brown eyes, I knew that I didn't want you to leave from my side. Cleo, I want you for my wife to have and hold forever and ever. Cleo Jones, will you marry me?

(*Cleo stood there as if she was in shock.*)

CLEO. Jake, oh, Jake, I do love you so. But before I say yes, there is something I have to tell you, something you need to know.

JAKE. Cleo, I'm sure there is nothing you can tell me that will change my mind about how I feel about you.

CLEO. Jake, my love, how can you love me so much and we have never slept together?

JAKE. Cleo, my love for you goes a lot deeper than that. When I'm with you, it's like a breath of fresh air. When I hold you, I feel like a child on Christmas morning that has just gotten everything he's asked Santa for. Cleo, I think about you day and night. I want to be your friend and your lover, as well as your husband. I want to be with you, to care for you, to provide for you, to protect you!

CLEO. Wow! Jake, I still must tell you this. This morning when I was sitting on you, I wanted you so bad. I felt you pressing against me. I wanted you, yet I couldn't go all the way. I … I … When I was thirteen, I was raped my momma's…

JAKE. My love, you don't have to explain. Cleo, all of that is behind you now. I'm here now, and I will take away all the fear and all the pain. I will put all the love you lost back into your life again. Baby, who am I? I'm Jake, and I will make all things better.

(*That very moment, Cleo fell into Jake's massive arms as if her whole body went limp.*)

CLEO. Jake, oh, Jake, yes, yes, yes, I will marry you. Happy birthday, Jake. Happy birthday!

JAKE. Yes, it surely is!

(Jake kissed Cleo like she had never been kissed before, a kiss like it was permanent, and a kiss that will last a lifetime. Jake picked Cleo up, and she wrapped her legs around his narrow waist, and she indeed returned his permanent kiss. But they both decided to wait until they were married before they would go any further.)

The Wedding

(The next morning, Cleo was so excited she knew that she had to call Sharon so that she could help her with her wedding plans.)

SHARON. Hello.
CLEO. Girl, he did it, he did it!
SHARON. What did he do, and who did it?
CLEO. Jake! He asked me to marry him.
SHARON. He did what? How did it happen? Where were you two? Did he get on his knees? Come on, tell me!
CLEO. If you will give me time. Wow! I'm so excited! My head is still spinning around!
SHARON. Did you two set a date? Who's going to be your bridesmaid?
CLEO. A date?
SHARON. Yes, a date for the wedding.
CLEO. A date? Wow. I guess through all the excitement we didn't get around to discussing a date.
SHARON. Girl, you had better. Wait a minute, what time is it?
CLEO. It's about five.
SHARON. In the morning? Are you out of your everlasting mind?
CLEO. Uh, yes.
SHARON. Okay, where's Jake?
CLEO. He's still in the bed.
SHARON. May I suggest that you get off this phone, go back to bed, and wait until in the morning? Talk to Jake, your husband-to-be, and you two discuss a date.
CLEO. You're right, I'm sorry for waking you up at this hour. I will talk to you in a few hours. I'm so excited!

SHARON. Me too! Call me after the sun comes up! Good night.

(Cleo hurried back into the bedroom.)

JAKE. Where have you been? No, let me guess, you called Sharon?
CLEO. Huh, yeah, I had to call my girl. I had to tell her the good news.
JAKE. How about waiting until we have discussed a date for the wedding?
CLEO. Funny, Sharon said the same thing.

(Jake and Cleo began discussing possible dates and plans. Jake not being one to wait, wanted to get married right away.)

JAKE. How about next week?

(Cleo didn't have to say a word all she had to do was to look at Jake.)

JAKE. I guess next week is out of the question?
CLEO. Jake, I want this to be a very special day, a day that I will always cherish for the rest of my life.
JAKE. I guess you're right. It's whatever you want within reason that is.

(Jake looked at Cleo, and Cleo looked at Jake he reach out to her and she did the same to him. They were like two teenagers in love for the very first time.)

The morning light seem to come quickly.

CLEO. Get up I want to start making plans for my wedding.
JAKE. Who's wedding?
CLEO. You know, our wedding! I'm so excited! I'm going to start making a list of things to do and a list of people to invite. Jake, about how much can we spend? I saw this beautiful wedding gown. Sharon and I was just talking about it. Where are we going to get married? Who are we going to get to conduct the ceremony? Jake, how come you are not saying anything?
JAKE. First of all, you are not giving me a chance to say anything, and second, I just have a few people that I want to invite.

(Jake, being a big family man but having no other family on his own, wanted so much for Cleo, her mother, and her aunt to be reunited.)

JAKE. I tell you what, why don't you and Sharon get together and discuss the colors and the rest of the details? And I can be working on who will be my best man. Hey, by the way, how many guys will I need?

CLEO. Let's see, there's Sharon, Candice, GG, and my home girl from back in the day, Gertrude.

(Jake was feeling kind of low, because he had no family members to invite. But he still had a plan; he knew exactly what he was going to do. First, he would pick some of his coworkers to be groomsmen. That was a given, but he still must put his plan in motion. Jake called on Aunt Brianna, Aunt Brea for short. Aunt Brea was Cleo's aunt, the one that took her in when she left home. Cleo had mentioned her several times, and she had taken Jake to meet her once. Jake quickly learned that she was not one to hold her tongue. She was not one to hold back her feelings, and she often spoke her mind, an old-school aunt for deep, deep, deep down in the country. Jake had only met her once, but she left an everlasting impression on him. Jake knew that if his plan was going to happen, then she would be the one to help make it happen. Jake decided to take that long drive to visit Aunt Brea. When he arrived, he saw a couple of old hounds lying around, but he knew not to get out of his car until Aunt Brea came out to tell them that it was okay. The first thing Jake saw sticking out of the door was the barrels of a double-barrel shotgun. Jake quickly rolled his window.)

JAKE. Aunt Brea, it's me, Jake, Cleo's man!

AUNT BREA. Boy, you done better tells who you might be. I might done mistaken you fur one of them there revenuers. They is still trying to catch me with my still. I mean they is still trying to say that I's got a still. I done told them that all I's got now is for my arthritis. Boy, you sho' is fine. What done brought you way out here anyhow? You wants a real woman now, huh?

JAKE. Aunt Brea, can you tell your dogs that I'm okay so that I can get out and talk to you?

(Jake knew not to get out until Aunt Brea told her two old hounds that he was okay.)

AUNT BREA. Blue, Boy, he ain't no problem. He cans come in.

(Jake got out of his car and walked toward the house.)

JAKE. What's the other dog's name? Aunt Brea, the reason I came out here was because I need your help.

AUNT BREA. The first one is Blue, and the other is Boy. That girl done left you?

JAKE. No, she hasn't. As a matter of fact, we're getting married.

AUNT BREA. Married! Boy, you sho' you don't want none of this before you get hitched?

JAKE. No thank you, Aunt Brea. But I would like for you to help me find and get Cleo's mother to the wedding.

AUNT BREA. Betty! That hoe, hell do Cleo knows what you doing?

JAKE. No, she doesn't.

AUNT BREA. How do you thank her would feels? Seeing her maw after all these years? After her maw calls her a liar and not believing that no-good stank Henry had his way with that innocence young child! But if you is determined to do, this I's help you.

JAKE. What, he did what?

AUNT BREA. I done says too much, huh? Well, it ain't fur me to tells you. If she wants you to know, she's tell you.

JAKE. Come on, Aunt Brea!

AUNT BREA. Naw, I ain't saying no more about it. Now come on in here and have you some possum stew. It's fresh. I killt the varmint yestada. I even made some dumplings. I hates to sit here and eats all this food myself. Well, I's do have my dogs.

JAKE. Aunt Brea, as good as that sounds, I must be going. I have other arrangements to tend to. I will check back with you next weekend.

AUNT BREA. You makes sho' you do that. Heck, next time I's be ready for you with your fine self, umm umm!

(Jake hurried back to his car and left. He dreaded going back to see Aunt Brea by himself, but he knew that she would be the only person that would be able to assist him. By the time Jake made it back to town, it was getting late in the evening. He wondered if Cleo was home and if she was busy. But instead of

just dropping by, he decided to run by his house first so he could clean up a bit and to call her. He decided to call her first.)

CLEO. Hello, who is this?

JAKE. What, have you forgotten me so soon?

CLEO. Jake, you know that I could never forget about you. You are my man. Are you coming over?

JAKE. I was hoping you'd asked. Let me take a shower, and I will be right over.

(*When Jake arrived, he saw that Sharon was still there along with Candice and GG, and when he walked in, he felt like a piece of meat hanging in a butcher's window. All eyes were on him.*)

JAKE. Hello, ladies.

GG, CANDICE, SHARON, AND CLEO: Hello, Jake! (*They all responded at the same time.*)

(*Cleo walked up to him and planted a kiss right on his lips.*)

CLEO. Ladies, uh, we can continue this in the morning. There are some things Jake and I have to take care of. Good night, ladies.

JAKE. Good night, ladies!

CLEO. Jake, let's discuss the plans we've made so far.

(*Although this was not what Jake had on his mind, he decided that to keep peace, he had better listen. After Cleo finished telling Jake all the plans she and her girlfriends had started, Jake felt extremely sleepy.*)

JAKE (*yawning*). I am extremely tried. I have had a very long day. I spoke with the guys, and they all agreed to be in the wedding, even Dennis.

CLEO. Who? Dennis? I can't believe you even asked Dennis!

JAKE. I'm even thinking about asking him to be my best man.

CLEO. What? I thought you couldn't stand Dennis. What changed your mind?

JAKE. My momma always told me to keep my friends close but keep my enemies closer.

CLEO. Oh, I see.

(Jake knew the next day he would be very busy, so he decided to cut it short.)

JAKE. My love, I must be off. I have an extremely busy day tomorrow— you know with planning our wedding and all.

CLEO. Jake, baby, I thought we would sit and watch a movie for a while.

JAKE. Cleo, as good as that sounds, I must be going.

CLEO. Okay, if you must. I love you.

JAKE. I love you more. See you tomorrow.

(All the way back to his place, Jake could not help but to think how it would be with Cleo seeing her mother for the first time since she was fifteen. He started to wonder whether he should try to do this or not. What was Aunt Brea talking about? He knew that if his mother was alive, he certainly would want her to be at his wedding. He would want her to meet her new daughter-in-law, I hope. Jake made it home, warmed up some leftovers, ate, and decided that it was time for him to go to bed. He went straight to sleep. The next morning, Jake went into the office.)

JAKE. Dennis, could you come in here? I really need to talk to you.

DENNIS. Jake, if it's about what I was talking about in the mall a few days ago, I am sorry. I should not have been talking about that fine a—.

JAKE. Dennis.

DENNIS. Naw, man, I was wrong, but Cleo is so damn—

JAKE. Dennis!

DENNIS. I mean she got all of the curves—

JAKE. Dennis, that's enough! I am beginning to wonder if I really want to ask you this.

DENNIS. Uh, you're not upset with me? Aw, man, I was just saying.

JAKE. No, Dennis, I'm not upset. I just want to know if you would be my best man.

DENNIS. What! You want me to be your best man? Not that I'm surprised or anything. Man I will take care of everything. I will be the best best man ever. Uh, do I get a chance to kiss the bride?

JAKE. Keep talking and your lips will be too swollen, too pucker up to do anything.

DENNIS. I was just joking, man. I'll be happy to be your best man. Uh, do I?

JAKE. Dennis, I have one more favor to ask.

DENNIS. Anything for you, Jake, anything at all. You know I will do anything for you. All you have to do is ask.

JAKE. Dennis, Dennis! I just want you to ride out to Cleo's Aunt Brianna's house with me this weekend.

DENNIS. Uh, no! You see, uh, I mean I would, but I promised that I take my grandmother to see *Super Fly*.

JAKE. You, taking your grandmother to see *Super Fly*? Okay, I get it.

(*After Jake spoke with the other guys, he took the rest of the day off. The days seem to fly by, and Jake dreaded doing what he knew he must do. As much as he dreaded it, he knew that he had to make that long drive out to Aunt Brianna's. All the way out there, he was thinking about how she kept looking at him, or was she? Because of her extremely cocked eye, it was hard to tell who or what she was actually looking at. Once again, as he was pulling up, the same ole mangy hounds stared at him as if he was a side of beef specially cooked just for them. Jake blew his horn and slightly rolled down his window.*)

AUNT BREA. Jake, is that you with your fine … Oh, that skinny niece of mine ain't in there, is she?

JAKE. Yes, Aunt Brea, it's me Jake and no Cleo is not with me. I was wondering if you had gotten word to Cleo's mother.

AUNT BREA. Boy, you know you sho' is fine!

JAKE. Thank you, but did you get word to her.

AUNT BREA. Yeah, I done got words ta her. How 'bout given yo Aunt Brea a hug and a kiss?

JAKE. Well, what did she say, will she come or what? And I don't think a hug and kiss will be proper.

AUNT BREA. I ain't trying to be no proper. Jake, you sho' is fine. I ever tells you that? Proper my butt!

JAKE. Yes, Aunt Brea. Well, what did she say?

AUNT BREA. She says that she gots to check her schujule. If you asks me, she ain't gots no schujule.

JAKE. Thank you, Aunt Brea! As soon as we get the final date, I will let you know. One question, how did you get in touch with her when you have no telephone?

AUNT BREA. You sho' you wants that niece of mines when you coulds haves all of this and a bag of chips?

(*We must keep in mind that Aunt Brianna is about one hundred years old. No one living knows for sure exactly how old she is.*)

JAKE. Thanks again, Aunt Brea, but I must be going. I will let you know the date, for sure. Thanks again.

(*Jake left.*)

AUNT BREA. Betty, you and Henry can comes out of the back. That fine Jake is gone. Betty, how comes you don'ts talks to this man? He gonna be marrying little Cleo.

BETTY. What can I say? What has she told him about me? I can see that she has done very well! He is a fine-looking man! Wow!

AUNT BREA. You just keeps in mind that he belongs to your daughter and me! And you Henry, you is supposed to be a man. Can't you control your woman? Makes one to thank what Cleo says back then was true.

HENRY. Now you has no right to brang that up. I's done told you that I's didn't do nothing.

AUNT BREA. Yeah, yeah, yeah, if this girl here believes you, so do I.

(*All the way back to town, Jake had an uneasy feeling, a feeling like he was being watched from Aunt Brea's back room. For a moment he thought, "Naw, it couldn't have been." As soon as Jake walked in, his phone started to ring.*)

JAKE. Hello. Oh, hi, Cleo. I was just thinking about you.

CLEO. I can't tell. I haven't heard from you all day. Jake, is there something wrong? Not having second thoughts, are you?

JAKE. About what?

CLEO. You know, marriage?

JAKE. No, never! I guess I never thought that so much planning went into getting married.

CLEO. Jake, baby, if you want, we can just have a very simple wedding. We can even find a Justice of the Peace to perform the ceremony.

JAKE. Now, Cleo, I wouldn't dare take this day from you only to hear about it for the rest of my life.

CLEO. Very funny, Jake, very funny.

(Meanwhile, back at Aunt Brea's house.)

BETTY. Henry, will you go out and get some more wood?

(Henry went out to get some more wood.)

BETTY. Aunt Brea, I feel like my daughter was telling me the truth and Henry was not.

AUNT BREA. Look a here, now you's knows good and well that that no good hairy stanky tail man done some'um to that baby, and you knows that the only reason you done stayed with him this long is because you done used your stanky coochie up with all those no-good fellows and none of them there other one wants you.

BETTY. When Henry is asleep, it's like he has a lot of demons. He tosses and turns. He talks, and sometimes he even screams.

AUNT BREA. Hell, gal, I needs to get me some popcorn and come sees that.

BETTY. Aunt Brea, I'm for real. It is like his soul is being tormented. He scares me!

HENRY. I's got the wood.

AUNT BREA. Don't just stands there. What, you scared to put it in the box?

BETTY. Aunt Brea!

(Back to Jake and Cleo.)

JAKE. We really need to come up with a date.

CLEO. I agree. How about a date in July? That will give us two full months to make sure we have everything together.

JAKE. How about July the 14th?

CLEO. That sounds good to me. July the 14th, so be it. Are you coming over? I really want to see you.

JAKE. I will be right over. *(Jake wanted to see Cleo just as bad as she wanted to see him.)*

CLEO. Enter, Mr. Martin! I've really been missing you. Hold me! Oh, it feels like you've been missing me also.

JAKE. I almost started to think that it was a mistake asking you to marry me. I was seeing more of you before I asked.

CLEO. You listen here, Mr. Martin. It is no way you are backing out on me now. I know with both of us trying to work and plan our parts of the wedding, we have been missing the most important part of all, and that's spending time with each other.

JAKE. Stop talking and just let me hold you in my arms.

(Cleo felt like butter melting in Jake's massive arms. Her body pressed against his, their lips touching each other's. He was looking into her eyes and she into his.)

CLEO. Wow, Jake, you really have been missing me!

JAKE. Cleo!

(That was all he had to say. She knew then what was exactly on his mind.)

CLEO. Oh, Jake, I love you, and I never want you to leave me.

JAKE. Leave you? Where in the world did that come from?

(Jake then picked Cleo up in his arms and put her down onto the bed, their bodies caressing each other.)

CLEO. Jake, we can't do anything, not tonight.

JAKE. I know, but we can do the most important thing of all. We can hold and caress each other. This is what makes it all worthwhile.

(Jake continued to lie there and hold Cleo the rest of the night. The next morning appeared to come quickly.)

CLEO. Jake, get up. We have to go to work.

JAKE. What time is it?

CLEO. It's about eight o'clock.

JAKE. What? Wow, I have to get out of here.

CLEO. Jake, is this how it's going to be? You know, like last night?

JAKE. I truly hope so.

(Jake made it to his office, and just as soon as he made it in, his assistant handed him a note stating that his supervisor wanted to see him, ASAP.)

JAKE. How long has it been?
ASSISTANT: Oh, about thirty minutes.
JAKE. Wow, I guess I better go and see him.

(You see, Jake's supervisor never wanted to see anyone unless he was going to fire them or promote them. And Jake knew that he was good, but he also knew that with him planning this wedding, he hasn't been working as hard as he should have. He also knew that that snake Dennis had been sucking up to the boss. Jake made it to the end of the hall, turned left, and knocked on the door.)

MR. JOHNSON. Come in.
JAKE. Mr. Johnson, you wanted to see me?
MR. JOHNSON. Jake, I'm giving you a raise starting immediately. That will be all.
JAKE. Yes, sir.

(Jake turned and walked out of the office, thinking to himself what just happened. As soon as Jake made it back into his office, he picked up his phone and called Cleo. Her office phone rang, and the operator picked it up.)

JAKE. Cleo Jones, please.
OPERATOR: Oh, you must be Jake. I've heard all about you, so you gonna marry that Cleo Jones, huh? I done heard a lot about you. Pam says that you is a mighty big man. I's would like to find out for myself.
JAKE. Thanks, but could you get me Cleo Jones, please?
OPERATOR: Well, I guess so!
CLEO. This is Cleo.
JAKE. Hello, Mrs. Martin!
CLEO. Jake. What caused you to call?
JAKE. Can I not call the woman I love, the woman that I'm about to marry, the woman that will one day have my children?
CLEO. Well, mister, since you put it that way, I guess you can.
JAKE. Oh, first of all, who is that operator?
CLEO. Why? Did that slut say anything to you? I will beat her...
JAKE. Cleo, calm down. No, I was just asking. She was polite.

CLEO. Yeah right, polite my butt, but if you say so.

JAKE. Besides, you know that you are the only one I have eyes for. Oh, my boss called me into his office today. I thought it was because I was late for work, but it wasn't. Take a guess why he called me in.

CLEO. Come on, Jake, you know that I hate guessing. And besides, I'm at work.

JAKE. Well, well, he gave me a raise!

CLEO. A raise! How much! When does it start?

JAKE. Calm down. I thought you were at work. As for how much, well, I kind of didn't ask him.

CLEO. You didn't ask him? How in the world? He tells you that you have a raise, and you don't ask him, man.

JAKE. Okay, I didn't ask him, but I'm sure that he will let me know. Better yet, I will just ask Dennis. I'm sure that he know. He knows everything that goes on around here. His head is so far up Mr. Johnson's...

CLEO. Uh, Jake! You never know who might be on the other end. Let's not mess up that raise.

JAKE. You're right. Can we celebrate tonight?

CLEO. Can we say more money to help with the wedding?

JAKE. I guess you are right. Boy, will I ever be glad when this wedding is over.

CLEO. Jake!

JAKE. I mean so I can see you all of the time and hold you every night.

CLEO. I'm sure that is what you meant. I will talk to you tonight, mister. Love you.

JAKE. Okay, love you too.

(Just as Jake got off of the phone, Dennis walked into his office. That made Jake wonder if Dennis was in the other office all the time and if he heard what he was telling Cleo.)

DENNIS. Well, Mr. Money Man. I wonder what someone did to get such a big raise.

(Jake, not knowing how much it was, thought he would sucker Dennis into telling him how big it was.)

JAKE. Now, Dennis, you know and I know that it's not all that big.

DENNIS. Not that big? I would have to work two months overtime for that type of money.

JAKE. Dennis, now surely, stop joking. You know that you probably can make this up in one day.

DENNIS. Jake, how can I make up a one-thousand-dollar-a-month raise?

(Jake's mouth flew opened. He was speechless. A word could not be spoken.)

DENNIS. You didn't know, did you? You mean a man gets a one-thousand- dollar-a-month raise, and he doesn't even know it? Wow!

JAKE. Get out, Dennis, just get out.

(Before Dennis would leave, he would hand an envelope from Mr. Johnson. Jake snatched it from him.)

Jake. Now get out!

DENNIS. Am I still your best man?

JAKE. Get!

(Jake opened the envelope.)

JAKE (*reading*). Congratulations, Jake, on your upcoming proposal. I know Ms. Jones. She is an upstanding woman. The missus and I have had the pleasure of meeting her, and I kind of look at her like a daughter to us, so I know that she will be *well* taken care of. I thought I would give you two an early wedding present because I know how it is when it comes to planning a wedding. Jake, I have also been watching you and your work. You are a very good worker, and I know that you will make a fine husband and good father. Once you two get settled, I know that you two will be looking for a good church home, so I just want to invite you to visit my church.

(Jake just sat back in his chair. He had no words; he had no thoughts. All he could do was to think, wow. Jake wanted to call Cleo, but he thought better.)

JAKE (*thinking*). I will just wait until we get off. I want to discuss a few things with that young lady. Plus, I have work to do. Don't want to lose my raise, yeah right. (*The more Jake thought about it, the less he was upset.*) So what if my boss knows my soonto- be wife? So what if he thinks highly of her? And so what if she is the reason for my raise? I should just be appreciative that I have such a fine lady and that my boss thinks highly of her. Yeah, and besides, I just got a one thousand-dollar-a-month raise! Yeah, baby!

(*After Jake got off, he went home, took a shower, and changed into an old pair of jeans. He then drove over to Cleo's.*)

CLEO. Come on in. I was waiting for you. I cooked dinner, and I hope that my man is good and hungry.
JAKE. Oh yeah, I'm good and hungry!

(*Jake grabbed Cleo and began kissing her forehead, her cheeks, her neck, her lips, her chest.*)

CLEO. Hold on, baby. In time, in time, we will have plenty of time for that.
JAKE. After dinner?
CLEO. No, more like after we are married. You are not mad, are you?
JAKE. No, I guess not. Let's eat.

(*Cleo had the table all set, and she also had the wedding and honeymoon plans all laid out in front.*)

JAKE. Is this the only reason you wanted me to come over?
CLEO. Now, Jake, you know that this is not the only reason. I wanted to see you and spend some time with you as well. We only have a month left before we get married.
JAKE. Okay, but can we eat first?

(*After dinner, Jake and Cleo went into the living room and sat down beside each other. Jake grabbed Cleo, and they started kissing.*)

CLEO. Oh, Jake, Oh, baby! No, Jake, not now. We have to … Oh, get our plans together. Jake, come on, stop. (*She was speaking as if she was out of breathes.*)

JAKE. Okay.

(*Jake was taught that when a woman says stop, that is what you do.*)

CLEO. Wow! Why did you stop?

JAKE. You told me to.

CLEO. Oh, Jake.

(*Since the mood was broken, they sat down and finalized their plans.*)

JAKE. Now that we have our plans finished, how about picking up where you told me to stop?

CLEO. Not now, Jake. I'm not fresh anymore, and besides, it is getting late, and we both have to be at work early in the morning.

JAKE. Okay, I can take a hint. I will see you tomorrow.

CLEO. Jake, please, don't be mad. After all, you were the one that stopped.

JAKE. Mad? I'm not mad, but you just wait until our wedding night!

CLEO. No, you just wait. I'm going to eat you up!

(*Jake got ready to leave, but before he left, he grabbed Cleo and kissed her, then he rubbed his hands over her bodacious behind, then down into her panties.*)

CLEO. Jake, what are you doing? I will see you tomorrow.

JAKE. Okay, I tried.

(*The next morning, Jake went to work, and as soon as he arrived, Mr. Johnson informed him that he needed him to work late.*)

JAKE (*thinking*). Well, I guess I won't see Cleo tonight.

(*Time seemed to fly by. It was only two days before their big day. And Jake knew that he had to go back out to Aunt Brea's place. That was a place that he dreaded to go. All the way out there, he tried to pep himself up for the visit. When Jake pulled into the yard, those old mangy hounds started barking.*)

AUNT BREA. Betty, you and Henry better gets into the back. My fine man Jake done pulled up.

(*Jake blew his horn and shouted out his window.*)

JAKE. Aunt Brea, it's me, Jake. Can you come and call off your hounds?

AUNT BREA. Blue, Boy get. Lets my fines man in. Jake, I done told you that you is one fine man. I cans sop you up likes you is some gravy. Man, you is fine!

JAKE. Thank you, but I come out here to find out about Cleo's mother, Betty.

AUNT BREA. That whore, yeah, what's about her?

JAKE. Well, will she be able to come? The wedding is in two days at one thirty at my boss's church, CCC. Do you need directions?

AUNT BREA. I knows where it's at. You sho' you don't wants none of this?

JAKE. No thanks, Aunt Brea, I must be going. The invitation I gave you have all the details on it. And please, if you all need a ride, you can call that number, and someone will pick you up. Oh, I forgot, you don't have a phone.

AUNT BREA. You means ta tells me that you ain't gonna be the one ta pick me up?

JAKE. Now you know that I have to be there early so that I can get ready.

AUNT BREA. Before you leaves, I gots one question. Is you having a bachelor party, and can I's come? I's can jump out of the cake.

JAKE. That's two questions, and the answers are I don't know if I'm having one, and *no*, you cannot come!

AUNT BREA. Blue, Boy, lets him out! Bye!

JAKE. Bye, Aunt Brea.

(*As Jake got back into his car, all he could do was breathe a sigh of relief.*)

AUNT BREA. Betty, you and Henry cans come out of hiding. Here you go, here's the invitation. You sho' you wants ta go?

BETTY. I's like to see my baby. Henry what do you think?

AUNT BREA. Hell, you's might as well ask Blue and Boy outs there!

BETTY. Aunt Brea! Stop it! Henry, what do you think?

HENRY. If you wants to go, then okay.
BETTY. Well, it's the day after tomorrow. I need to wash my hair.
AUNT Brea. That ain't all you needs ta wash.

(*When Jake made it back home, he received a call from his best man, Dennis.*)

DENNIS. Hey, my man, Jake, how's it going?
JAKE. Dennis, what do you want?
DENNIS. Jake, why so sour?
JAKE. I just came from Aunt Brianna's house, and it just didn't feel right.
DENNIS. When does it feel right coming from her house?
JAKE. No, I mean it felt like someone else was there.
DENNIS. Oh, I see. Hey, I got a great bachelor party planned for you!
JAKE. Dennis, I told you that I didn't want a bachelor party.
DENNIS. What kind of best man would I be if I listen to you and didn't throw you a party?
JAKE. Okay, where will it be?
DENNIS. Tomorrow night at the old hotel in the curve at about nine o'clock. Man, do I have a surprise for you!
JAKE. Nine? What time is this thing going to end? You do remember that I am supposed to get married the next day? And you are supposed to be the best man. I will see you there, and you better not get too drunk! I got to go, going to see my lady for the last time before she becomes Mrs. Martin. Dennis. Yeah, you better hit it now because … Hello, hello, hello, sucker, done hung up on me.

(*Yeah, Jake had hung up on Dennis because he didn't care to hear what that clown had to say. Jake decided to call Cleo.*)

CLEO. Hello, Jake, are we still going to the movies?
JAKE. Yeah, if that's what you really want to do.
CLEO. Uh, what is it you want to do?
JAKE. Well, I thought we could get an early start on our honeymoon.
CLEO. Jake, as good as that sounds, uh, no. We have waited all this time. What difference does two more nights make?
JAKE. Wow, I guess you are right, but I must warn you, the night of our wedding, I will show you no, not any at all, mercy!

CLEO. I must warn you also that goes both ways!
JAKE. Huh? I'm on my way. Be ready, okay?
CLEO. I'm ready.

(Jake picked up Cleo, and as they drove, they enjoyed each other's company and conversation. They made it to the movie. It was a drive-in. Cleo slid close to Jake. He put his arm around her shoulder, and from that moment on, they didn't see any of the movie.)

CLEO. Uh, Jake, I think the movie is over.
CLEO. Jake, I told you that we had to wait until after our wedding. And stop putting my hand on the humongous thing.
JAKE. What, I'm not doing anything.
CLEO. Come on, Jake, it's time to go.

(Jake and Cleo drove off. He took her home.)

JAKE. Do you want me to come in?
CLEO. Yes, but no, I know what might happen if you do. So I guess we had better just kiss each other good night right here. Good night, Jake.
JAKE. Good night. Are you sure?
CLEO. Good night, Jake.

(It was the day before the big day. Jake got up bright and early as always.)

JAKE. Wow, what am I going to do today? I'm off from work with nothing to do until tonight, the bachelor party. I know, I'll just wash and wax my car again and make sure that it's cleaned on the inside.

(Cleo was still in bed, but she knew that she had to get up real soon. She had her hair appointment. She wanted to get her nails done again. Plus, she wanted to make sure everything was perfect. Cleo decided to get up and call Sharon.)

SHARON. Hello.
CLEO. Sharon, get up. Let's get started.
SHARON. Girl, you are late. I've been up waiting for your call.
CLEO. Okay, girl. I'll be over soon.

(As Jake and Cleo went on with their busy day, time was quickly passing. Jake was at home, relaxing, thinking this will be the last day by himself. Jake had been keeping himself busy, trying to help time pass. He was actually getting a tad bit nervous. He started to wonder what was taking the day so long. But before he knew it, the phone rang.)

DENNIS. Jake, my man, how does it feel knowing that in less than twenty-four hours, your freedom will be taken away?
JAKE. What is it, Dennis?
DENNIS. Jake, I know. You haven't forgotten about your party?
JAKE. No, I haven't forgotten. It's only eight. What eight o'clock!
MAN, where has the day gone. I guess I will see you in a few.

(Jake jumped in the shower, looked in his closet, and grabbed a pair of blue jeans and a designer T-shirt, and headed for the hotel, thinking they are probably going to have some lame stripper. Jake decided to turn on some music, but all he could think about was him standing in front of that preacher, holding Cleo's hand, saying "I do." Jake made it to the hotel, and Dennis was standing outside, waiting for him.)

DENNIS. Man, what took you so long? I've already done had three dranks.
JAKE. Smells and sounds like you've had more than three. What have you been drinking?
DENNIS. Malt liquor, that ole blue bull and that funky monkey, and some gin. I just done had three dranks!
JAKE. Look, man, you had better not mess up my wedding tomorrow!
DENNIS. Relax, man, I's got this. I's got this all under control. Come on in and get you some dranks!

(Jake went in with Dennis. All of the fellows from the office were there, all but Mr. Johnson. All of the fellows shouted for Jake to have a drink, but Jake refused because he didn't drink with just anybody, and besides, if he was to drink anything, he wanted to be at his house.)

DENNIS. Jake, is you sho' you don't want some dranks?

(Jake didn't say a word. He just looked at Dennis, and Dennis shut up and didn't ask if he wanted a drink again.)

FELLOWS. Bring her on, bring her on, bring her on!

(The room got dark, and music started playing. They sat Jake down in the chair of honor. All of a, sudden a figure shaped like a Coke bottle appeared. Jake looked. It was her, he thought. It was the girl from his dream. It was Faye. It was her.)

JAKE. Dennis! Give me a drink and make it strong!
DENNIS. Huh?
JAKE. I said give me a drink!

(Dennis gave Jake a drink, and he swallowed it down as if it was water. Jake called Dennis close to him.)

JAKE. Dennis, what is her name?
DENNIS. You worried about a name. Man, look at that booty.
JAKE. Name, Dennis, what is it?
DENNIS. Hell, Plew, Phad, Pray, something like that.
JAKE. Is it Faye?
DENNIS. I thank so. So what, look at that booty!

(Jake was in shock. He didn't know what to think. He was just ready for the party to end. But he didn't want to spoil it for the rest of the guys, so he pretended to enjoy it just as much as the rest of them. Faye danced. She twisted, and then she started to sit on Jake's lap. Jake got up.)

JAKE. Man, I have to use the bathroom.

(Jake went into the bathroom, knowing that he could not let that girl sit on his lap. After all, it was Faye, the girl from his dream. He wondered how. The party went on without Jake. The fellows seemed to have all but forgotten about him. They enjoyed the entertainment. Time was quickly passing, and they only had their dancer for two hours. Man, Jake was never so happy to see a woman leave.)

JAKE. Wow! I like to thank all of you for the wonderful party, but I think that we all need to call it a night so that I can get married tomorrow. Dennis, I'm going to drive you home! I want to make sure that you are able to get it together by tomorrow.

(Jake drove Dennis, stopping almost every other block, allowing him to throw up until he made it to his house. While Jake was on his way home, he started having crazy thoughts.)

JAKE (*thinking*). I wonder if she knew me. I wonder if she liked me. I wonder if I could have gotten that.

(Jake thought, "Scratch that last one." Jake just started laughing. When he made it home, he pulled out his tuxedo. He looked at it for a while, then he decided to take a shower and go to bed. Morning came, and Jake was somewhat excited, but at the same time, he was nervous. He got dressed and later went to the barber shop.)

BARBER. Jake, my man, today is your day, huh? The old ball and chain, ha, ha, ha!
JAKE. What do you mean by that?
BARBER. Never mind. You want the usual, shaved head and shaved face?
JAKE. Yeah, but do a good job this time, ha, ha, ha!
BARBER. Since today is your day, this one is on me.

(Jake went back to his house. He called Dennis.)

DENNIS. Hello, hello.
JAKE. Dennis, get your butt up!
DENNIS. Jake? Man, what time is it? Have I missed it? I'm so sorry! You shouldn't have let me drink so much!
JAKE. Man, shut up! You haven't missed it, and besides, if you did miss it, you would be missing! It's about eleven o'clock, and I want us to be at the church around twelve thirty, so get your stinky behind up. Take a shower and be there on time.
DENNIS. Look, my brother, you know that you can count on me. Uh, what time, and where is the church?
JAKE. Yeah, I can count on you all right. twelve thirty, and you know where the church is located! Dennis, don't make me do something to you!

(After Jake got off the phone with Dennis, he called the other guys, making sure that they would all be there around twelve thirty. It was time. Jake grabbed his tux, shirt, and shoes and head out the door.)

JAKE. My socks, I almost forgot my socks.

(Jake turned around and went back into the house. His phone would ring.)

JAKE. Hello.
AUNT BREA. Hey, Jake! You needs some help getting dressed?
JAKE. Aunt Brea, what is it? What do you want?
AUNT BREA. Relax, fool, I's just wants you to know that we is here and will be at the church shortly. We had to stop at this here gas station.

(Jake didn't know if he should be getting excited or terrified. Jake grabbed his socks and again headed out. He checked and made sure that he had the ring. Jake finally arrived at the church. The first person he looked for was Dennis.)

JAKE. Dennis, you are here!
DENNIS. I know, you weren't worried. I told you, man, that I'm cool like that.
JAKE. Yeah, cool. Well, fellows, let's get dressed.

(They all went into the male dressing room that the church had set up. All of a sudden, Jake heard Aunt Brea.)

AUNT BREA. We is here. Where that fine Jake is?
DENNIS. Jake, man, is that who I think it is?

(Jake just held his head down and wondered if it was a mistake to invite Cleo's family. But it was too late now. It wasn't long before the usher would come in.)

USHER. We have ten minutes. Just ten minutes before you march out, and make sure that things are done like we rehearsed.
DENNIS. Yes, um, Captain!

(Jake and his groomsmen went out and lined up at the door. The groomsmen's music started to play. They began marching in. The music changed, and it was finally time for Jake. When Jake marched in, all got quiet, and all eyes were on him. You would have thought that the president of the United States was marching in, and the only thing missing was "Hail to the Chief." The audience fell into a deep silence. Jake made it to the front and turned around. The first

person he saw sitting on the front row was Aunt Brea. She was winking and blowing kisses at him. He could have fainted, but he didn't. He just wondered who the lady and the fat guy sitting there beside her were. He thought that it couldn't be Cleo's mother, Betty. Cleo told me that she was a picture image of how her mother—well, what her mother used to look like. She said that her mother also had a beautiful body. Wow, what happened? She looked used up! That fat guy sitting next to her, who in the world? It couldn't be, uh! All of a sudden, the bride's music started. Jake looked up, and all he saw was a goddess! You would have thought she was an angel floating on clouds. For a minute, Jake's eyes look off Cleo and into the crowd. He saw the fat man sitting next to her mother. He was sweating. He was sweating something awful.)

JAKE (*thinking*): I know it's not hot in here because I'm about to freeze and I have on this tux. (*Jake look at him again, and he couldn't sit still. He was being a distraction. It was as if he had ants underneath his clothes and they were all biting him. Jake knew then that this must be Henry and his own conscience was biting his butt. As Cleo walked down the aisle, the only thing in her sight was her man Jake. He stood like a mountain. He looked like a man who owned everything and mastered all.*)

CLEO (*thinking*). My man, I'm going to tear him up tonight. I'm going to put it on him like hot sauce on fried catfish. I'm going to be on him like white on rice. I'm going to give it all to him. I hope he's ready!

(*Cleo made it to Jake, and they joined hands. Cleo had Mr. Johnson, Jake's supervisor, to give her away. The ceremony started, and it quickly ended.*)

PREACHER: You may kiss your bride. Okay, Jake, that's enough. Jake, Jake.

(*After Jake and Cleo kissed, they both turned around with smiles on their faces, but just when Cleo turned around, she looked down and saw her mother and Henry sitting there. The smile left her face. She gripped Jake's hand like a vise. Her heart started to race as if it were to jump out of her chest. Jake, sensing something was terribly wrong, wrapped his massive arm around Cleo's tiny waist and rushed her on out.*)

Fulfilling His Purpose

(*With tears in her eyes, she pulled away.*)

JAKE. Cleo, I am truly sorry. I was just trying to get you and your mother together. I thought you would have wanted her to be here.

(*Jake walked up to Cleo; she grabbed him, wrapped her arms around him, and kissed him.*)

CLEO. Jake, I want to thank you! You don't know how much this means to me! Not only do I get to see my mother. I can finally let go of my past hurt and give you all of me, and all of this you are going to get. Come on, let's get these pictures out of the way.

(*Cleo and Jake went to enter back into the sanctuary, but just when they opened the door, there stood aunt Brea.*)

AUNT BREA. Don't I's get a chance to kiss the groom? You wants teeth in or out? I's can do it both ways. I's like out better.

JAKE. You better keep them in, Aunt Brea.

(*Jake grabbed Aunt Brea, hugged her, and gave her a smack on her lips.*)

AUNT BREA. Shucks, you sho' you don't wants none of me? Cleo, you had better holds on to him, 'cause I's be a waiting if you don't.

JAKE. Aunt Brea, I want to thank you from the bottom of my heart. If I had not had your help, I could not have pulled this off.
AUNT BREA. What is you pulling off? I wants to see!
CLEO. Aunt Brea, I want to thank you as well. Not just for this, but for taking me in, for making sure I stayed in school, for letting me know that I did nothing wrong. Thank you, Aunt Brea!

(Cleo hugged Aunt Brea.)

AUNT BREA. Enough, Cleo! Cans Jake thank me again?

(Jake and Cleo both smiled and turned Aunt Brea around as the three walked back in. They made it back up to the front of the church. Cleo turned around, looked at her mother, and walked over to her. She grabbed her mother and hugged her. At first, Betty just stood there as if she was in shock. Standing there with tears in her eyes, she slowly returned the hugged.)

CLEO. Momma, I am so happy to see you. I have missed you so much! I love you, Momma.
BETTY. Cleo, my baby, I is sorry, I is so sorry!

(Betty looked over her shoulder at Henry. He could not look at her, nor could he look at Cleo. He just sat there, sweating and twitching.)

BETTY. Excuse me, Cleo, I's got to do something.

(Betty walked over to Henry. She sat down and whispered to him.)

BETTY. Henry, you stanky low-down dirty dog. If I's ever sees you again, I's gonna cut your pecker off and stuff it down your lying throat! You hurt my baby girl. You separated us. If you don't get out of here right now, I just might…

(Henry got up, and before he turned to walk away, he look at Cleo and mouthed sorry. Cleo looked and nodded. Jake then stepped in front of her. He looked at Henry like a pit bull about to maul a Chihuahua. Henry turned and ran out of the church. As the festivities were coming to an end, Jake and Cleo were looking into each other's eyes like two carnivores stalking their prey. They both knew their honeymoon was next! Jake escorted Cleo out to their car. He

opened the door for her. He walked around the car at a very fast pace, opened the door, got into the car, and leaned over and kissed his new bride.)

AUNT BREA. Shuck, you two ain't gonna go to no room? I remember when me and da mista gots married, we didn't wait to get no room before he done—

BETTY. Okay, Aunt Brea, love you.

AUNT BREA. Yeah, uh-huh.

(Jake and Cleo drove off. They really didn't plan a big honeymoon. Instead, he just decided to drive to this resort that was about an hour or two away. Jake had made reservations without telling Cleo.)

CLEO. Where are we going?

JAKE. I decided to make reservations at this resort.

CLEO. Jake, as sweet as that is, I didn't bring any clothes.

JAKE. I know!

CLEO. Jake, I tell you what, let's just swing by my place so I can get some things.

(What Jake didn't know was that Cleo had gone shopping just for their special night and she had packed a suitcase. They swung by her place, and she ran in and came right back out.)

JAKE. How did you know?

CLEO. I knew my man would do something besides just go back to the house.

(As Jake drove, Cleo grabbed Jake's hand and placed it on the inside her thigh. Jake's foot pushed harder on the gas pedal. Before he knew it he was speeding.)

CLEO. Going kind of fast, aren't we?

(Jake looked down, and he was driving about 90 mph. He slowly took his foot off the gas, and Cleo removed his hand from her thigh.)

JAKE. Cleo, I want you to know that this will be my first time.

CLEO. I know!

JAKE. Why did you say it like that, and why did you look at me like that?
CLEO. Just get us there.

(They finally arrived at the hotel. Jake pulled up to the front. The valet opened Cleo's door and assisted them in checking in. They took the elevator to the seventh floor; they exited the elevator, found their room, and went in. Jake grabbed Cleo, picked her off her feet, and kissed her at the same time. They made it over to the bed. He tried to put her down gently, but it was as if he lost all his strength at once. Both of them fell onto the bed. Cleo started to get undressed as well as Jake. Jake ran his hands up and down her body. He kissed her on her forehead, on her neck, and then on her lips.)

JAKE. Oh, Cleo.
CLEO. Now, Jake, now!

(Two minutes later, it was over.)

CLEO. Now that we got that first one out of the way, let's take a shower, and I can slip into something that I purchased just for you. Better yet, you go take yours first.
JAKE. Cleo, I'm…
CLEO. No, Jake, don't say a word. Just go and take your shower.

(Jake got up and went into the bathroom; he was feeling like he had let Cleo down. He got into the shower, finished up, and went back into the bedroom to wait for Cleo. When Cleo returned, she was wearing a transparent teddy. It was as if she was wearing nothing at all. Jake's little BIG man stood up immediately. He knew that he had to do a better job than he did the first time. Cleo lay beside Jake.)

CLEO. Jake, please, just take it easy?

(Jake wondered what she was talking about. But not for long, because once he got on top of Cleo, he was like a man with a new sports car. He didn't want to get out.)

CLEO. Jake, oh, Jake, I need a break!
JAKE. Not yet.

(Jake tried to go all night long. Finally, he finished. Cleo could not get up. Her legs were too weak, and they were numb.)

CLEO. Jake, I think I'm paralyzed! I can't move my legs. My man, Jake, wow, did you ever make up for the first time. We have to call room service for some more sheets, these are all wet. Jake, say something.

(Jake didn't say a word. He just lay beside her with a rather large smile on his face.)

CLEO. Jake, can you at least get up and get some dry towels?

(Jake tried to get up, but his legs were weak also. So he just rolled off the bed and crawled to the bathroom. He returned with the towels. Jake and Cleo both started to laugh. Morning came.)

JAKE. How are we going to explain to room service that we need more sheets and towels?

CLEO. Explain? They might as well leave us extra sheets and towels. They know that we are on our honeymoon!

(Jake sat up with a smile on his face. The weekend ended, and it was time for Jake to start moving Cleo's things from her place into his.)

CLEO. We have been moving every day since we came back. How about you go hang out for a while and I will cook you a delicious home-cooked meal?

JAKE. Sounds good to me. The guys should be off from work and at the pub by now. I think I will go by there and catch up on what's been happening at work.

(Jake left and went to the pub. When he made it, the first person he saw was Dennis.)

DENNIS. Jake, my man, we haven't seen you since the wedding. I'm surprised you still can walk. That fine woman of yours must be putting it on you. Man, if that was my woman, I would—

JAKE. Dennis, you are about to say a little too much!

DENNIS. Okay! I was just saying that she is a fine woman!

JAKE. I bet you were. Come on, fellows, I will buy you all your first round of beer.

(All five of the guys cheered as they sat down and ordered their beer. While they were sitting down, that woman came in.)

DENNIS. Man, look at all that BOOTY! Damn! That small waist and those tits, oh bitties! Man, I sho' like to get on that.

JUSTIN. Jake, you know who that is. You remember the stripper we had at your bachelor party? Nah, you probably wouldn't remember. You stayed in the restroom the whole time.

(With his back to the door, Jake didn't see her come in. But he remembered the stripper that was at his party. Jake turned around slowly. It was her. It was Faye, the girl from his dream. As he turned around to look at her, a certain feeling came over him. It wasn't lust; it was a feeling like he has never felt before, like he really knew her, a feeling from deep within. Jake knew that he had to go talk to her, but he thought, "What will I say?" Jake got up to walk over to her.)

DENNIS. Jake, where the hell do you think you are going? Jake, sit your butt down, man. Don't you know a fine stripper like that gots to have a pimp!

(Jake didn't pay any attention to what Dennis was saying; he just kept walking toward the lady. Jake approached her as if he was a cat walking on a hot tin roof.)

JAKE. Uh, excuse me.

LADY: Yeah, what do you want, and how much money do you have?

JAKE. No, it's not like that. I was just wondering about your name.

LADY: My friends call me...

JAKE. Faye.

FAYE. How did you know? You do look kind of familiar. I know, I did your bachelor party. How can I ever forget a man of your stature? Wow, you are thick!

JAKE. Thank you, but I felt like I knew you even before then. Where were you born?

(All of a sudden, this guy started walking up to Faye. He was dressed like a circus clown. He had on an oversized lime-green trench coat, too-tight lime green pants with a matching vest. He had to be about five feet five, but with his shoes on, he appeared to be six feet.)

PIMP. Look at here, Faye, is this a customer, or is he just wasting your time and my money?

JAKE. Uh, I'm over here, you can talk to me.

PIMP. Boy, when I want to hear from you, I will address you. Until then, you can just shut the hell up!

(Jake stood up from the bar stool. The pimp pulled back his coat and showed a pearl handle what looked like it belonged to a .45-caliber pistol.)

PIMP. Like I said, boy, when I want to hear from you, I will pull your chain, but until then, shut the hell up!

(Jake was no fool. He knew that it would be to his best interest to sit back down and shut up, for now.)

FAYE. No, baby, we were just working out the details. He was just asking me if I was the one that danced at his bachelor party. Honest, baby, would I lie to you?

PIMP. Shut up before I slap the taste out of your mouth! This conversation is over!

(They got up and walked out, with Faye walking behind him, she glanced over her shoulder to look back at Jake.)

DENNIS. Man, are you crazy? Ain't no booty worth getting killed for. Wait a minute, didn't you just get married? Creeping already, huh?

JAKE. Dennis, you wouldn't understand if I told you! I know her.

DENNIS. Oh, you already hit that, huh?

JAKE. I will see you guys later.

(Jake started home. But he just could not get Faye out of his mind.)

JAKE (*wondering*). She has to be the one that was in my dreams. She just has to be. Everything about her, even her name, even the pimp, he reminds me of that Mr. Eli. What could this mean?

JUSTIN. Jake, will you wake up, man? Jake, now you know that that sorry sucker Dennis is going to make sure everyone on the job finds out about that girl.

JAKE. So let him!

JUSTIN. Even Mr. Johnson?

JAKE. You are right. And I know Dennis. He is going to try and make it seem like more than what it was.

JUSTIN. Jake, what was it?

JAKE. I really don't know. I really don't know.

JUSTIN. Jake, man, I don't know how you gonna handle it, but my advice to you is to handle it.

JAKE. Yeah, I hear you. I will just have to try to figure something out. Later, man.

JORDAN. Jake, my brother, my advice to you is for you to go home and tell Cleo what just happened so when Dennis blabs his mouth to Mr. Johnson, Cleo would already be aware of the situation. But surely, Mr. Johnson would address you first, and knowing him, he wouldn't dare say anything to Cleo without first speaking to you.

JAKE. Wow, I never really heard you talk before, but when you have something to say, I guess you really say it.

JUSTIN. Later.

JAKE. I will see you guys later.

(*Jake made it back home.*)

CLEO. Jake, how was it? Was that so-called best man Dennis there? I bet the guys were happy to see you? Jake, is everything okay. You haven't said a word.

JAKE. Yeah, everything is okay. I'll be right back. There's something I have to do.

(*Jake left the house to look for Faye, but he didn't know why. He knew that her pimp wouldn't be hard to find. He was driving a Lincoln with a diamond in the back and a sunroof top, and it had a certain lean to it. It was like something inside of him was pushing him. Jake searched for hours but could not find them. He searched until it started to get dark. He thought to himself, "I better be getting home. I don't want Cleo to think that I'm out doing something.")*

CLEO. I'm glad to see you back. Is there anything wrong? Jake, you look like you have seen a ghost. You do know that you can talk to me, right?

JAKE. Yes, baby, I know that I can talk to you. I love you, Cleo, and you are the only one for me.

(Jake reached over and grabbed Cleo; he picked her up and started kissing her.)

CLEO. Hold on, have you eaten anything? I cooked us some beans, cornbread, fried chicken, and for dessert, I cooked a nice rice pudding.

JAKE. Wow! You cooked all of my favorites, but for dessert, I thought I would have you!

CLEO. Well, we will see. If you are good and clean your plate, we will see if I can accommodate you.

(Jake sat down, and before Cleo was finished talking good, he had finished.)

JAKE. Come on with it!

CLEO. Not now, I'm not fresh. Plus, I have to clean my kitchen. You know that I do not leave my kitchen dirty.

(Cleo ran her dish water and started to wash the dishes. Jake walked up behind her. While pressing his body against her, he kissed her on the back of her neck. He then turned her around and kissed her. Cleo put her arms around his neck and returned the kiss.)

CLEO. Oh, Jake, let me finish these dishes and take a shower, and I promise you that I'm going to make you scream for mercy!

JAKE. What? I can't believe my sweet lady just said that.

CLEO. Believe me, you haven't seen anything yet. You just go and get ready for this whipping I'm about to put on you!

(Jake went and got into the shower, but before he was finished, Cleo came and got in with him. She stood between him and the water.)

JAKE. Aw, this is what I'm talking about, my lady.
CLEO. Jake, I love you so.
JAKE. And I love you.

(*After Jake got out of the shower, he decided to turn on some music. Teddy Pendergrass was singing "Turn off the Lights," and that is exactly what Jake did. He turned off the lights and lit some candles. And when Cleo got out of the shower, she walked in with this transparent red thigh-high negligee. She was very sexy. Jake picked her up and placed her on the bed; he caressed her body and kissed her all over. Jake looked up at the clock. It was only eight, but when it was all over, it was twelve.*)

CLEO. Jake, you've done it again. I can't move. Oh, what a feeling, wow! We better hurry and get up, or we are going to soak right through the mattress pad and all. And this time, we can't call room service.

(*Cleo and Jake both crawled out of their bed, pulling the sheets and mattress cover off.*)

JAKE. We got up just in time.
CLEO. When I get my feeling back in my legs, I'll make the bed. Wow!

(*After the bed was made, they decided to call it a night. Cleo placed her head on Jake's massive chest as he placed his hand on her bodacious rear end.*)

CLEO. Good night, superman.

(*Jake couldn't answer because he was already sleeping. The next day was Jake's last day off.*)

JAKE. We need to finish with the rest of this moving today. I don't want to be moving every day after I get off from work.
CLEO. How about getting the guys to come help you?
JAKE. That's okay. I'm just about finished now. I just have small items now.

(Jake left heading back to Cleo's old place, but on his way, he saw the Lincoln. It was the one all right. He decided to follow it. The car stopped in front of this daycare. The door opened, and a fair-skinned female got out with two young children. He couldn't believe his eyes. Jake thought to himself, "This gun-toting, hard-talking, funny-dressing punk of a pimp has a family, it doesn't figure." Jake drove on and went on to finish his moving. That night, Jake was talking to Cleo.)

JAKE. I've been having some weird feelings lately, feelings I can't explain.

CLEO. Weird like what?

JAKE. I can't explain them right now, but I assure you, as soon as I can, I will.

(Jake and Cleo decided to turn it in, because they knew that they had to go back to work the next day. But Cleo could not help but to wonder what he was talking about.)

CLEO. Good morning, Mr. Martin.

JAKE. Good morning, Mrs. Martin. How did you sleep?

CLEO. I slept great. Your body is so warm, and it felt wonderful feeling you beside me, just wonderful.

JAKE. Well, I will see you this evening.

(Jake reached and grabbed Cleo, giving her a kiss. He wrapped his arms around her, and she pressed her tender body against him.)

JAKE. Uh, we better move on before something happens, and we both are late.

(Jake drove to work, not knowing if his friend Dennis had said anything to Mr. Johnson about what happened at the pub. Jake made it to work.)

MRS. BROWN. Good morning, Mr. Martin. Mr. Johnson asked to see you as soon as you walked in.

JAKE. Good morning, I think.

(Jake slowly walked down the hall to Mr. Johnson's office. He walked into the outer office.)

JAKE. Good morning, Ms. Thomas.
MS. THOMAS. Good morning, he said for you to come right in.

(The palm of Jake's hands were dripping wet with sweat. He opened the door to see Mr. Johnson sitting at his desk with his back to the door. But before he turned around, he spoke.)

MR. JOHNSON. Jake, my boy, how's everything going? Did you get all your moving done, or were you too busy hanging with the fellows? I was told by a certain person that you were hanging out and you almost got killed. Look here, have you gotten your life insurance changed over, because if you are going to be messing with people like that, I want to make sure that Cleo is taken well care of. Jake, I must say that I was certainly shocked to hear that you were trying to solicit from that young lady. Now that I have said all of that, I want you to know that I didn't and don't believe one word of it. Jake, what was going on?

(Jake looked completely shocked; his color slowly returned, and he was able to breathe again.)

JAKE. Mr. Johnson, I will not lie to you. There is one part of that that's true. I was out buying the fellows a drink, and it was Cleo who suggested it. Mr. Johnson, we were at the pub when this certain lady came in. Well, the best way to explain it is to tell you from the beginning, but it might take a while.
MR. JOHNSON. Wait one minute.

(Mr. Johnson buzzed Ms. Thomas.)

MR. JOHNSON. Ms. Thomas, hold all of my calls until I tell you otherwise, and call down to Jake's office and tell Mrs. Brown that Jake will be out until further notice. Now, go right ahead, Jake.
JAKE. Well, Mr. Johnson, it all started when I was home and I had decided to go to college. The night before, I was so excited that I even dreamed about it, but it felt so real. It felt like it actually happened. I dreamed that I woke up and went to

college, but when I got there, I discovered that I didn't know anything about going to college, so I ran away. When I ran, I met this guy. He was dressed in a lime-green leisure suit and large-brimmed hat with a feather in it, and he had on a pair of stacks which heels and soles were at least six inches, and he asked me to work for him.

MR. JOHNSON. What about the girl?

JAKE. I'm going to come to her. I'm telling you about all this because it all ties in together. So while I was working for him, I met this young lady who was known by Faye. She was fine. She was so fine that she would have put a Coke bottle to shame. Oh, anyway, I met her, and right away, I fell for her, and I thought she had fallen for me. So one day I was walking home, and she met me about halfway. I went into the woods with her, and she did something's to me that if I close my eyes right now I still can feel.

MR. JOHNSON. Jake, keep your eyes opened.

JAKE. Well, it only happened the one time. The next day, I decided to tell this stooge Lenny. He also worked for this sharp-dressed man, but he said that he was going to tell him. You see, I was warned to stay away from her by Mr. Eli. This is the sharpdressed man's name. I then found an old jack handle and killed

LENNY. I ran and hid. I found Faye, and she took me in and cleaned me up. I ran home to discover that my mom had died also. I later woke to discover that all of this was a dream. My mother was alive, and I never left the old house to go to college.

MR. JOHNSON, I took all of this to be a dream until the night of my bachelor party. There she was. I saw her. It was Faye. It was her, the girl in my dream.

Mr. Johnson. Wait a minute, you had a bachelor party, and I wasn't invited? How do you know it was her? Did you ask her name? How do you know?

JAKE. I told you, by the way she made me feel, I would know her from anywhere. And besides, I asked her name the other day, and it was Faye.

MR. JOHNSON. Wow, have you discussed this with Cleo? And have you and Cleo found a church home yet?

JAKE. A church home? What does that have to do with anything I've been telling you?

MR. JOHNSON. Jake, my boy, I believe you, but there is something more going on here something. I don't think you are ready to handle. I believe this young lady was placed into your life for a reason.

JAKE. In my life? What are you talking about? How can someone just be put in your life? What can I do? Who am I?

MR. JOHNSON. Jake, I know where you can find all of your answers, but let me strongly advise you, please do not attempt to contact her again until you are fully ready.

JAKE. So you think I should go get a gun?

MR. JOHNSON. No, my son, a gun will only get you killed. It will not accomplish what needs to be accomplished.

JAKE. I really don't understand.

MR. JOHNSON. Once again I ask, have you spoken with Cleo on this matter and have you two found a church home?

JAKE. No! How can I tell her that I've seen the girl that I dreamed about, a girl that made me feel like a man, a girl that when I close my eyes I still can feel her, a girl...

MR. JOHNSON. Jake, my son, I know that you are brighter than that. You have been hanging around Dennis far too long. Jake, you are going to have to discuss some of the details, but you should know what details to leave out. I assure you Cleo is more advanced than you know.

JAKE. Advanced?

MR. JOHNSON. Jake, after you talk to Cleo, I want you to report back to me.

JAKE. Yes, sir.

(*Jake got up turned around to walk out the door.*)

MR. JOHNSON. Oh, I didn't tell you when to report to me.

JAKE. You told me after I talk to Cleo.

MR. JOHNSON. I meant day after tomorrow. Jake, I told you before you married Cleo that she is like a daughter to me, and if this young lady is that important to you, you really need to have a talk with Cleo. It's not for me, it's for you and Cleo.

JAKE. I understand, and I will talk to her.

(Jake walked out.)

MS. THOMAS. Mr. Martin, is everything okay?

(Jake didn't say a word, because he didn't really hear her, but just before he exited, he quickly replied.)

JAKE. Aw, yeah, everything is okay.

(When Jake made it back to his office, he told Mrs. Brown to continue to hold all his calls and that he didn't want to see anyone unless it was an emergency. The day seemed to last forever, but it seemed to fly by.)

MRS. BROWN. Uh, Mr. Martin, are you leaving for the day, or are you staying late?

JAKE. Mrs. Brown, I really don't know. This is one of those times that I don't know if I'm coming or going. I guess I had better go. I will see you tomorrow, I guess.

MRS. BROWN. Mr. Martin, all will work out. He will not allow more on you than you can handle. Just call on his mighty name, and all will work out. Mr. Martin, Philippians 4:13 says, "I can do all things through Christ who strengthens me." Simply just call on his name, just call on his name. Good evening, Mr. Martin.

JAKE. Good evening, Mrs. Brown.

(Jake, being one who didn't really know the Word, had little ideal of what she was trying to say. Oh yeah, he knew of God, but he didn't really know God. He knew Psalms 23, and he knew the Lord's Prayer. His mom made him learn that. You see, when he was young, his mom took him to church, but he didn't really pay attention, and when it came time for him to give his life to Christ, well, let's say the deacons really confused him. Jake got up in front of the church to confess his life to Christ and the deacons. I guess they didn't know any better; they just wanted him to say that he believed in Jesus Christ. Jake had so much more to say. He wanted the people to know that he loved the Lord and that he felt truly blessed to have lived his life for twelve years, but they interrupted him as if that really didn't mattered. They just wanted to say that he accepted the Lord Jesus Christ. That really hurt Jake, and it made him feel like it was all just one big show, but he did get baptized. Jake started home. He

thought he should take the long way. He felt like the weight of the world was on his shoulders.)

JAKE. If I am weak, maybe I won't make it or if I just forget all about Faye and told Mr. Johnson that I decided to just leave the whole matter alone. (*He didn't know what to do. He pulled up in front of his home. He sat there in the car for a while. Cleo who had already made it home looked out of one of the windows and saw that he had made it. She wondered what was taking him so long to get out. She decided to go outside; she walked up to the car.*)

CLEO. Jake, is everything okay? How was your day? Did anything happen?

(*Jake snapped back.*)

JAKE. What! That Mr. Johnson called you, didn't he?

CLEO. No, he didn't. Why, should he?

JAKE. Oh, he didn't. I'm sorry, I shouldn't have snapped at you like that. I've had such a trying day.

CLEO. Jake, come in, and we will get you something to eat, and then you can relax.

(*Jake got out of the car, and Cleo grabbed him, wrapped her arms around him, but much to her surprise, the hug wasn't returned. Yeah, he put his arms around her, but she knew that he wasn't his usual self. She knew that something was seriously wrong.*)

CLEO. Jake, why don't you go in there? Take off your shoes and get comfortable. I will bring your plate to you. I think that old junkman and his son is just coming on.

JAKE. Okay.

CLEO. Jake, do you feel like talking?

JAKE. Talking about what?

CLEO. Uh, maybe about what's going on?

JAKE. Well, I guess this might be as good as a time as ever, and besides, as soon as I get it out, the sooner I get it over, right?

CLEO. Get what over?

JAKE. I never told you how I came to be here in this city. I'm going to try to make a long story short. Before I came here, I was living at home with my mom. I had just graduated from high school and had thoughts of going to college. I was excited about going too. I was so excited that the night before I had a dream about it. I dreamed that I went off to college, but when I got there, the paperwork and the whole process was too much for me, so I ran and ran until I saw this pimp, Mr. Eli. He was dressed sharp. He had on a lime-green leisure suit, an oversized green-brimmed hat with a feather sticking in it, and a pair of platform shoe that soles and heels had to be six inches.

CLEO. Excuse me, sharp-dressed?

JAKE. Yeah, funny, huh? Well, anyway I ran into him, and I started working for him, yeah, delivering drugs. Until one day I met this young lady. Remember, this was a dream. I met this young lady. She was okay. I met her, and I kind of liked her, and I thought that she kind of liked me. So one day, I decided to tell Lenny, who was also working for Mr. Eli, and Mr. Eli had already told me to leave Faye, the young lady, alone. I became upset. I picked up a jack handle and killed poor old Lenny.

CLEO. Okay, what's the problem? You said that this was a dream.

JAKE. Well, it was, until the night of my bachelor party. You see, Dennis went against my wishes and hired a stripper. I didn't stay in the room, but I did see the stripper before I left out. It was her. It was Faye!

CLEO. What? How do you know it was her? Did you ask her name or something? What happened?

JAKE. Hold on. No, I did not ask her name. I didn't even see her dance, but the other day, when you told me to go and hang out with the fellows at the pub, she came in. I then felt compelled to go over to talk to her. I wasn't attracted to her, but it was like I was supposed to talk to her. It was like a gut feeling—not a lusty feeling, a feeling that I can't really explain. So I got up and went over to her and asked her name, and before she told me, I answered Faye. But before we were able to say anything else, her pimp came over, and that was the end of the conversation.

CLEO. Wow! A person can live their whole life and not have happen to them what you've encountered. Jake, we have to get you in a good church. We have to get you into the Word before you do anything else.

JAKE. You sound like Mr. Johnson. What does the church have to do with anything? What does getting into the Word has to do with it?

CLEO. Jake, I can try to explain this to you, but you might need more than me explaining it. You see, when we are born, we all have a purpose in life, and our purpose is to a person or to people. Some of us may have several, but a lot of us might not ever realize who that person is, or we might not even know if we have fulfilled our purpose, but we somehow do. Do you understand me?

JAKE. You lost me a long time ago.

CLEO. I tell you what, Sunday we are going to start visiting churches.

JAKE. Why don't we just go to Mr. Johnson's church?

CLEO. Jake, you have to understand—you don't pick the church, the church picks you.

JAKE. If you say so.

CLEO. Come on, let's go take a shower so I can rub your back and help you relax.

(That night, Jake thought that he was going to be able to sleep, but he was wrong. He had a dreamed that he was in a hot steaming jungle and he kept hearing someone calling his name. There was a waterfall, and all of a sudden, he saw this body falling. He couldn't see the face, but he saw tears falling from her eyes. He thought, "Why did I assume it was a female? I couldn't see the face." When Jake woke, the whole side of his bed was wet from his head to his feet. It was wet with sweat.)

CLEO. What's wrong?

JAKE. Nothing. I guess I was just too hot.

(Cleo knew that something was wrong, because the air was blowing and he had only a sheet on him.)

CLEO. Okay, let's take the sheets off and see if the mattress cover is wet also. If not, we will just put new sheets on the bed.

(The next morning, Jake couldn't wait to get to work and tell Mr. Johnson that he had spoken to Cleo. He got up, kissed Cleo, ate his breakfast, and hurried out. But on his way, he saw Faye. He saw her, and he wanted to stop. He

wanted to say something to her. He wanted to pick her up. But he thought to himself, "She is fine and sexy, but I don't want her. It feels like I need to help her." Jake decided to continue driving. He remember what Cleo and Mr. Johnson told him that he was not ready. Jake made it to work.)

JAKE. Good morning, Mrs. Brown!

MRS. BROWN. Good morning, Mr. Martin. How are you this morning?

JAKE. Great, just great! Would you ring Mr. Johnson's office and see if he can pencil me in?

MRS. BROWN. Yes, sir. I'm glad to see that things are better for you.

MS. THOMAS. Mr. Johnson's office.

MRS. BROWN. Mr. Martin wants to know if Mr. Johnson has time to see him today.

MS. THOMAS. Girl, let me check. Mr. Johnson, Mr. Martin wants to know if you have time to see him today.

MR. JOHNSON. Sure, tell him now is the only time I will have today.

MS. THOMAS. Girl, he said that the only time he has is right now. Send him right over!

MRS. BROWN. He said that you can come right over.

JAKE. Thank you.

MR. JOHNSON. Jake, my boy. I trust that you had a talk with Cleo last night?

JAKE. Yes, sir. We had a long conversation, and basically, she said almost the same thing you told me, not to do anything because I'm not ready. Oh, by the way, I did see Faye this morning, and once again, I had that feeling, but I didn't stop.

MR. JOHNSON. Jake, my boy, you will find that the feelings you are having are the ones confusing you. One is spirit, and one is flesh. Jake, I can tell you that we are three-part being. We are spirit, we have a soul, and we live in this physical body. You need to know that our bodies will only do what it's trained to do. That will be all. Oh, find yourself a good church home. You are going to need it.

(On his way back to his office, Jake thought to himself, "What in the world was he talking about? We are going to start looking for a church home, and it won't be Mr. Johnson's." Sunday came, and Jake was being a man of his word.)

JAKE. Okay, get up, beautiful, we are going to church.

(Jake and Cleo both got ready, and they went to this one church. The choir was pretty good, but then the pastor got up.)

PASTOR. We is here today to give honor to God. Speaking of giving, ushers, make sure everybody got they little brown envelope. We got to pay our dues. Remember to humble yourselves. When we pay our dues, we don't expect nothing in return. We got to give. We got to give until it hurt, for the building fund. God likes a cheerful giver. It is better to give than it is to receive. Ain't that right, Deacon?

(Jake and Cleo just looked at each other. Jake leaned over to Cleo.)

JAKE. We will not be coming back here.

(Another week went by, and yet again another church. Once again, the choir was okay, but then the sermon.)

PASTOR. Mary had a little lamb, his fleece was as white as snow. When we say *white as snow*, that means not one blemish was on it. That's how we should be, white as snow. And da Jack and Jill went up the hill. Jack fell down and da Jill fell behind him. We don't need to fall, but if we do, we need to get up. And da Mary, Mary was quite contrary. She needed to have a stable mind. We needs a stable mind. I want ta send y'all home with this. Humpty Dumpty sat on the wall, Humpty Dumpty had a great fall, but unlike Humpty, we ain't got to stay down.

(Once again, Jake looked at Cleo. This time, they both shook their heads and whispered, "We will not be coming back." Another week passed, and yet again another church. This time, the choir—well, let's just say they shouldn't have been called a choir. The pastor got up to deliver the sermon.)

PASTOR. Brothers and sisters, I'm here to tell you that our Jesus died on the cross. He died. Yes, he died. He died. Didn't he die? He died for our sins. They stabbed him in his side, and he died.

Yes, he died. Awwwww, he died. Yes, he died. They hung him on the cross and struck him in his side. He died. Yes, he died.

(After church, Jake looked at Cleo, and they both started laughing.)

CLEO. He died. Yes, he died! Well, Jake, my love, what now?
JAKE. Okay, next Sunday we will visit your church.

(Sunday came, and they went to Cleo's church, Canaan Christian Center. The choir was called a praise team, and praise was what they did. It was very good. After the singing, they even asked for the visitors to stand, and then the pastor got up. He was a tall fellow. He even introduced his wife as beautiful. Jake felt that this was the place for them; it was a feeling deep inside, a feeling in his gut. After that, it was offering time. He explained that when we give we should expect a return because when a farmer sows seed, he expects a harvest. Okay, after the offering was the sermon. But first, the pastor prayed.)

PASTOR. Lord, I want to thank you for being present in here today, and, Holy Spirit, you have the right to walk up and down every row, touching each one as you see fit. Now let's get into the Word.

(After the sermon, Jake wanted to join, but something stopped him from doing so. Jake instead left out feeling like he had just missed the opportunity of his life. All week long, something inside of Jake wanted to go back to that church. Sunday seemed like it would never come. Finally Sunday, Cleo was taking her time getting ready.)

JAKE. Cleo, are you ready yet?
CLEO. Give me five more minutes.
JAKE. You said that ten minutes ago.
CLEO. Okay, mister, I'm ready.
JAKE. Wow! You look great. Now let's go!

(When Jake arrived, he didn't want to hear the praise team sing. He didn't want to hear the pastor preach. All he wanted to do was to satisfy that burning inside of him, that burning he felt to join. After the sermon and when the preacher begun to asked if anyone needed a church home, Jake's hand flew up. Jake walked up to the front with Cleo by his side.)

PASTOR. So you want to join? Tell everyone your name.

JAKE. Jake Martin, and I believe you all know my beautiful wife, Cleo.

PASTOR. We certainly do. Jake, we accept you into this body of Christ. All we ask is that you give us a year, and if your life hasn't made a drastic change for the better, that means we have not done you a service. So, Ms. Cleo, you finally got him here? This is your Jake? Everybody put your hands together and welcome Jake into this body of Christ.

(Jake stood there with tears in his eyes. He didn't know why, but for some reason, they just started to flow. On the way home after church, Cleo wanted to talk.)

CLEO. Jake are you okay?

JAKE. Yeah, I'm good.

CLEO. Are you hungry?

JAKE. Yeah, I could eat something.

CLEO. What do you want?

JAKE. Whatever.

(Cleo drove to get a bucket of chicken. They made it home, they ate, and Jake decided to take a nap. When he woke up, he went into the kitchen, grabbed Cleo from behind, and started kissing her on the back of her neck. It became so intense that she had to stop what she was doing to make sure that she satisfied her man. After they were finished, they both were lying on the den floor out of breath.)

CLEO. Wow! I guess you liked what you saw?

JAKE. Now you know that you can't wash dishes with just an apron on and expect me not to notice. I really liked what I saw. Can't you tell?

CLEO. I can tell. Besides, there were not any dishes to wash.

(Jake started laughing.)

JAKE. So this was all planned?

CLEO. I thought you would never get up. I waited until I heard you moving around, then I pretended to be washing dishes. I see it worked.

JAKE. Yeah, it worked all right!
CLEO. And you worked it too!

(The next morning, Jake made it to work.)

MRS. BROWN. Good morning, Mr. Martin. Mr. Johnson wants to see you immediately.

(Jake walked do the hall.)

JAKE. Good morn—
MS. THOMAS. Go right in.

(Jake walked into Mr. Johnson's office.)

MR. JOHNSON. Jake, my boy, how are you?
JAKE. I'm fine. As a matter of fact, I never felt better.
MR. JOHNSON. Good. That will be all.

(Jake left out feeling puzzled. He didn't know what to think. All of the rushing to his office and all he wanted was to ask me how am I. Jake went back to his office and started to work. Before long, Dennis walked in.)

DENNIS. Jake, my man, you going to lunch?
JAKE. Is it lunch time already?
DENNIS. Yeah, come on, I will let you treat me to lunch.
JAKE. Treat you, I should beat you. You came back and told Mr. Johnson about Faye. And besides, twice I was with you, and twice I saw her.
DENNIS. Come on, man, there's this new place opened up. You can eat all that you want.
JAKE. I am kind of hungry. Who's driving?
DENNIS. Uh…
JAKE. I'll drive. I am kind of hungry.

(After they made it, they walked in. Jake paid, and they both got their plates. And just when Jake went to sit down and pick up his fork, he saw Faye.)

FAYE. Well, hello, are you following me?

(*Jake slowly looked up.*)

JAKE. Well, hello and how are you?

(*A man walked up behind her.*)

MAN. Uh, they can wait their turn. I'm paying you now.
JAKE. Nice seeing you again.
FAYE. Nice seeing you too. I hope to be seeing more of you.

(*Jake turned and looked at Dennis.*)

DENNIS. Well, who would have thought? Pass me the salt.

(*Jake didn't say a word. But in his mind, he thought she was fine.*)

JAKE (*thinking*). Wow, her body is out of this world. Man, she's fine. What did she mean she hope to be seeing more of me? Stop it, Jake, you are a married man. There's nothing wrong in looking. Man, she is fine. I can't be thinking like this. But why is it that she keeps popping up in my life? Is this what Mr. Johnson was talking about when he said that my confusion was coming from my spirit and my flesh?
DENNIS. Jake, are you okay? And pass the salt.
JAKE. Here, Dennis!
DENNIS. Are you going to eat or what?

(*Jake picked up his fork, and they finished eating. As soon as Jake made it back to his office, he knew that he had to talk to someone, but who? He couldn't talk to Mr. Johnson. He was way too close to Cleo. He didn't think that he had been in church long enough to call and speak with his pastor, and surely, he knew not to talk to Dennis on a matter such as this. He didn't know what to think.*)

MRS. BROWN. Jake, you have a call from Mrs. Martin.
JAKE. Hello, my love, what's up?
CLEO. Oh, nothing. Does something have to be up for me to call my husband?

JAKE. No, of course not. It's just … never mind. I'm fine. What about you?

CLEO. Jake, is there anything wrong?

JAKE. No, I'm just sitting here, thinking.

CLEO. About me, I hope.

JAKE. You know it. Hey, I have to go. I will see you in a few.

CLEO. Okay, I love. Oh, he hung up.

JAKE (*thinking*). Did I just hang up in my wife's face? Man, what am I doing? I need to call her back, but I can't. She doesn't work near a telephone. I will just talk to her tonight.

(*Later that evening.*)

CLEO. Hello, Jake. How was your day? You know you hung up on me.

JAKE. Yeah, I know, I'm sorry. I had a lot on my mind.

CLEO. The pastor called. They want to have lunch with us tomorrow. I told them that we would be delighted.

JAKE. Well, if you already told them. (*Then Jake thought to himself.*) This would be the best time for me to try to speak with him.

Cleo. Now what were you so busy doing that you hung up on me?

JAKE. Uh, you know I had a deadline to make and stuff.

CLEO. And stuff, yeah right.

(*After Cleo's comment, there wasn't too much more to say. Jake just sat down, turned on the TV, and waited for Cleo to call him to dinner. He waited and waited and waited. He waited until he couldn't wait anymore.*)

JAKE. Cleo, my love, what's for dinner?

CLEO. Oh, I got a little busy doing some stuff.

JAKE. Okay, I get it.

(*Jake wrapped his massive arms around her, picked her off her feet, and kissed her like it was their very first kiss.*)

JAKE. I love you, Cleo Martin. I love you, and I apologize.

CLEO. What do you want for dinner? My treat!

JAKE. I tell you what, you cook dinner, and then you can treat me to dessert.

CLEO. Sounds like a plan to me. I don't know if I can wait until after dinner. How about eating your dessert first?

JAKE. Uh, baby, I think I'm a little too hungry for dessert first.

CLEO. Okay, I'll cook first, but you are going to owe me big time!

(The next morning Cleo and Jake got up and got ready to meet their pastor and his wife for lunch.)

JAKE. Did the pastor say why they wanted to meet with us?

CLEO. No, they probably just want to get to know you better.

JAKE. I see. Are we going to meet them or what?

CLEO. No, they said that they would pick us up.

JAKE. What time?

CLEO. My, why all the questions? Are you nervous?

JAKE. Uh, no, I just want to know.

CLEO. Well, they thought it would be better if we did an early lunch, about eleven or so.

JAKE. Eleven! Do you know what time it is?

CLEO. It's only nine thirty.

JAKE. Yeah, but you know how long it takes you to get ready.

(Time passed. There was a knock on the door. Jake answered.)

PASTOR. Hello, brother Jake. Are you and the missus ready?

JAKE. I am. Let me check.

CLEO. Here I am, let's go.

(As they got into the vehicle everyone spoke to each other and had idol conversation while on their way to the restaurant. They made it to the restaurant they went inside they all were seated they ordered got served and ate.)

PASTOR. So, Jake, have you given it any thought of how you might want to serve in the ministry?

JAKE. Uh, no, I haven't.

PASTOR. Jake, you haven't said two good words. Is there anything wrong?

JAKE. Wrong? No, there's not anything wrong.

(The pastor looked over at his wife, and she at him. He nodded, and she knew that he needed to be alone with Jake.)

PASTOR'S WIFE. Cleo, why don't we go powder our noses and go look in the gift shop?
CLEO. Sounds great to me.

(Cleo and the pastor's wife got up, leaving Jake and the pastor alone to talk.)

PASTOR. Okay, Jake, I cleared it out for you. Spill the beans.
JAKE. Well, I really don't know how to say this.
PASTOR. We don't have that much time. Do you need an appointment to come and talk with me?
JAKE. That would probably be better.
PASTOR. I tell you what, we can leave, and you and I can meet at the church today around two o'clock. How does that sound?
JAKE. Sounds good.

(Jake and the pastor got up and went to meet their wives.)

PASTORS. You ladies ready to go?

(They all loaded up and left. They dropped Cleo and Jake off, and the pastor told Jake that he would see him around two.)

CLEO. Oh, you have a meeting with the pastor?
JAKE. Yeah, I guess it's something he wants to talk to me about.
CLEO. I guess I'll let you go. Besides, I have some house cleaning to do.

(Time quickly passed, and Jake met the pastor at the church.)

PASTOR. Come on in. Have a seat.
JAKE. I know you're wondering what's going on. Well, the only way I can tell you is to start from the beginning. It all started when I was home and I had decided to go to college. The night before, I was so excited that I even dreamed about it, but it felt so real. It felt like it actually happened. I dreamed that I woke up and went to college, but when I got there, I

discovered that I didn't know anything about going to college, so I ran away. When I ran, I met this guy. He was dressed in a lime-green leisure suit and large-brimmed hat with a feather in it, and he had on a pair of stacks which heels and soles were at least six inches, and he asked me to work for him. I'm telling you about all of this because it all ties in together. So while I was working for him, I met this young lady who was known by the name Faye. She was fine. She was so fine that she would have put a Coke bottle to shame. Oh, anyway, I met her, and right away I fell for her, and I thought she had fallen for me. So one day, I was walking home, and she met me about halfway, and I went into the woods with her. She did something's to me that if I close my eyes right now I still can feel. Well, it only happened the one time. The next day, I decided to tell this stooge Lenny. He also worked for this sharp-dressed man, but he said that he was going to tell him. You see, I was warned to stay away from her by Mr. Eli. This is the sharp-dressed man's name. I then found an old jack handle and killed Lenny. I ran and hid. I found Faye, and she took me in and cleaned me up. I ran home to discover that my mom had died also. I later woke to discover that all this was a dream. My mother was alive, and I never left the old house to go to college.

PASTOR. Okay, what does this have to do with your life now?

JAKE. Well, you see, all of that was a dream, but when my coworker Dennis gave me a bachelor party, he hired this stripper, and as soon as I saw her face, I knew it was her, the girl from my dreams. It was Faye.

PASTOR. Could it be that you're overreacting? She could have just looked like her.

JAKE. Yeah, I thought about that also, but once again we were at the pub, and she walked in. This time, I had to be sure. I approached her, and I asked her name.

PASTOR. Don't tell me it was Faye.

JAKE. Yes! I was about to engage her in conversation, but her pimp showed up and started to act stupid. He said that I was wasting his time and stopping her from making money. But the strangest thing of all is that I feel something on the inside of me when I see her. It's not like I want her sexually, but a deep burning inside of my stomach.

PASTOR. Jake, I have to tell you that all of us have a purpose here on this earth, and that purpose could be to a person or to people. The way you are explaining this to me, it sounds like you and this Faye woman are connected in some kind of way. No, I'm not saying that you two should get together, especially not at this point. You may not be strong enough to resist what you see.

JAKE. I don't understand. You sound like Mr. Johnson. How are we connected?

PASTOR. Jake, that answer will reveal itself.

(Jake got up, shook the pastor's hand, and thanked him for his time.)

PASTOR. Jake, you're a grown man. I can't tell you what to do, but my job is to give advice, and my advice is, you need to stay away from this young lady until you are stronger, and I'm not talking physically.

JAKE. I understand.

(Jake understood, but he felt that he just had to do something. The burning desire inside of him was telling him that he had to do something. His mind shifted because he knew that when he made it back home, Cleo would be ready to ask a thousand questions, just as soon as he walked in.)

Cleo. So how did it go? Did you two accomplish anything? What did he want with you, and what did he say?

JAKE. It went okay. We had a pretty good conversation, and he said that he will see us tomorrow at church.

(While laughing, in his mind, he thought, "I'm good!" The weekend was over, time for another week of work. Jake pulled out and headed for work, but on his way, he saw her. It was Faye. He wanted to stop, but he remembered what the pastor had said. But he still wanted to stop. He passed by her. He went about a block before he turned around. He just felt like he had to say something to her. He pulled up beside her.)

Meeting Faye

FAYE. What's your pleasure? Wow, it's you! I can't just stand here and talk. My boss is watching.

JAKE. Well, how much would be for a little time?

FAYE. It's a hundred for an hour.

JAKE. A hundred dollars to just talk to you? I tell you what, I get paid Friday. I really want to get with you.

(*As the week went by, Jake was trying to figure out how he was going to get with Faye without causing any confusion in his home and without being seen by anyone. He thought that he would just pick her up in his car and take her for a ride. Then he thought someone might see them, and then he thought that he would ask her to meet him in a public place but he thought better maybe a motel room. I will just have to figure it out later. That night at home.*)

CLEO. Jake, come here and rub my back. That feels so good. Lower, lower, a little lower. Don't it feel good and firm to you?

JAKE. Yeah, it does.

CLEO. Come on, Jake! Wow, what's the problem? Is there anything wrong? You're not your normal self. A night like this usually brings out the animal in you. What's wrong?

JAKE. Oh, nothing, I'm just a little tired. Come here and give me a big kiss with your fine butt!

(*Jake knew that he had to do something to make up for his poor performance. He thought, "This is really starting to affect my life. I have to do something I have to get this Faye out of my head." Friday at last. Jake thought, "I will just go and get a motel room. After all, all we are going to do is talk. I can control myself. I wouldn't dare mess around on Cleo, especially with a prostitute. I love my wife. I will just keep an extra hundred out of my check, go get the room, and all will be fine. Now all I have to do is to find her. That wasn't hard. I guess she remembered what I said." He pulled up beside her.)*

FAYE. I thought you were going to talk yourself out of it?
JAKE. No, I told you that I wanted to talk with you.
FAYE. Talk, yeah right. You mean that you can look at all of this, and all you want to do is talk? Well, it's your money. If you want to give it up so we can talk, so be it.
JAKE. Come on, get in.
FAYE. Uh, not so quick. I have to see the money first.

(Jake pulled his wallet out of his back pocket and pulled a hundred dollar bill out.)

JAKE. Now get in.
FAYE. Where are we going?
JAKE. I thought that we would go get a room.

(Faye started to laugh.)

JAKE. What's so funny?
FAYE. A room, huh? To talk, huh? If we are going to get a room, I have this place that won't cost you but twenty dollars for fifty minutes.
JAKE. Fifty minutes? What happen to the other ten?
FAYE. The other ten minutes are used to get the room ready for the next customer.
JAKE. Where is this place?
FAYE. Uh, just turn the corner. Okay, here we are.
JAKE. What is this place? I thought this place was abandoned.
FAYE. No, now get out. Pay the man and let's do this. The time is ticking.

(Jake quickly got out of his car, paid for the room, and went inside.)

FAYE. This is your first time, huh?
JAKE. What do you mean my first time?
FAYE. You know, with a prostitute. I won't bite, unless you want me to.

(*Faye started to take off her clothes. Jake looked at the curves.*)

JAKE. Stop! No, I said we were here to talk, and that's all we are here for. Faye, why are doing this?

FAYE. Well, I make pretty good money, and believe it or not, most guys don't want sex. They mostly want me to fulfill some wild fantasy for them. This one guy told me that he always like that little white doll with all of the outfits, so he buys several outfits and have me to change into one after another one while he takes care of himself. Now how about you tell me a little about your life?

(*Faye and Jake both burst out laughing.*)

FAYE. Will you promise to not say anything if I tell you this? But first, let's hear about you.

JAKE. I promise. Okay, I was born deep in the Delta. My dad, Jacob, died when I was five. He was a good man. He worked in the saw mill. I was a little older when I finally got out of high school. I moved here, met my wife, and it was love at first site.

FAYE. You say you were born in the Delta and your dad's name was Jacob? What's the last name?

JAKE. Martin. Why?

FAYE. Oh my, no reason. You promised, remember? The guy that was with you at the pub the other day, he was the one who hired me for your party. He's my best customer.

(*Faye seemed to be in deep thought.*)

JAKE. You mean to tell me old Dennis likes the dolls, huh? Wow!

(*Jake burst out laughing. He laughed so hard the person in the other room knocked on the wall.*)

JAKE. I said that we were going to talk, and I meant it.

FAYE. Well, we only have five minutes left before Dennis will be here.

JAKE. What! I have to get out of here! I will talk to you later. If he sees me in here or even around here, my life won't be worth crap!

FAYE. Relax, there's something I need to tell you. We really have ten minutes, but I thought you might want to know. I had a great time laughing with you and…

JAKE. What is it you wanted to tell me? I really need to go. Faye, I want to invite you to my church.

FAYE. On Sunday? That's one of my busiest days. When all the women go to church, I really rack up!

JAKE. What! Well, we have an eight-o'clock service and a ten o'clock. Wednesday nights are at seven.

FAYE. If I do come, it will have to be an eight o'clock. What's the name of it anyway?

JAKE. Canaan Christian Center.

FAYE. That's the church that's on TV. I saw it once or twice when things got slow. You know, on those special Sundays, first of the year, Easter, Mother's Day, and days like those, those family Sundays where the husband tries to be a good little husband and goes to church with his family. Hey, you better be getting out of here. Dennis is never late.

JAKE. Okay, later.

FAYE. You had better go out the side door. It will take you right to your car without taking you back by the front. Bye.

(Jake hurried out, got into his car, and drove home.)

CLEO. Jake, is that you?

JAKE. What if I said it wasn't? Then what?

CLEO. I guess that was kind of dumb, huh?

JAKE. Uh, yeah.

(Jake grabbed Cleo, picked her up, and gave her a kiss, a kiss as if it had to last her for the rest of her life.)

CLEO. Jake, you have to be gentle with us.

JAKE. What do you mean with us?

CLEO. Sometimes I think you don't listen to me at all.

JAKE. What? What's for dinner?

CLEO. I don't know, get it yourself!

JAKE. What? What did I do now?

CLEO. Jake, do you not listen? I said that you have to be gentle with us.

JAKE. With us? Wait a minute, you mean, you are, what, when, how, who?

CLEO. I know that you know the answer to all of those. Yes, we are going to have a baby!

JAKE. Wow! A baby! Wow.

CLEO. Jake, is anything wrong?

JAKE. No, I'm overwhelmed!

(But Jake wasn't being truthful. He was excited about the baby, but he only wished that he had some family to share the news with.)

CLEO. I told Mom, and she was so excited that she was going to be a granny. I even told Aunt Brea.

JAKE. Aunt Brea! Oh my lord, what did she have to say?

CLEO. Wait a minute, how come you only reacted when I said that I told Aunt Brea?

JAKE. Do you really need to ask?

CLEO. Well, Aunt Brea said that she was ready for one herself and for you to come visit her but for me to stay home.

JAKE. If you don't come over here and let me plant a kiss on you, I just might take her up on her offer.

CLEO. Uh, if you don't plant a kiss on me, you just might have to take her up on her offer.

(They both kissed, and afterward, they had a good laugh.)

JAKE. I am so happy! We are going to have a baby! When is the due date? How far along are you? Is it a boy or girl?

CLEO. Slow your roll, my love, all of your questions will be answered soon enough. Right now, I want to go in the bedroom and make our baby good and strong.

(Cleo went over to Jake and kissed him. He picked her up, and she wrapped her legs around him, and he carried her to the bed. The next morning, Jake decided to get up and wash his car. While he was washing it, Dennis came by.)

DENNIS. Jake, my man, what are you up to?

JAKE. Dennis, what does it look like?

DENNIS. Uh, Jake, can I ask you a question?

(Jake started to sweat. He didn't know if Faye had said anything or if Dennis saw him. But he knew it was very unusual for Dennis to come by his house.)

JAKE. Dennis, what is it?

DENNIS. Jake, I need to ask you something.

JAKE (*thinking*). He knows that I went to a motel room with Faye. I wonder, did she tell him, or did he see me leave? Is he going to try and blackmail me? Is he going to tell Cleo? What does he want?

DENNIS. I want to know.

CLEO. Oh, hello, Dennis. What brings you this way?

DENNIS. Well, I was going to ask Jake something, but you might need to hear this as well.

JAKE. Cleo, why don't go and get Dennis something to drink?

CLEO. Dennis, do you want anything to drink?

DENNIS. Nah, that's okay, maybe I shouldn't say anything.

JAKE. Well, if you feel that way, maybe you shouldn't!

CLEO. Jake, stop it. If Dennis feels like he needs to talk to us, at the least we should be willing to listen.

DENNIS. Thank you, Cleo. Well, it started last night.

JAKE. Are you sure you don't want anything to drink?

CLEO. Jake!

DENNIS. I'm good. You see, it's this girl.

(Jake pretended that while he washing his car he sprayed Dennis by mistake.)

CLEO. Jake, watch it! What's wrong with you? Dennis, I'm so sorry. I'll go and get you a towel.

DENNIS. No, Cleo, that's okay. I see that my friend doesn't want to hear what I have to say.

CLEO. I wonder why. Dennis, you go right ahead and tell us what you want us to know.

DENNIS. Well, like I was saying, yesterday evening I went to see my friend, and when I arrived something was different. When I got there, she was there but—

JAKE. Dennis, how about a beer? Cleo, how about going in and get Dennis and myself a beer?

DENNIS. A cold beer sounds good, but it's a bit early even for me. Like I was saying, I went to see my friend, and she mentioned that someone else had come to see her.

(*Cleo looked at Jake, and Jake looked at Dennis.*)

DENNIS. She said that this person made her laugh and had made her feel good about herself. What I want to know is. Well, I'm almost too embarrassed to say it. You know that they say that you can't make a whore into a house wife, but I can't help it, when she was telling me that someone else made her laugh and made her feel good about herself, I knew then that I loved her.

JAKE. Man, that's all!

CLEO. Jake! Dennis, I understand exactly how you feel. First, I need to know, does she feel the same about you, and does she have a name?

DENNIS. That I'm not sure about. You see, in her line of business, she might tell a lot of men that she loves them and that they are her favorite. Her name is Faye.

(*Cleo looked at Jake. She looked at him because she remembered the story that he told her about the Faye in his dream and about his bachelor's party. She wondered, could this be the same person?*)

CLEO. How does she tell you, before, during, or after?

DENNIS. Sometime before, sometime during, and sometime after. Yeah, when I'm leaving, she looks into my eyes, and then she tells me that she loves me and if only things were different.

CLEO. Dennis, you fool. Forgive me, but, Dennis, she is crying out to you. She is crying out for help.

DENNIS. Well, why don't she just come out and say it?

CLEO. What is it you want her to say?

DENNIS. Well, I guess you're right. What can I do now? She has a pimp and a crazy one at that.

CLEO. Well, it's not too much that you can do.

DENNIS. What? What do you mean it's not too much I can do?

CLEO. It's obvious that you really like this lady.

JAKE. Uh, who is she?

DENNIS. Uh, Jake it's funny you should ask.

JAKE. Never mind, I really don't want to know.

CLEO. Jake, why don't you just stay out of this? Now come on, Dennis. We need to figure out what we are going to do.

JAKE. Hold on, you say that this lady has a pimp? I'm all for love, but when it comes to my wife taking chances, that is where I draw the line. No one will be putting my wife's life in danger!

DENNIS. He's right, Cleo. It just might be too dangerous.

CLEO. Uh, I'm a big girl, and I know when to back off, and besides, my big strong man will protect me.

(Jake looked up with a surprised look on his face, but he knew that she was telling the truth. He knew that he would do whatever it took to protect his wife and his baby. After Dennis helped Jake with his car, all three went in and started to try and figure out how they were going to handle Dennis's situation. While all of the time Jake was wondering if Dennis actually knew that he was the one who made Faye laugh and who made her feel good about herself, Jake suddenly started to laugh.)

DENNIS. What's so funny?

JAKE. Oh, nothing.

(Jake had just remembered what Faye had told him about how Dennis likes for her to dress up like a doll. They sat around all morning until Dennis said that he had to leave.)

JAKE. I'll walk you out.

(When Dennis and Jake made it out, Dennis looked at Jake.)

DENNIS. Jake, I just want to thank you. If it had not been for you, I would not have known how much I really cared for Faye.

(Jake just looked at Dennis. He didn't know if he was just talking or if he actually knew about him seeing her yesterday. So he just took it as if he didn't know.)

JAKE. So Dennis you want to go get a beer?

DENNIS. Well, I would, but I left my wallet.

JAKE. So you drove over here without your wallet? I really don't believe that.

DENNIS. Funny, huh?

JAKE. Come on, man. Let's just go. You don't even have to drive. This new pub just opened up around the corner.

(*After Jake and Dennis walked about a mile and a half, they arrived.*)

DENNIS. Man, I thought you said that it was around the corner! I'm going to need at least a pitcher, and I'm talking about for myself.

JAKE. This is why we walked. I'm thinking I will have a beer or two myself. And why are you breathing so hard? So when was it you said you saw Faye?

DENNIS. I saw her yesterday, right after you.

(*Jake spit half of his beer out.*)

JAKE. Uh, so you knew all of this time!

DENNIS. Hey, man, you are wasting good beer. Relax, I'm glad you saw her. You see, this way, I know that I can trust her. She tells me about all of her clients.

JAKE. Huh?

DENNIS. Even the ones that are supposed to be leaders in the community. The stories I could tell. The ones that hold their heads up so high and look down on people like us. The men with their so-called perfect family life, they all sneak around. Jake, how can I take her away from all of this?

JAKE. Dennis, are you in church?

DENNIS. I want to be, but I hear about so many of these preachers, even the deacons, they're all customers.

JAKE. I beg your pardon. I can show you one that I know is not a part of this. And besides, I'm pretty sure that it's even more than just him who are not customers. What you have to do is to focus more on the Lord than on man.

DENNIS. You know what's funny? We sit here in a pub, drinking beers and talking about the Lord.

JAKE. Well, you know what they say, if the mountain won't come to Mohammad, then Mohammad must go to the mountain. Dennis, it doesn't matter where you get him in as long as you get him in. I must be all things to all people.

DENNIS. Jake, I really want to believe you.

JAKE. No, don't believe me. Believe in the Lord.

DENNIS. Jake, how can I change? How can she change?

JAKE. Dennis, Roman 3:23 reads, "For all have sinned and fall short of the glory of God."

DENNIS. If we all fall short, what's the purpose?

JAKE. Yes, we do fall short but, Psalm 136 reads "Oh, give thanks to the Lord, for He is good! For His mercy endures forever." Dennis, you see, even though we have sinned, we still have his mercy.

DENNIS. Okay, we have his mercy, but now we are sinners with mercy?

JAKE. Dennis! Isaiah 53:5 reads, "But He was wounded for our transgressions, He was bruised for our iniquities: the chastisement of our peace was upon Him, and we are healed by His wounds." So you can see that all sin died with him, and he defeated it when he rose back up.

DENNIS. Jake, how do you know all of this? How about another pitcher?

JAKE. I think you have had enough. Besides, I'm not going to carry you all the way back to my house.

DENNIS. Yeah, I forgot we got to walk ten miles.

JAKE. Now I know you had enough. Come on, let's go.

(They were on their way back.)

DENNIS. Jake, how can I learn more about the Lord? I love her, you know. I want her to be my baby momma. I mean my wife. I love her, man. She is my doll.

(Jake started to laugh.)

DENNIS. What is you laughing 'bout?

JAKE. Oh, nothing, man. Are you going to make it back? Dennis, man, I suggest to you that both of you get into a good church. As a matter of fact, I want to invite the both of you to my church. We have two services, an eight o'clock and a twelve o'clock. I know I will probably have to invite you again when you sober up.

DENNIS. She tells me that she don't even sleeps with all of them, some just like to watch her dance. She even said that one just want to suck her toes. I'd never be able to suck her toes again.

JAKE. Uh, Dennis, you are probably talking too much.

DENNIS. Jake, talk to her, man. Talk to her about the Lord. You know how he done died for our sins. This one preacher told her that all she got to do is to repent. She asked him, so should I repent after we are finished, after each customer, or at the end of each day? I thought that was funny.

JAKE. Well, Dennis, we should thank God for his forgiving and try to live righteously. Hebrews 9:15–18 reads, "And for this cause he is the mediator of the new testament, that by means of death, for the redemption of the transgressions that were under the first testament, they which are called might receive the promise of eternal inheritance. For where a testament is, there must also of necessity be the death of the testator. For a testament is of force after men are dead: otherwise it is of no strength at all while the testator lives. Whereupon neither the first testament was dedicated without blood." So, Dennis, you see that when Jesus died, he died for the redemption of our sin so you can see that if we continue to repent over and over. It would be like in the Old Testament before they had a redeemer. You either believe or you don't.

DENNIS. So are you saying that I can do whatever I want?

JAKE. Well, yeah, I guess that is what I'm saying but, Hebrews 10:15–19 says, "Where of the Holy Ghost also is a witness to us: for after that he had said before. This is the covenant that I will make with them after those days, says the Lord, I will put my laws into their hearts, and in their minds will I write them; and their sins and iniquities will I remember no more. Now where remission of these is, there is no more offering for sin. Having therefore, brethren, boldness to enter into the holiest by the blood of Jesus, by a new and living way, which he hath consecrated for us, through the veil, that is to say, his flesh; you see that once we receive Him as our Lord and saver he, to put it this way he will not judge us according to our sin." But—

DENNIS. I knew it had to be a catch in there because it sounds too good to be true.

JAKE. Dennis, I'm not expecting you to understand—not now at least. But what I have just told you is the gospel.

DENNIS. What is?

JAKE. I will tell you later, but first I have to tell you that Matthew 6:33 says, "But seek first his kingdom and his righteousness, and all these things will be given to you as well." Dennis, I know that I'm giving you a lot of scriptures. Dennis, I just want to wet your appetite. I want you and now Faye to know that it is so much more that our Lord Jesus Christ wants for us.

DENNIS. You said us.

JAKE. Yes, us. I know that I am truly blessed and am walking in the blessing, but there is so much more. Well, we are here. Now that wasn't too painful, was it?

DENNIS. Man, my drunk is gone.

JAKE. Good. Now you can go home after you wash your face.

DENNIS. I can't help it. I need to ask you one question. How come you didn't get drunk?

JAKE. I only took that one drink, and you made me spit it out, remember?

(The next day was Sunday, and Jake and Cleo went to church. Jake continued to look around as if he was looking for someone.)

CLEO. Jake, why are you looking around so much?

JAKE. I was hoping Dennis would come, but I guess he's not ready.

CLEO. Continue to work on him and don't give up.

(Time was flying by. Before they knew it, nine months had passed.)

JAKE. Cleo, are you okay? Is it time yet? Are you ready? You got everything together? Where's your suitcase? Do I need to take off? Maybe I should call in?

CLEO. Jake! Calm down. Everything is just fine. We still have some time yet. You go on to work. We will be just fine.

JAKE. Make sure you keep the phone handy. Call my office if you need me.

CLEO. Go, Jake. Get out of here and go to work.

(Jake kissed Cleo, and then he bent over and kissed her stomach. I love you. I love you both.)

CLEO. We love you too.

(Jake was on his way to work, but he decided to go the back way again in hope of seeing Faye. He drove slowly through the gut-wrenching neighborhood. There were empty buildings with broken windows, rats looking like rather large cats, stray dogs with litter of puppies following closely behind, and prostitutes and drug dealers on what appears to be every corner. A prostitute walked up to Jake's car.)

PROSTITUTE. What's happening, big daddy? How about an early morning snack? Looking at you, hell, I will even give it to you half price.

JAKE. No, thank you. I'm looking for Faye. Do you know her?

PROSTITUTE. That hoe! Hell, what she got I don't got? I ain't her keeper!

(Jake drove of slowly in hope of seeing Faye. And when he was just about to leave, he saw this silhouette—a silhouette he knew oh so well, but there was something wrong. He pulled up.)

JAKE. Faye, Faye, is that you? Wow! What happened? Oh, Faye.

(Faye's eyes were swollen, and her lip was burst.)

FAYE. I can't stop. He's watching me. He's watching me.

(Jake pulled out his money.)

JAKE. Get in!

(Faye got into the car with Jake.)

JAKE. Now, Faye, would you tell me what happened?

FAYE. I told him that I wanted out. I told him that I found someone that I truly want to be with. But the worst part is that he thinks it's you.

JAKE. Me?

(As Jake and Faye spoke, the pimp approached the car.)

PIMP. Look here, we got the lovely couple.

(Faye reached around Jake and handed him the money. Jake looked him in the eye. He looked at Jake and pulled his chrome-plated pistol out. He pointed it at Jake.)

PIMP. Look at here Mr. Big Man. Let me tell you something that hoe over there is mine, and she can leave when I say she can.

(What he didn't know was that Jake had heard all he wanted to hear. And he made one little mistake. He put the gun a little too far inside the window. Jake grabbed the gun. It went off. The projectile hit the window shield. Jake wrestled the gun out of his, and while letting the window up on his arm, Jake quickly got out of the car and punched him in his ribcage, breaking three ribs. The pimp started coughing and begging for is life.)

PIMP. Please, please, please, don't kill me!

FAYE. Jake! Jake! Jake! That's enough. Enough, Jake. Don't become like him. That's enough.

(Shaking, Jake stood over him like a predator stands over his down prey. Soon Jake saw the blue lights of a police car. The car pulled up, but when the officer got out, Jake couldn't believe his eyes. How could this be? It was that officer, the one in his dream, the ole fat officer that called him a boy and slammed his face onto the hood of his vehicle.)

OFFICER. Hold it right there. What the hell is going on here? Looks like you boys can't play together without trying to kill one another. Oh, I see. Hey, Faye, why don't you tell me what done happened here?

FAYE. We were in the car when he pointed a gun at us.

OFFICER. Now, Faye, you must be mistaken. Have you done forgot who this fella is? Who you work for?

FAYE. No, Officer, I haven't forgotten. And I don't work for him no mo'!

OFFICER. So you still saying that this fella pointed a gun at you, and this fella, did he shoot it, or was he just showing it to y'all?

JAKE. Officer, are you going to arrest me? Better yet, are you going to arrest anyone?

OFFICER. Look a here, nig—

JAKE. Be careful, sir.

OFFICER. Look a here, mister. I got the right to arrest who I see fit to arrest, and as I see it, ain't no real damage been done.

JAKE. So are we free to go.

OFFICER. We? Faye, gal, I would thank long and hard before I get back in that car with that fella.

FAYE. I bet you would. Come, Jake, let's go.

(Jake and Faye got back into his vehicle and drove off. After going about a block or so, Faye broke into tears.)

JAKE. Faye, are you okay?

FAYE. I'm going to be just fine. I just have to find a real job and probably move out of my downtown apartment. What about him? Am I going to have to look over my shoulder every time I do something? Oh, Jake, what am I going to do?

JAKE. Faye, all I can say is live. You have to try and find a way to live. I can help you find a different JOB. HEY, WHAT ABOUT ALL OF YOUR USED-TO-BE CLIENTS?

FAYE. Now, Jake, do you seriously think I would be able to work for one of them? I would feel like a sheep among wolves.

JAKE. Yeah, I guess I didn't think that one out. Hey, I have to get my window fixed.

FAYE. Jake, where are you going? Turn left and go to my friend Lenny.

JAKE. Lenny?

FAYE. Yeah, Lenny. Do you know him or something? Well, anyway, he repairs and replaces windshields.

(As they drove, they laughed and had conversations. They acted like they had known each other all of their lives.)

JAKE. Faye, where are you from?

FAYE. I'm from—oh, here we are. Pull in here. There's Lenny.

(Jake looked like he had seen a ghost. Lenny had a striking resemblance to the one in his dream. He was tall and skinny. He even sounded like him.)

LENNY. Hey, Faye. What can I do you for?

FAYE. Lenny, this is my friend, Jake.

LENNY. Friend, huh?

FAYE. No, seriously, he is a friend—a real friend. So don't give him the special that you give the rest of my friends. Give him my price.

LENNY. You for sure? Let me see if I got one to fit this car. Yeah, I got one. You is in luck.

(Faye and Jake went into this old broken-down shed to wait for Lenny to finish. They sat beside each other on this lumpy couch that smelled like old used motor oil.)

FAYE. Jake, how long have you been here?

JAKE. Well, I moved here right after high school.

FAYE. Oh, so you've been here since you were eighteen or nineteen?

JAKE. Uh, it took me a little longer to get out than that. I was twenty-one when I moved here.

FAYE. Wow!

JAKE. Hey, wait a minute, it was my early years. I was foolish and thought I didn't need an education. I thought I would work in the saw mill like my dad did.

(When Jake mentioned working in the saw mill, Faye's facial expression suddenly changed.)

JAKE. Faye, what's wrong?

(Lenny walked in.)

LENNY. All finished.

JAKE. Okay, my man, how much do I owe you?

LENNY. No charge.

JAKE. What no charge?

(Jake looked over at Faye. She looked down at the ground.)

LENNY. Yeah, no charge, now get out of here.

(As Faye and Jake drove away, Jake looked at Faye and asked something.)

JAKE. Was the reason for it being no charge because he was or will be one of your clients?

FAYE. Jake, just because I know a man doesn't mean I've slept with him. I introduced Lenny to his wife.

JAKE. Faye, I shouldn't have said that.

FAYE. Why not? You were thinking it. At the time I met Lenny, he was in the shoe business. He tried to get with me, but I told him my price, and he apologized for wasting my time. He's a nice guy, so I would go by every now and then. One day I went by, and I had my friend Hope with me. It was love at first site. He looked at her, and she looked at him. It was like magic. You see, Hope was left this repair business by her father, so now it's her and Lenny's place.

JAKE. Oh, Faye, I almost forgot I have to get to work, my wife!

FAYE. What your wife got to do with you getting to work?

JAKE. You see, she is pregnant, and it's really close to time, so I need to be by the phone.

FAYE. Well, my place is right around the corner. You can drop me off.

(Jake pulled around the corner. He saw this high-rise. His mouth flew opened.)

JAKE. You live here? My, you do make some money. No wonder I could never find you. I never would have thought it.

FAYE. Jake, I told you that my customers were high class, and at five hundred dollars a setting, it's not hard.

JAKE. Wait a minute, you were charging me one hundred.

FAYE. Yeah, I know. There was just something about you.

JAKE. I must be going. Oh, will I see you at church Wednesday night or Sunday morning?

FAYE. Do you ever give up?

JAKE. Never.

(Jake went on to work wondering if Cleo had called. He made it to work ran in and asked Mrs. Brown if his wife had called.)

MRS. BROWN. No, Jake, she has not. You have been asking me the same question for a whole month now. I can tell you when the baby is coming.

JAKE. Oh yeah, when?

MRS. BROWN. When he gets here. No, really, when is the next full moon?

JAKE. That's tomorrow!

MRS. BROWN. Well, you had better be ready, because he's coming.

(Just as soon as Mrs. Brown finished talking, the phone rang.)

MRS. BROWN. It's your wife!

(Jake grabbed the phone.)

JAKE. Is it time? I'm on my way! Do you think we need an ambulance? How much time do we have? Are you okay?

CLEO. Jake, Jake, calm down. No, it's not time yet. I just called to tell you to bring me some ice cream this evening.

JAKE. Oh, I guess I do need to get a grip on myself.

CLEO. Yes, you do. But I love you anyway.

JAKE. Okay, baby, I love you too.

(Just as soon as Jake hung up the phone, there was a knock on his office door.)

JAKE. Come in. Dennis, how come you always come at the wrong time?

DENNIS. Rough day, huh? You mean to tell me that you just got to work? Wow, you must have a real rough morning.

JAKE. Dennis, if only you knew the half of it. Dennis, why don't you visit my church Sunday? For some reason, I believe you will be pleasantly surprised.

DENNIS. Do you ever give up? And besides, Sunday is five good days away. Now what happened to you this morning, you look like you've been hit by a bus.

JAKE. Well, I was on my way to work this morning, and I just happened to run into Faye.

DENNIS. How did you just happen to run into her? Her strip is on the other side of town, and the only way you happen to run into her is if you purposely went that way!

JAKE. Yeah, I know. Dennis, it's just something about her. I find myself attracted to her Dennis. What! Here I trust you, telling you how much she means to me.

JAKE. Hold on, let me finish. I'm attracted to her in a way that I can't explain.

DENNIS. I can. It's called your dick!

(Dennis started to walk out of the room but stopped short of the door. He turned around.)

DENNIS. Jake, man, I'm sorry. I had no right to accuse you, and after all, she is a prostitute.

JAKE. Dennis, stop. Don't you ever speak about her like that again. Proverbs 18:21 says, "Death and Life are in the power of the tongue: and they that love it shall eat the fruit forever more."

DENNIS. Now, what in the heck does that supposed to mean?

JAKE. Dennis, the words you say will paint the picture you see. You speak positive, and things will be positive.

DENNIS. So you're saying that things will never go wrong for me if I only speak positive?

JAKE. No, I'm not saying ever. One reason is because of what you just spoke into Faye's life. It says death and life is in the power of the tongue, not just your tongue. For example, a mother or father calling their child stupid all his or her young life now, when that child gets older, they can't understand why he acts so stupid. The reason being they planted that stupid seed in him as a child.

DENNIS. Wow, you know that actually makes sense. You know what, I think I will visit your church Sunday.

JAKE. Great! Hey, bring Faye with you.

DENNIS. I'll try, if she will come.

JAKE. She will. I have a strong feeling things are going to be different from now on.

(Dennis turned and walked back toward Jake. He held his hand out, and they shook hands as if they were meeting for the first time. Before Dennis was able to walk out, Jake's phone rang.)

JAKE. Mr. Martin speaking, how—

CLEO. It's time!

JAKE. Time for what?

CLEO. It's time!

JAKE. Oh, it's time! On my way!
CLEO. No hospital!

(Jake hung up the phone but remembered and picked it back up.)

JAKE. Oh, love you!
DENNIS. What is it, man?
JAKE. It's time!
DENNIS. Time for what?
JAKE. Cleo, it's time!
DENNIS. I'll drive! Where are your keys?
JAKE. In your hand!
DENNIS. Where's the car?
JAKE. Outside! Look, Dennis, I appreciate you offering to drive, but uh, I want to make it there in one piece.

(Jake and Dennis both ran out, telling Mr. Johnson that it's time.)

MRS. BROWN. Already taken care of it, and he has already left.
JAKE. Dennis, where are you going?
DENNIS. I am the best man!
JAKE. Oh hell, come on.

(When Jake and Dennis made it to the hospital, they ran into Mr. Johnson.)

MR. JOHNSON. I thought you weren't going to make it in time, and why didn't you just take the day off? They just took her back. Don't just stand there, go get cleaned up and put on your scrubs.

(The nurse escorted Jake into a locker room, where he put on the too small scrubs and mask.)

NURSE. Are you ready?
JAKE. I think so.
NURSE. If you feel faint, try taking deep breaths. If that doesn't work, you might need to leave the room.

(She escorted him into the delivery room. Jake looked. He saw Cleo lying on what looked like a table, with both of her legs up in the air and a sheet hanging between them. The doctor walked in.)

Doctor. Okay, Mrs. Martin, I see we are ready to bring this little one into this world.

(The doctor raised the sheet up, and Jake saw the crowning of his baby's head, and his knees got weak.)

NURSE. Mr. Martin, are you okay?

(Jake didn't say a word. He just stood there, looking like a skyscraper that was about to fall. He then saw the shoulders, chest, midsection, and then there it was, a boy he was so excited he forgot about the rest of the delivery. He had a smile on his face so wide it would have made the Los Angeles freeway look like a narrow dirt road. The rest of the delivery went smoothly. Jake walked out of the delivery room with his chest swollen and a very wide grin.)

MR. JOHNSON. It's a boy!
DENNIS. How do you know?
MR. JOHNSON. Look at the grin on his face, but most of all, look how his chest is stuck out. It's a boy I tell you.
JAKE. A son, I have a son. I have a son, a large healthy son.

(It took a while before the nurse would bring him to the window, but she eventually showed him. He looked just like Jake's father, Jacob.)

DENNIS. Oh, man, look at little Jake. Wow, he has eyes like my girl, Faye.
MR. JOHNSON. Have you two decided on, Jake, as his name?
JAKE. We haven't, but if you ask me, I really don't want to name him Jake Jr. Cleo and I will make that decision, Cleo! I almost forgot, I need to get in there to see how she is holding up.
NURSE. Okay, Mr. Martin, you can deflate your chest now. Your wife wants you, and we will be bringing your son in there in a few minutes. You do want him circumcised?
JAKE. Yes, please do.

(Jake went back in and looked at Cleo, and for a woman who just had a baby, she looked great. He went over to her bedside, bent over, and kissed her.)

JAKE. Thank you, you birth me a son.

(Cleo grabbed Jake's hand. He looked into her eyes and kissed her again. The nurse walked in.)

NURSE. Mr. Martin, you do realize that it will be at least six weeks before she is able to perform, right?
JAKE. Six weeks! Yeah, I know, wow, six weeks.
NURSE. We are just about finished with baby, Martin. Have you two decided on a name?

(Cleo opened her eyes and spoke his name.)

CLEO. Jacob, his name is Jacob.

(After she spoke, she went back to sleep.)

JAKE. I guess Jacob it will be. My son Jacob Martin, a son. What more can a man ask for?

(Jake just sat there, holding Cleo's hand.)

NURSE. Mr. Martin, would you be a little more comfortable in the recliner?
JAKE. No, I'm just fine.

(The hospital let Cleo out after two days but told her to take it easy. The days flew by; Jake could barely wait to take his son to church to show everyone. But until then, he just kept a picture with him and showed everyone. He was extremely proud of him.)

JAKE. Mrs. Brown, guess what little Jacob did this morning. I was changing his diaper, and he shot a laser beam right into my face. He's my boy all right.
DENNIS. I know. Guess what little Jacob did this morning. Look, when are you two going back to church? I think I've talked

Faye into going to church with me. She seem rather excited to meet little Jacob. I told her that he has her eyes.

JAKE. Well, you tell her that he will be at church Sunday. You might want to stop saying that he has her eyes, at least around Cleo that is.

(All that week, Jake seemed more excited than he was already. He felt good on the inside. He was getting Dennis and Faye to come to church. Saturday.)

JAKE. You want to do something today?

CLEO. No, not really. Jacob kept me up all night.

JAKE. Funny, I didn't hear him.

CLEO. I bet you didn't. With your snoring, a bomb could have gone off. But I love you anyway.

JAKE. I must have been really tired. Oh, I love you too. I'm going outside. I need to cut the grass and wash the car. I want it to be clean for tomorrow.

CLEO. What do you want for dinner? I was planning on frying a chicken, some brown beans, corn bread, and a peach cobbler.

JAKE. Sounds good to me.

CLEO. Jake Martin, that's what I like about you. Whatever I cook sounds good to you. Give me a kiss and get out of here.

JAKE. How long has it been? Is it time yet?

CLEO. No, not yet. Now get out of here.

(Jake went outside to wash his car, but before he could start, Dennis walked up.)

JAKE. Dennis, my man, how are things going?

DENNIS. Jake, you know Faye and I are supposed to be coming to church tomorrow. Well, I'm kind of nervous.

JAKE. Why? Let me guess. You're thinking about what other people are going to think and say. I have one question, do you love her?

DENNIS. Yes, very much!

JAKE. Well, the hell with everyone else.

DENNIS. Thanks, Jake. I knew you would make it better.

JAKE. Dennis, you can't live your life worrying about what others are saying or thinking about you. As long as you live your life as a righteous man, you don't have to be concerned about others.

Proverbs 20:7 says, "The just man walks in his integrity: his children are blessed after him."

DENNIS. Yeah, but how can I live good enough?

JAKE. You can't. Romans 3:23 says, "For we all have sinned and fall short of the glory of God."

JAKE. Hold on. Before you ask, 2 Corinthians 12:9 says, "And he said unto me, my grace is sufficient for thee: for my strength is made perfect in weakness. Most gladly therefore will I rather glory in my infirmities, that the power of Christ may rest upon me." So you see, if you are born again and believe in Christ, the anointed one, you are righteous.

DENNIS. So what you're saying is that I can do anything I want to do because he has already saved us?

JAKE. You can, but we go back to Proverbs 20:7, "The just man walks in his integrity: His children are blessed after him."

DENNIS. How can I go all day and do nothing wrong?

JAKE. Dennis, you are so funny. You don't have to go all day. All you have to do is to live your life and keep his words in your heart. As a matter of fact, if you just keep his greatest commandment, then you will do fine.

DENNIS. Wow, which one is that?

JAKE. I glad you asked. Matthew 22:37–38 says, "Jesus replied: 'Love the Lord your God with all your heart and with all your soul and with your entire mind.' This is the first and greatest commandment." So, Dennis, you see, if you love God, how can you do wrong?

DENNIS. I'm beginning to see what you're talking about, wow. You mean to tell me that all this time, all I had to do is to love God.

JAKE. Well, yeah, but I have to tell you the second greatest commandment. It also comes from Matthew 22:39, which says, "And the second is like it: 'Love your neighbor as yourself.' All the Law and the Prophets hang on these two commandments." Yes, loving God is the most important, but loving your neighbor is just as important.

DENNIS. Okay, who are you calling my neighbor?

JAKE. I'm going to let you figure that one out for yourself, but I will leave you with this. Go read Luke 10:25–37. It's a book in the New Testament, your Bible that is.

DENNIS. Okay, thanks, and I know where Luke is.
JAKE. Now get away so I can get my work done. Hey, I will see you two at church tomorrow?
DENNIS. Yes, you will!

(*It was a beautiful Sunday morning. The sun was in the sky. Birds were singing, and so was Jake.*)

JAKE. I'm walking in the favor of God. His grace and mercy has brought me this far.
CLEO. Jake, are you singing? Wow, it is going to be a good day.
JAKE. No, it is a great day. I just feel like something great is going to happen today! I feel good.
CLEO. Oh, from church to James Brown, what a combination.
JAKE. It's all good.

(*Jake and Cleo loaded their baby and his gear into the car and headed to church. When they arrived, Jake started to look around.*)

CLEO. Who are you looking for?
JAKE. Dennis is supposed to be coming.
CLEO. What! How did you manage that?
JAKE. Well, to be honest, I told him that we were giving away free wine.

(*They both started laughing.*)

CLEO. Yeah, that will do it.
JAKE. Come on, let's go in. I want everyone to see Jacob!
CLEO. Okay, calm down. They will see him soon enough.

(*Jake wouldn't let Cleo carry him. He scooped him up and headed in. He was so busy showing everyone his son he didn't see Dennis and Faye walk in. Praise and worship started, then the announcements and welcome.*)

SISTER ROZ. Are there any first-time visitors?

(*Dennis and Faye both stood up.*)

SISTER ROZ. Don't sit down. I like to welcome you and ask how you came to be here with us today.

DENNIS. My name is Dennis Seward, and I was invited by my friend and coworker Jake Martin.

FAYE. My name is Phaedra Martin, and I was invited by my older brother Jake Martin.

(There was not a sound. Jake turned around. He looked at Faye, then he looked back at Cleo.)

JAKE. What did she say? Did she say older brother? What did she mean?

SISTER ROZ. On behalf of our pastors here at Canaan, we like to thank you for coming. And I see that we also have a new soon-to-be member, little Jacob Martin.

(They both sat down.)

DENNIS. Why did you call him your brother?

FAYE. Because he is.

DENNIS. What! You mean Jake, Jake Martin is your brother?

(Jake got up and walked back to where they were sitting.)

JAKE. Why did you say that?

FAYE. I tried to tell you, but you had to go, remember?

JAKE. We will talk after church.

(Looking like he had seen a ghost, he got up and walked back to his seat.)

CLEO. Well?

JAKE. She said that she is my sister.

CLEO. This is great, I think.

(Church seemed to go on forever. After church, the pastor walked to Jake.)

PASTOR. So this is Jacob. He's a good-looking baby. He has your sister's eyes.

JAKE. Thank you, Pastor.

CLEO. You know he's right. He does have your sister's eyes.

(Jake turned and looked at Cleo. She didn't say another word. Instead, she walked over to Dennis and Faye and invited them to dinner. They accepted.)

JAKE. What did you do that for?

CLEO. So you and Faye can talk. If she is your sister, we need to get to know her, and if she's not, we will find that out too.

JAKE. You know that is why I love you. Are you sure it's not time yet?

CLEO. Jake, come on, and no, it's not.

(Dennis and Faye followed them home. They ate dinner, and Jake and Faye sat down and talked.)

JAKE. Faye, I'm going to let you go first.

FAYE. Jake, I know this is hard to swallow, but my mom told me that one day my dad Jacob Martin came by.

JAKE. Hold on, Jacob Martin is a common name!

FAYE. Please let me finish. We lived about eight blocks from you. She said that one day while our dad was on his way home, he saw her trying to fix her fence. He asked, "Don't you got a man to help you with that?" At that time, she was twenty and had curves like that old coon-creek road. She said that he started stopping by helping her with the fence, but one day, he came and she was just finishing up washing her long black hair. She said that her dress was wet, and it being hot, she didn't have on any underclothes. He saw right through it. She said that he grabbed her, and his little man was as hard as a two-by-four and almost as big. She said that she wanted him bad and he wanted her. That is when she got pregnant. She said after that he would come by, but he told her that he was married and he loved his wife and son very much. About a month later, she told him that she was pregnant. He told her that you were about two months old. She told me that he was a very good man and she should have not tried to get him that way. She knew he was coming by, and that's why she wet up her dress like that. He would still come by and bring my mom money for me and spend time with me, but she said that they never slept together again. You see, I too remember him as a good man and a loving dad.

(After she finished, Jake just sat there with tears in his eyes.)

JAKE. Why didn't he tell us? Why did he have to do it?

CLEO. Faye, welcome to our family. I guess you should be saying that to me. Anyway, welcome.

FAYE. Thank you. Jake, are you okay?

JAKE. How come he didn't tell us? He could have told my mom if no one else. Here it is, I'm thinking I'm an only child. All these years, I have no one to share things with.

FAYE. Jake, may I say something? We can't help what happened then, but we can move forward now.

JAKE. I guess. So I know you're looking for a new job?

FAYE. I guess it's time to put this degree to work for me.

JAKE. Dennis. and Cleo. What! You have a degree?

FAYE. Yes, in accounting. What? You thought I was dumb?

CLEO. But why?

FAYE. Well, you see, it was my senior year in college, and I didn't have enough money to finish up. I met my pimp. I made the money. My first month, I made over $5,000, and it was easy money.

DENNIS. Easy, huh?

FAYE. Dennis, you don't have anything to worry. That life is completely behind me, and I've completely closed the door on it.

DENNIS. Completely?

FAYE. All but one.

(Dennis stood there with a large smile on his face.)

JAKE. You mean to tell me that you have a degree in accounting? Have you not read the papers? They are looking for accountants every day.

FAYE. Yeah, Jake, but have you forgotten what I told you about working for some of these guys?

JAKE. Surely there has to be someone that you feel comfortable working around.

FAYE. Jake, it's not my feelings that concern me.

JAKE. Oh, I see. How about I ask Mr. Johnson if he has an opening? It is safe to say that you have not had him for a client.

(Faye started laughing.)

FAYE. It's safe.

CLEO. Enough, let's go in and play a hand of spades, ladies against you two.

DENNIS. I didn't like how you said that.

JAKE. Aw, shut up, Dennis. You better know how to play. I hate losing!

DENNIS. You must be crazy. I'm the spade king. I can't be beat. I can't beat. I can't lose!

CLEO. Okay, spade kings, how about putting your money where your mouth is? If you two lose, you two take us two shopping and to dinner, not any cheap places. Oh, and we get a full-body massage.

DENNIS. It's on bet!

JAKE. We had better not lose!

DENNIS. How about when we win?

CLEO. Faye. Anything you want!

DENNIS. Jake. Anything?

JAKE. Anything?

(They sat down and started their game. It only took four hands.)

FAYE. I can't be beat, I can't lose, and I'm the spade king. What happened, spade king? Girl, when do you want to go shopping?

(Jake sat there, looking at Dennis. He looked at him like he just took the last can of beer that he didn't buy. Dennis couldn't look up.)

DENNIS. I guess I'm a little rusty. There is no way they can beat us two games.

JAKE. Dennis, shut up. I refuse to play with you again. How about me and Cleo against you and Faye?

CLEO. How about Dennis and I against you two?

DENNIS. Yeah, we are going to beat the socks off of you two. Jake, you will owe me an apology for not wanting to play with me. I tell you what. After we beat you two, you will treat me to lunch for a week, and if we lose, I will treat both of you to lunch for a week.

JAKE. Bet!

(Once again, it only took four hands.)

CLEO. Dennis, you have got to be the worst spade player in the world! I had at least six books in each hand. Why did we go for ten four hands in a row? Can you not count your books?

JAKE. All I know is that my little sister and I are going to be treated to free lunch for a week!

DENNIS. Cleo, can a brother get a little help?

CLEO. Uh, no. You made your bed, now lie in it.

FAYE. Come on, Dennis, we better be leaving before you owe your whole pay check.

DENNIS. Yeah, I guess you're right. Uh, do you want to go back to my place?

(Jake looked at Dennis.)

DENNIS. I mean just to hang out.

FAYE. Sure.

DENNIS. You don't have to if you don't want to.

(Faye grabbed Dennis's face.)

FAYE. Dennis, I said sure. I want to see your place anyway.

DENNIS. Great. I guess we will be going. See you at work tomorrow, Jake.

JAKE. If not at work, at lunch for sure.

DENNIS. Jake, my friend, you're not going to hold me to a silly bet like that, are you?

(Jake looked at Dennis.)

DENNIS. I will see you for lunch tomorrow.

CLEO. Faye, you don't forget, we have a free shopping date with these two men.

FAYE. For sure. Oh yeah, don't forget about the full-body massage.

CLEO. Girl, with our bodies, they will benefit from that more than we will.

(Dennis and Jake looked at each other as Cleo and Faye started to laugh. After they left, Jake started kissing Cleo on the back of her neck.)

CLEO. Oh, Jake, you might need to stop. It has only been five weeks, and the nurse said six. But don't stop just yet.

(Jake continued kissing her neck while slowly working his way around to her lips.)

CLEO. Oh, Jake.
JAKE. Wow, I have a sister!
CLEO. Jake! What happened? I know you didn't do me like this?
JAKE. Like what?
CLEO. You know, and you will pay for it.

(Later that night, as they were in bed.)

JAKE. You know it's funny, the dreams I had were telling me of my purpose.
CLEO. What are you talking about?
JAKE. Our pastor said that our purpose in life is related to a person or to people. Here it is. I dreamed about my sister. Even in my dreams, she needed help, but it was me who perverted that dream. I was being led to her all of this time.
CLEO. So do you think that you have fulfilled your purpose?
JAKE. I think that this is only the beginning and I have so much to do. You know, like that Shakespeare fellow said, "All the world's a stage, and all the men and women merely players: they have their exits and their entrances; and one man in his time plays many parts, his acts being seven ages." I feel like that. I still have parts to play. There once was this young man who would work from Sunday to Sunday just to try to have something and to try to make ends meet. He wasn't a bad guy. After all, he went to church when he wasn't working. There was one problem with that. When he did make it to church, he was fighting so hard to stay awake that he didn't get much out of the service. So he worked, paid his bills, and took care of his children. This would go on for months at a time. He wanted to spend more time with them, but he figured that if he worked and just took care of them, that would be enough.

But it seemed like no matter how much he worked and the amount of money he made, it just wasn't enough, so he would try to work some more. Until one Saturday, he was not able to get up to do much. His body had physically shut down. It was that day that he slowed down enough to talk with God, saying, "God, I will not work anymore part-time. If I'm going to make it, it will be because of you. I can't keep living like this." That young man had to come to the realization that it didn't matter how much he worked the only thing that he had to do was to turn to God and be willing to obey him, and things would fall in place. The young man continued to work his regular job and cut out all the other side jobs. He was able to attend church on Sundays—and not only attend, he was able to start to receive the messages that were being taught. Oh, how were his finances? Well, let's just say that he did spend more time with his children, and neither he nor his children wanted for anything. One thing that we must remember is that we can only do so much within our own, but remember Philippians 4:13. "I can do all things through Christ which strengthens me."

Tragedy Strikes

(*A few years have passed. Jake had moved up on his job. Little Jacob was now three. Faye and Dennis were about to announce their engagement, and Cleo was once again expecting.*)

CLEO. Jake, I was hoping that you would stay home a few extra hours to help me with Jacob. I'm not feeling too well this morning.
JAKE. What's wrong? Is it something you ate?
CLEO. No, I think it is more like something you did.
JAKE. I did? What do you mean?
CLEO. Think about it, Jake. It's in the morning, and I am sick.
JAKE. Okay, you're sick. Wait a minute. You are sick, and it's early in the morning. You mean you're pregnant? Wow!
CLEO. Jake, do not ask me who, when, and how again.
JAKE. I'm so excited. How far along are you?
CLEO. Well, I'm not really sure yet. I have an appointment later this week.
JAKE. I will be there.
CLEO. I didn't even tell you when.
JAKE. It doesn't matter. I will be there. Now what do you want me to do this morning?
CLEO. Will you dress and feed Jacob for me?

(*Across town, Dennis and Faye were having a conversation.*)

FAYE. Dennis, are you sure you want to get married? Marry me?
DENNIS. Am I sure. How can you ask me that? We have been together for about two years now. We practically live together.

I want you for my wife. I want to have all of you, and I want you to have all of me.

FAYE. Dennis, you have all of me now. Are you not worried about what everyone will say? After all, you know what the fellows say, "You can't make a whore into a house wife."

DENNIS. Faye, don't you ever let me hear you say that again! You are not a ho'. Think about it. We all were something or someone else before we became who we are now. Remember, when the people were trying to stone the prostitute, Jesus said that those without sin cast the first stone. He then told her to go and sin no more. Well, you have been there, and now you are here.

FAYE. I know, but...

DENNIS. But what? What is it, Faye?

FAYE. Well, you do remember before I met you, I had a pimp. I just have this feeling that if we announce our engagement, there might be trouble.

DENNIS. Trouble? I tell you what, you just let me handle that.

(Dennis soon left for work; once he arrived, he met up with Jake.)

DENNIS. Good morning, my brother.

JAKE. Dennis, how many times have I told you that I am not your brother?

DENNIS. Jake, that's what I kind of want to talk to you about. You see, Faye and I have been together for about two years now, and seeing that you are her older brother, you being my best friend, and since y'all dad is dead, I want to ask you what would you think about me and Faye getting married?

JAKE. Married? You and my sister getting married? Dennis, are you for real? Dennis, I thought you were the ladies' man? I thought that you once said that no one woman can tie you down. You want to marry my sister, why?

DENNIS. Come on, Jake. You know that all of that other stuff was just talk, and besides, I love her.

JAKE. You love her. Do you even know what love is? Dennis, I'm going to break it do to you. This word for *love* doesn't refer to warm feelings but to a deliberate attitude of good will and devotion to others. Love gives freely without looking at whether the other person deserves it, and it gives without expecting anything back. So you say that you love my sister, I ask you this, do you like her?

DENNIS. I said that I love her.

JAKE. I know that. I want to know, do you like her? Because sooner or later that warm feeling that you call love is going to leave, and she is still going to be there. Can you live with her after that warm feeling is gone?

DENNIS. I see what you mean, and my answer is still yes. She brings me such joy. I love her, and I like her. She is everything I want.

JAKE. Dennis, are you forgetting what she used to do for a living? And besides, she shouldn't be the one to bring you joy. She should make you happy, because unlike happiness, joy is gladness that is completely independent of the good or bad things that happen in the course of the day. In fact, joy denotes a supernatural gladness given by God's Spirit that actually seems to show up best during hard times. This is a product of fixing your focus on God's purposes for the events in your life rather than on the circumstances.

DENNIS. I understand. My joy is in the Lord and not in a person. Now how can I forget what she used to do for a living? I was her best customer, remember?

(*Jake and Dennis both laughed.*)

JAKE. Well, if you can live with that and you love and like her like you say you do, then I will be more than happy for you to marry my sister. Now get to work before you won't have a job to support my sister.

DENNIS. Jake, there is one other thing. Faye was kind of worrying about what might happen once we announce our engagement.

JAKE. What do you mean?

DENNIS. Well, she mentioned something about a pimp.

JAKE. Oh, I see. I remember that sorry sucker. We haven't seen or heard from him in a while, but I tell you what, I don't think you two will have to worry about him.

DENNIS. Okay, Jake, I will see you at lunch.

JAKE. Yeah.

(When Dennis left the room, Jake started to think about Faye's former pimp. I truly hope that he is not foolish enough to try to stop her wedding or, even more, stupid enough to attempt to do something to her. Jake decided to go to Mr. Johnson's office. He knew that if anyone could offer any positive advice, Mr. Johnson could. Jake met Mr. Johnson in the hall.)

JAKE. Mr. Johnson, I was just coming to see you.

MR. JOHNSON. Oh yeah, I owe you a congratulations, or has Cleo told you yet?

JAKE. Oh, I guess you know about Dennis and Faye as well?

MR. JOHNSON. Jake, you are about the only one who's just finding out. Now how can I help you?

JAKE. Mr. Johnson, I have a concern. I know you know about the type of work Faye did before she came to work for you.

MR. JOHNSON. Yes, I know. Well, now with her and Dennis wanting to announce their engagement, you are concerned that this pimp might want to show his foul head and try to spoil it for them. Jake, my boy, the best advice I can give you is for all of us to pray. Pray that he doesn't act a fool. Pray that we don't have to bust a cap in his sorry butt!

JAKE. Mr. Johnson! I'm shocked to hear that from you!

MR. JOHNSON. Jake, my boy, I'm human as well, but I know that the right thing to do is to let the Lord fight our battles.

JAKE. Okay, Mr. Johnson, one other thing. You said congratulations. What was that for?

MR. JOHNSON. Oh, Cleo hasn't told you? She hasn't told you that she might be pregnant?

JAKE. Yeah, she told me this morning. Might I ask you, when did you find out?

MR. JOHNSON. Oh, she told me and my wife last week.

JAKE. It figures.

(Feeling better, Jake went back to his office. It wasn't long before Dennis walked back in.)

DENNIS. Jake, are you ready for lunch?

JAKE. Lunch, so soon?

DENNIS. Yeah, it's time. Where do you want to go? How about that pub around the corner from your house. That way, you can go in and check on Cleo and Jacob before we come back to work. Uh, you do know that she might be pregnant again?

JAKE. And when did you find out?

DENNIS. Last week.

JAKE. Dog gone it. Everybody knew before me. I guess Ms. Brown already knew as well? Will we have enough time to go all the way over there?

DENNIS. Jake, you are the man. Besides, I have already told Mr. Johnson that you needed to go check on Cleo.

JAKE. I'm the man, huh?

DENNIS. Well, hell yeah. You think he would have said go ahead for anyone else?

JAKE. Yeah, you are probably right. Man, let's go.

DENNIS. Jake, you want to drive or you want me to drive?

JAKE. Dennis, you don't have a car.

DENNIS. I know. I can drive yours.

JAKE. That is perfectly okay. I will drive. Besides, I have seen you drive before.

(Jake and Dennis left for lunch. They stopped by Jake's home to check on Cleo and Jacob, and then they went on to the pub.)

JAKE. Dennis, remember, no alcohol. We have to go back to work.

DENNIS. You don't have to remind me. I'm a grown man.

WAITER. Hey, Dennis, you want your usual two beers and a burger?

DENNIS. Who me? You must have me confused. I have to go back to work.

WAITER. I know, but that's what you usually get when you come in for lunch.

DENNIS. Well, uh, not today. I've turned over a new leaf on life. I'm getting married.

JAKE. Grown man, my butt. Dennis, I'm starting to wonder if I made a mistake saying you can marry my sister, Faye.

DENNIS. Jake, you are a man of your word.

JAKE. Yeah, I know.

(What Jake and Dennis didn't know was that Faye's former pimp was sitting in the booth behind Jake. And when he heard that Dennis was going to marry Faye, he grabbed a knife and gripped it as if he was getting ready to jump up

and stab someone, but he remembered the beating he had gotten from Jake before. So instead, he thought, "So Faye is big man's sister. I will make their lives miserable, and I will get even with all of them." So he just played it cool until they left. He walked out behind them to see what type of vehicle they were in. And when he saw it, he thought, "Wait a minute, I've seen that car before. That's the car that is parked around the corner from Willie's house. That must be big man's place. Got you!" From that moment on, all he did was plot to take revenge on Jake and his entire family. Jake and Dennis made it back to work, and the day soon ended. Jake got off and hurried home. When he made it home, he parked his car and went inside, but what he didn't notice was this tall slender man standing across the street, hiding behind the big oak tree.)

JAKE. Cleo, I'm home.

JACOB. Daddy, where you been?

JAKE. It's *where have you been*, and the answer is I've been at work so I can provide for you and your mommy, well, until mommy goes back to work.

CLEO. I am glad you cleared that up because you know that I'm going back to work just as soon as the repairs to our building are finished. Jake, did you see a strange person hanging around outside?

JAKE. No, why do you ask?

CLEO. Well, I was talking to our neighbor, and she said that she saw this slender-built man hanging in the neighborhood. It probably was nothing.

JAKE. Yeah, you're probably right, and besides, you know how nosy Karen is.

(Jake knew in his heart that Karen wasn't wrong; he knew that something wasn't right. Later that night.)

CLEO. Jake, are you coming to bed?

JAKE. I'll be there in a few. I think I'm going to stay up and read for a while.

(As Jake sat in his recliner, he thought he heard a noise, so he rushed to the front window. It was nothing. He thought to himself, "I have to get a grip. I can't be jumping at ever sound." He thought, "Lord, I need your peace. I need

your holy peace." Jake pulled out this booklet that Mr. Johnson had given him. It had "Fruit of the Spirit" written in it; he started to read the one on peace.)

JAKE (*reading*). Peace, it's not the absence of turmoil but the presence of tranquility even while in a place of chaos. It is a sense of wholeness and completeness that is content knowing that God controls the events of the day.

(Jake thought, "Yes, Lord, that is the peace I need right now. I have to have your peace so that I can rest." He continued to sit in that recliner until his mind was at eased. The next morning came.)

CLEO. Jake, you stayed up mighty late last night.

JAKE. Yeah, I know, I was reading.

CLEO. Jake, what's the matter? I know when something bothers you.

JAKE. Oh, it's nothing. I just couldn't sleep, so I decided to sit up and read for a bit.

CLEO. Jake!

(Jake hurried and kissed her and rushed out the door. Cleo, being no fool, got on the phone and called Faye.)

CLEO. Faye, this is Cleo.

FAYE. Oh, hey, Cleo, I guess you've heard the great news.

CLEO. News, what news?

FAYE. Jake didn't tell you? Dennis and I are finally getting married!

CLEO. That is great news! No, he didn't tell me. Faye, I hate to ask you this, but was there anything else that could have happened?

FAYE. Girl, I don't know. What do you mean? Unless … no, Dennis didn't mention anything.

CLEO. Unless what?

FAYE. Well, I was concerned that once we announced our engagement my former employer would try to stop the wedding, but Dennis assured me that nothing like that would happen.

CLEO. Now, I'm concerned. This explains why Jake basically stayed up all night. If I know Dennis, and I do know Dennis, he left you and went straight to Jake with that concern.

FAYE. So you are saying that Jake was acting funny? I knew it was wrong. I never should have tried to have a normal life.

CLEO. Faye, stop with all the foolish talk! You deserve a normal life just like anyone else.

FAYE. I don't want to cause you and my brother any headaches.

CLEO. Girl, listen here. If we have any headaches, it will not be because of you and Dennis.

(When Jake made it to work, he went straight to Mr. Johnson's office.)

JAKE. Mr. Johnson, I might need to take off for a few days.

MR. JOHNSON. What's the matter?

JAKE. Well, let's just say that I might have some personal business to take care of.

MR. JOHNSON. Does this business have anything to do with Dennis and Faye getting engaged?

JAKE. You can say that. You see, last night, Cleo told me that our snooping neighbor Karen saw this tall thin man standing behind that old oak tree, the one that is across the street from my home.

MR. JOHNSON. Jake, how do you know if what she was saying is true?

JAKE. I really don't, but I want to make sure that if it is true, I will be there to protect my family.

MR. JOHNSON. Jake, I understand how you feel, but you can't be there 24/7. You can go ahead and take a few days off, but you alone cannot predict when, where, or if something is going to happen.

JAKE. Mr. Johnson, I know, but I will feel better if I could be there at least for today.

MR. JOHNSON. Okay, Jake, my boy. I will see you when you get back.

(Jake left work, but he didn't go straight home. Instead, he drove through the neighborhood where he had encountered Faye's former pimp. He was hoping to see him. He drove up and down each street, and then he thought, "I remember where he lived." Jake drove to where he saw the pimp's family live, but much to his surprise, when he made it there, it was abandon. The windows were boarded up, and two boards were across the front door. "Maybe I'm thinking too hard. Maybe nothing is going to happen." He decided to go on home.)

CLEO. Jake, you're home early.

JAKE. Yeah, I took the rest of the day off.

CLEO. Is there anything wrong?

JAKE. Well, you know that I didn't get much sleep last night, so I took off so I can get some rest, but I can't get that with you asking all these questions.

CLEO. I only asked one question, and you didn't answer it! Jake, what is it? I spoke with Faye a few minutes ago, and she told me that she and Dennis were planning on announcing their engagement. She also told me that it was a concern about her former employer.

JAKE. I guess I might as well tell you. Yes, I'm concerned. Karen said that she saw a tall thin man standing across the street. Well, Faye's pimp was a tall thin person. I even drove by where he once lived, but the house was boarded up. I don't know what to do.

CLEO. Jake, one thing you can't do is to worry about something that hasn't happened.

JAKE. You don't understand. I don't want anything to happen to any of you!

CLEO. Calm down, honey. I'm on your side here.

JAKE. I know, but I guess I'm just a little bit tense.

CLEO. I know how we can work that stress off. Besides, Jacob is asleep and I'm horny.

JAKE. You do know how to relax me.

(*After Cleo relaxed Jake, he decided to go back to work. But as he was pulling out of his driveway, he thought that he saw someone sitting in a parked car, so he decided to drive by the car really slow. He looked over, and it was one of his other neighbors sitting in their car. Jake waved and continued to work. But what Jake didn't know was that he was being watched, and not only was he being watched, so was his family.*)

MR. JOHNSON. Jake, I see that you decided to come back to work.

JAKE. Yeah, Mr. Johnson, I decided that I shouldn't worry about something that hasn't happened yet.

MR. JOHNSON. So you decided all by yourself?

JAKE. Well, I did talk to Cleo, and we came to that conclusion.

MR. JOHNSON. I knew my girl would help you to be at ease. Now go in there and make us some money.
JAKE. Mr. Johnson, I just want to say thanks.
MR. JOHNSON. Just go make us some money.

(Cleo was at the house, cooking, when she heard a knock at the door. She went to the door and peeped out. It appeared to be the postman with a package. She opened the door, and much to her surprise, she was attacked. He slapped and punched her in the face several times.)

PIMP. Your man took away my best girl. I lost my family, and I lost my life because of him. Now I'm going to take something away from him!

(He tore Cleo's clothes off her and begun to rape her. He raped her over and over. He had been watching. He knew what time Jake got off, so each time he was ready, he would rape her again. Cleo didn't want to scream because she didn't want Jacob to wake up and start crying. When he thought that he had enough, he raped her once more, and then he pulled out and ejaculated all over her face. And then he stuck the head of Jacob's toy baseball bat in and out of her, damaging her insides.)

PIMP. Tell your big man that I'm not finished!

(He left. Cleo crawled to the telephone and called the police. When the police and ambulance arrived, their neighbor picked up her phoned and called Jake's job to inform him that an ambulance was at his home.)

KAREN. I need to speak to Jake Martin, please.
MS. BROWN. May I ask who is calling?
KAREN. This is his neighbor Karen.
MS. BROWN. I'll see if he is available. Mr. Martin, you have a Karen on the phone. She says that she is your neighbor.
JAKE. Oh, send her through.
KAREN. Jake, this is Karen. You need to get home right away. They done put Cleo on a stretcher. The police and ambulance is here! I have got to go.

(Jake rushed in and told Mr. Johnson.)

JAKE. I have to go. Something has happened to Cleo!

(*Mr. Johnson grabbed his hat and ran out with Jake.*)

MR. JOHNSON. I will drive. I want you to make it there alive.

(*By the time Jake and Mr. Johnson arrived, the ambulance was already gone but the police remain.*)

OFFICER. Hold it. Who are you?
JAKE. I'm Jake, Jake Martin. I live here. This is my home! Where is my wife? Where's my son!
OFFICER. Sir, your wife has been taken to the hospital, and your son is…
JAKE. To the hospital! What happened!
OFFICER. Sir, your son is in the car with another officer.
JAKE. What happened to my wife!
MR. JOHNSON. Jake, calm down. They can't talk to you until you calm down.
JAKE. Mr. Johnson!
MR. JOHNSON. Jake, is there anyone you can leave Jacob with? Because we probably should be headed to the hospital.

(*Just at that moment Karen walked up.*)

KAREN. Jake, I's be more than happy to keep him for you.
JAKE. Thank you, Karen. I will be back as soon as I can.
KAREN. You don't have to rush. We will be just fine.

(*Jake jumped back into the car with Mr. Johnson. They rushed to the hospital.*)

MR. JOHNSON. Jake, you need to calm down.
JAKE. Did you see all of that blood? Why couldn't they tell me what happened?
MR. JOHNSON. Jake, first of all, they are not doctors. They are only officers.
JAKE. Mr. Johnson, go faster!
MR. JOHNSON. We're going fast enough. You want to make it there alive, don't you?

JAKE. I guess so. Do you think she is … ?

MR. JOHNSON. Jake, don't even think or say it. We both know that life and death is in the power of the tongue!

JAKE. Yeah, I know.

(They arrived at the emergency room. Jake jumped out before the car was at a complete stop. He ran into the emergency room, yelling for Cleo. The armed officers that had followed the ambulance and the hospital security grabbed Jake and tried to get him to the floor, but they were not able to get him off his feet. A nurse grabbed a needle with a sedative and stuck him in his arm. Jake soon calmed down, and when he opened his eyes, there were two officers, two security guards, Mr. Johnson, and a doctor sitting in a room with him.)

DR. PATRICK. Mr. Martin, I'm Dr. Patrick. I'm the emergency room doctor. Mr. Martin, I'm not going to sugarcoat this. Your wife is in bad shape. If she makes it through the night, then we might have a chance. Let's just pray she survives the night. And your baby, I put it like this—if she survives, your baby just might survive. Can I now speak to Mr. Martin alone?

(Everyone left the room.)

DR. PATRICK. Mr. Martin, I have to be honest with you. Your wife was raped, and she was raped multiple times. She was even penetrated with some type of object, which the police think was your baseball bat. It's a wonder she's still alive.

(Jake could only sit there with tears in his eyes; he was still feeling the effect of the shot. He called for Mr. Johnson. Mr. Johnson grabbed his hands and started to pray.)

MR. JOHNSON (*praying*). Our heavenly Father Lord Jesus, we know that there is nothing too hard for you. You are the fixer of all things. Lord, you told us to come boldly before your throne, and now we want to thank you for the healing of Cleo Martin's body. We want to thank you for saving her baby. Lord, we also pray for the person or persons that did this to her. We pray that you have mercy on them. We pray that the police find them before we do, but if they don't, we pray for your forgiveness for what we are going to do to them. Heavenly Father, we pray this in our Lord Jesus's name. Amen.

(Jake looked at Mr. Johnson.)

JAKE. We, what do you mean *we*?

MR. JOHNSON. Jake, while the doctor was talking to you, I just happened to overhear him tell you that it looks like Cleo had been raped repeatedly and then they had repeatedly jammed what the police found out was Jacob's baseball bat in and out of her.

JAKE. Mr. Johnson, I need to see her.

MR. JOHNSON. I'll as the doctor if will it be okay for you to see her.

(Mr. Johnson left the room and found the doctor at the desk.)

MR. JOHNSON. Doctor, Mr. Martin wants to know if he could see his wife.

DR. PATRICK. I really don't think it would be wise, but since he is still feeling the effect of the shot and we still have the officers and security here, I guess we can let him in to see her, but he can't touch her. She probably won't be able to respond, but he can see her. I will have the nurse to make sure that she is covered up. The less he sees, the better it will probably be.

(The nurse came into the room where Jake and Mr. Johnson were waiting.)

Nurse. Mr. Martin, if you would come with me, I will take you to your wife.

(Jake nervously got up and slowly walked with the nurse toward room number 7, while the officers, security, and Mr. Johnson followed behind. The nurse opened the door. With tears in his eyes, Jake slowly walked in. He was the only one besides the doctor and nurse who was allowed to go in. He walked to her bedside, and he looked at her beaten and bruised face and upper body. He could not believe that it was her; she didn't look anything like herself. Jake bent over and whispered.)

JAKE. Cleo, my love, I am truly sorry that I was not there for you, but I will hunt down the low-down dirty dog that did this to you, and I will make him wish that he had never been conceived.

(Much to everyone's surprise, Cleo opened her eyes and said with extremely low voice, "No." Then her eyes closed again as she rested. The doctor and nurse looked at each other as if a miracle had just happened.)

NURSE. Can you believe she opened her eyes? Can you believe that she was able to speak or even make the motion to speak? I wonder what she said.

(As they walked out of the room, Jake looked at Mr. Johnson and told him what happened.)

JAKE. After I told her about me getting even with the person who did this to her, she opened both of her eyes and whispered, "No."

(With tears in his eyes, Mr. Johnson looked at Jake and told him that it would be to our best interest to do like she asked.)

MR. JOHNSON. As hard as it might be, we need to let the law handle him.

JAKE. So you also know who did this?

MR. Johnson. There is not a doubt in my mind he did this, but we must respect her wish.

JAKE. Mr. Johnson, what am I to do?

MR. JOHNSON. First of all, you must remember that you still have Jake to take care of, and then there is Jacob and finally Cleo.

JAKE. Finally, what do you mean finally?

MR. JOHNSON. Jake, look around you. There are doctors and nurses around here to look after Cleo, but who is there for Jacob, your neighbor? As a matter of fact, we might want to get over there and get him.

JAKE. You don't think that he would … not Jacob. He couldn't. He wouldn't.

MR. JOHNSON. Jake, all I'm saying is that we need to go and get him. He can stay with me and the missus until Cleo comes home.

JAKE. But wouldn't that be putting your and your wife's lives in danger?

MR. JOHNSON. Let me worry about that, plus he probably wouldn't think of looking for Jacob over at my house anyway. Let's go get him.

JAKE. Mr. Johnson, I really want to thank you for being here for me. You are more than a boss. You are a father figure and a true friend. Thank you, Mr. Johnson.

(As they turned down Jake's street, they saw an unusual number of officers. Jake looked at Mr. Johnson.)

MR. JOHNSON. Jake, let's not jump to any conclusions. They could just be still here at your house.

(Mr. Johnson had to park four houses down. Jake jumped out and hurried to Karen's house. He knocked on her door.)

KAREN. Who is it?

JAKE. Karen, it's me, Jake.

(Karen slowly looked out the side front window. She saw that it was Jake. By that time, Mr. Johnson was standing with Jake.)

KAREN. Jake, who is that with you?

JAKE. Karen, this is Mr. Johnson, my boss. Open the door, I come to get Jacob.

(Karen opened the door, and on the inside with her was an officer.)

JAKE. What are you doing in here?

OFFICER. Jake, just relax.

JAKE. How do you know my name, and who told you that you could call me by my name?

OFFICER. Listen here, Jake. I'm here to protect you and your baby boy!

JAKE. You are here to protect me and my son? How's that, and you're in here drinking coffee and smoking cigarettes? Shouldn't you be out there trying to find the person who did that to my wife? Officer. Person, you said person. How do you know that it was only one person?

JAKE. How do you know that it wasn't?

OFFICER. Mr. Martin, do you know who did this?

JAKE. No, I do not know.

OFFICER. Well, Mr. Martin, if you happen to get any information, why don't you just call this number and ask for me or Detective Williams, and one of us will be more than glad to assist you.

(*The plain-clothes officer left out of the front door.*)

MR. JOHNSON. Jake, why didn't you tell him about the pimp?

JAKE. Mr. Johnson, I will explain it to you on my way home. Karen, I want to thank you very much for helping with Jacob.

KAREN. He was no problem at all. He's a good child.

JAKE. Thanks again.

KAREN. Jake, how's Cleo?

JAKE. She's in pretty bad shape, but the doctor says that if she makes it through the night, then she might be okay.

KAREN. We will all be praying for her. Jake, if you need me to keep Jacob while you go to work or the hospital, I will be more than happy to.

JAKE. Thanks again.

(*Jake, Jacob, and Mr. Johnson left. But while they were leaving, little Jacob woke up.*)

JACOB. Daddy, where is Mommy? Is she at home?

(*Jake looked at Mr. Johnson, and Mr. Johnson looked at him.*)

JAKE. Well, Jacob, you see, Mommy had a little accident, and she got hurt, so Mommy has to stay at the hospital for a while.

JAKE. When she coming home?

JAKE. It might take a while for Mommy to get better.

JACOB. Can I see her?

JAKE. Not right now. That too will be a while.

JACOB. Daddy, I want Mommy!

JAKE. I do too.

(*Jake looked at Mr. Johnson.*)

MR. JOHNSON. Jake, pray for self-control.

JAKE. Self-control? What do you think? I'm going out on my wife at a time like this?

MR. JOHNSON. No, Jake. Self-control is more than sexual. It's ... our fleshly desires. Scripture tells us we are continually at odds with God's Spirit and always want to be in charge. Self-control is literally releasing our grip on the fleshly desires, choosing instead to be controlled by the Holy Spirit. It is power focused in the right place.

MR. JOHNSON. And I know right now everything inside of you want to hunt this skinny pimp guy down and beat him like the lowdown dog he is. How do I know this? Well, because I feel the same exact way. But two things. First, we are not 100 percent sure that he was the one, and second, in Romans 12:19, the Lord says, "Dearly beloved, avenge not yourselves, but rather give place unto wrath: for it is written, Vengeance is mine; I will repay, saith the Lord." So, Jake, you see that we must do our best to restrain from taking the law into our own hands.

JAKE. I see where you are coming from, but...

MR. JOHNSON. No buts, Jake.

JAKE. What I was about to say was that I wouldn't be avenging myself but my wife.

MR. JOHNSON. Jake, if you avenge your wife, you will be avenging yourself as well. You must remember you two are one.

JAKE. How come I knew you were going to say that? I need to get Jacob some clothes together so I can take him back to Karen's.

MR. JOHNSON. Back to Karen's? You will not do such a thing. Didn't I tell you, you are going to let Mrs. Johnson and myself keep Jacob? After all, what are godparents? If we can't keep him in a time of crisis, what good are we?

JAKE. Mr. Johnson, are you sure? You have not even talked with Mrs. Johnson.

MR. JOHNSON. Jake, you just go in there and get his stuff together.

JAKE. Mr. Johnson, I can't thank you enough. Oh, I'm going to need some time off. I will be spending time at the hospital.

MR. JOHNSON. Jake, consider it already done. You are going back to the hospital to night.

JAKE. Yes, I am. What did you think?

MR. JOHNSON. Oh, nothing, just asking.

(Jake went into Jacob's room and got his stuff ready.)

JAKE. Here we go.

JACOB. Daddy, where we going? We going to see Mommy?

JAKE. No, Jacob, you are going to spend time with your godparents, Mr. and Mrs. Johnson.

JACOB. Daddy, I don't want to go with them. I want to go see Mommy. Why can't I go see Mommy? I want Mommy!

JAKE. Jacob, shut up!

MR. JOHNSON. Jake, calm down. Let me handle this. Jacob, your Mommy isn't feeling too good right now, and she needs a lot of rest.

JACOB. Mommy is taking a nap?

MR. JOHNSON. Yes, your mommy is napping right now.

JACOB. Yeah, Mommy is taking a nap.

MR. JOHNSON. So we don't need to make any noise, right?

JACOB. Right.

MR. JOHNSON. So you are going home with me, and Daddy can go and make sure that no one does anything to stop Mommy from taking her nap.

JACOB. Okay, bye-bye, Daddy. I love you.

JAKE. I love you too, Jacob.

(As soon as Jacob and Mr. Johnson left, Jake went back into the house and broke down crying.)

JAKE. Lord, give me the strength. Give me the strength to not look for this guy!

(Jake soon got things together and started back to the hospital. He wondered if Dennis and Faye had made it there. Jake was back to the hospital.)

JAKE. Dennis, how's everything. Any changes?

DENNIS. Not that I know of. We've been here, and no one has come out to talk to us.

FAYE. Well, Jake, my brother, you know what they say, no news is good news.

JAKE. Yeah, Faye, that's what they say. Dennis, may I have a word with my sister?

DENNIS. Yeah, sure, I'll just step outside.

JAKE. Faye, I'm afraid.

FAYE. Jake, you're not afraid of anyone.

JAKE. I know, it's not that I'm afraid of anyone. I'm afraid that I won't be able to protect my family. I was not there for Cleo, and what if something was to happen to Jacob, you, or Dennis? Hell, now Mr. and Mrs. Johnson are involved. What can I do? Faye. Jake, first of all, you need to pull yourself together. I want you to know that you are not the savior of all. You do have a responsibility to your wife and child, but we are all grown, and we make our own decisions, so if we choose to stand by the people you love, so be it. Now having said that, I can understand your concern, but don't you ever let the word *fear* come out of your mouth again, because our God does not give us the spirit of fear, and I know that you are a godly man.

JAKE. Faye, I am glad that you are my sister, and I'm happy that we had this talk.

(*The nurse rushed into the room.*)

NURSE. Mr. Martin, the doctor will be in to speak with you all in a minute.

JAKE. Is everything all right? How is she? What's going on?

NURSE. Mr. Martin, the doctor will be here in a moment.

(*The doctor entered the room.*)

DOCTOR. Mr. Martin, I have some news. It looks like wife and child might survive, but we need to put her into a medically induced coma. She is fighting so much that it's hard for her to heal.

JAKE. Do it then!

DOCTOR. Mr. Martin, there is one thing. Your child, if we put her in a coma, your child might not survive.

JAKE. A decision has to be made.

FAYE. Jake, think about it. You and Cleo can make another baby, but you have only one Cleo.

JAKE. I guess you're right. Go ahead, Doc. Do what you must.

(The doctor left the room.)

FAYE. Jake, I see that look in your eyes. You can't do it. Jake, you just can't do it.

(Jake stormed out of the room.)

Keeping His Promise

FAYE. Dennis, go with him. You can't let him do anything he might regret. I will stay here. You can call, and if there are any changes, I will let you two know. Dennis, I love you.
DENNIS. I love you too.

(*Dennis swallowed really hard and loud and walked out behind Jake.*)

DENNIS. Where are you going? I'm going with you. Faye asked me to go with you and keep you out of trouble.
JAKE. How are you going to keep me out of trouble? But if you must, come on.

(*Dennis had no idea where they were about to go, but before they made it out of the hospital doors, their apostle and pastor arrived. The apostle looked at Jake and Jake at him. It was as if Jake was a child; he started to cry. He cried like he had been holding tears back his whole life. The apostle grabbed him and just held him. He didn't have to say a word. But what he felt was not all hurt; it was anger and confusion. After Jake finished crying, they all walked back to the waiting room.*)

APOSTLE. Hello, Faye.
FAYE. Hello, Apostle, Pastor. I'm glad to see you two.
PASTOR. I sense that we arrived just in time. Faye, how's Jake holding up?
JAKE. I'm right here. You can ask me.
APOSTLE. Faye, how is Jake holding up?
FAYE. Well, under the circumstances, I think he's doing very well.

APOSTLE. That's what we want to hear. Jake, I sense that Satan desires to sift you as wheat. He wants to make a martyr of you. You must be strong, and you must listen to your wife.

(Mr. Johnson was pulling up at his home.)

MR. JOHNSON. Emma, I have a surprise for you.

EMMA. Jacob, little Jacob, is he going to spend the night with us?

MR. JOHNSON. Well, it's like several nights. Something has happened.

EMMA. My god, what?

(Mr. Johnson whispered.)

MR. JOHNSON. Well, Cleo has been attacked, beaten, and raped.

EMMA. No, is she going to be okay?

MR. JOHNSON. I'm more concerned about Jake. I feel that Satan desires to sift him as wheat. I must keep him from doing something that he will regret for the rest of his life.

EMMA. You mean to tell me that he knows who did it?

MR. JOHNSON. I think we both do, but the funniest thing happened. Jake made a promise to Cleo that he would get the person who did that to her, and while she was lying there unconscious, she opened her eyes and said, "No."

(Back at the hospital, the apostle and pastor continued to speak with Jake and the rest. They prayed for the family and stayed for a while, but they had to leave, so they said their good-byes and well-wishes and left. As they were leaving, Jake called for Dennis.)

JAKE. Dennis, are you coming?

(Jake and Dennis left the hospital.)

DENNIS. Jake, do you want me to drive?

(Jake didn't say a word. He just looked at Dennis. Dennis got in on the passenger's side; he once again tried to make conversation.)

DENNIS. Hey, Jake, where are we going?

(Once again, Jake didn't mumble a word. He just drove; it wasn't until he turned down the street where he lived that Dennis knew where they were going. He remembered that Jake told him that he had brought a .357. They arrived; Jake sat there for a while. Dennis dared not to say another word. Dennis looked at Jake; he looked like a person with death in his heart. Dennis tried once more.)

DENNIS. Jake, are you all right?

(Once again, Jake didn't utter a word. Jake opened his car door and put one foot on the ground and then the other. He then stood up and looked back at Dennis as to say, "Are you coming?" Dennis got out, and they slowly walked toward front door. There was yellow police tape from pole to pole. Jake simply broke the tape and continued on to the front door. Dennis thought to himself, "Should we even be here?" Jake put his key in the lock and opened the door. When they walked in, there was a bloodstain on the floor. Jake felt like his head and chest were about to burst opened. He felt like pressure was pulling him down. But then all of sudden, he spoke.)

JAKE. Sit down.

(Dennis sat down. Jake went to the laundry room and got some cleaning supplies; he returned and started to clean the bloodstained floor. After he finished, Jake walked to the back room. Dennis didn't know what to do. He looked at the bar. He thought, "Maybe I should pour myself a drink." Then he looked at the fridge and thought, "Maybe I should go get me a cold beer." He did neither. He simply did what Jake told him to do; he sat down. Jake made it to the bedroom. He went into the closet. He reached into his Converse shoebox and pulled out his .357. He looked at it, and then he looked in the dresser drawer and picked up six rounds and began to load the gun. And then he sat down and put the barrel of the gun in his mouth, but it was then that the heard a voice coming from inside of him.)

VOICE. Jake, instead of putting a gun in your mouth, let words come out of your heart.

(Jake pulled the barrel out of his mouth, and he began to pray.)

JAKE. My heavenly Father, Lord Jesus, I know you said that you would never leave me nor forsake me, but now it feels like you have. Lord, I can't do this by myself. I need you. I feel like the weight of the world is on my shoulders. I feel like my head is about to explode. Lord, I need you right now! Lord, years ago in my dreams you showed me having to kill to protect my sister Faye. Was that dream a thing that I must do, or was it a thing that I took into my own hands and did?

(*As he was praying, part of the Psalm 23 came to his recalling.*)

JAKE (*praying*). Yea, though I walk through the valley of the shadow of death, I will fear no evil for you are with me. Your rod and your staff, they comfort me.

(*Jake continued to pray, but then something happened as he was praying. He went from words that he understood to words and sounds that he did not know the meaning of, but he continued and then the tears that were in his eyes started to dry up. The weight that he felt on his shoulders started to lift. The pressure in his head started to leave, and he felt like he was floating and being carried away. He felt like a small child being picked up by his father. Just as the praying and vision stopped, he heard that voice from inside of him telling him to write and do what he heard next. Jake jumped up, forgetting all about the gun he once put in his mouth. He picked up a pen and paper and started to write.*)

HOLY SPIRIT. Satan comes to sift you as wheat. He wants you to stand in defeat. The words that he speak are full of lies and deceit. You listen to the words that come out of your mouth, but I hear the words that are deep in your heart. I shaped and formed you when you were in your mother's womb. I placed a path out before you. Some will follow, and some will not. I am God, and I give you free will, yet I do love you still. When you look in the mirror and see your face, just remember that you are blessed and saved by grace.

(*After Jake wrote those words, he went to get Dennis. It was during this time that Dennis felt a peace come over him; he was so relaxed that he drifted off into a deep sleep.*)

JAKE. Dennis, come on.
DENNIS. What come on? Where are we going?

(Dennis looked at Jake's hands to make sure that he didn't have anything in them.)

JAKE. Come on, Dennis. We have to get back to the hospital.
DENNIS. What, did someone call?
JAKE. No, we just have to get back there. I know now what Mr. Johnson was talking about. We must trust in God and take ourselves out of the situation.
DENNIS. How is that going to solve anything?
JAKE. Dennis, let's look at it like this—I could go and hunt down that no-good sorry a … Oh, forgive me, I have to watch my words. I could go hunt him down and cut his balls off and shove them down his throat, but I have to think about it. With me doing that, will that help Cleo to heal? Would I get any pleasure out of it? Uh, I probably would, but in the long run, what good will that do?
DENNIS. Jake, what has happened to you?
JAKE. Well, Dennis you know all of the time we've been in church I have never heard God's voice until now. Oh I thought I knew him, you know with me being a Deacon and everything. But it's not until God shows you your own heart and speak words to you that you get to know him. The Holy Spirit spoke to me and most important I spoke to him.
DENNIS. What did you say to him?
JAKE. I really can't tell you.
DENNIS. Why, is it a secret or something?
JAKE. No, it's no secret. I just don't know what I was saying.
DENNIS. I'm confused.
JAKE. Yeah, I don't doubt it, but for now, let's just get out and go in.

(Jake and Dennis had arrived back at the hospital. They went to the waiting room where Faye was waiting.)

FAYE. Thank God you are here. I would have called you, but I didn't know where you were.
JAKE. Is there something wrong?

FAYE. No, but the doctor did come in here about thirty minutes ago and said that something just happened. He said that he had never seen anything like this before.

JAKE. What happened?

FAYE. Well, you remember that they said that they were going to have to put Cleo in a medically induced coma so that her body could get some rest and so that she could recover?

JAKE. I remember, now get to what has happened!

FAYE. Well, the doctor said that when they were putting Cleo in the coma, she woke up and said that my god has supplied all of my needs! Then he said when they checked her vital signs, everything was normal!

JAKE. What? So what does that mean?

FAYE. He said that he would wait until you get here to explain the rest.

(*Faye picked up the phone, and the nurses' station phone rang.*)

FAYE. This is Faye Martin. I'm here in the waiting room, and the doctor told me to let you all know when my brother, Jake, made it back. Well, he's back.

NURSE. Okay, Ms. Martin, the doctor will be right in to speak to you all.

JAKE. What is it, Faye? Has something happened to Cleo?

FAYE. Jake, calm down. All I know is the doctor came in and asked if you were here and, if not, to let the front desk know when you returned. That's all I know.

DENNIS. Come on, Jake, man, don't take it out on Faye. Hey, look at he bright side. She said that the doctor will be coming in and not the preacher.

JAKE. I guess you're right. I really don't want to lose my Cleo or my baby, but if it comes between my child and—

DENNIS. Jake, don't go there.

JAKE. Yeah, I guess you're right again. Dennis, this has to be a record.

DENNIS. What has to be a record?

JAKE. You've been right two times in a row.

DENNIS. That's very funny, Jake.

(*The atmosphere calmed, but as soon as they heard the doctor on the outside of the door, their hearts began to race.*)

DOCTOR. Mr. Martin, family, I want to tell you all that Mrs. Martin's vital signs are as well as can be expected. After she woke up, we did go ahead and put her in the coma, but I can tell that she is fighting to resurface.

JAKE. What about my baby, Doc? And Faye said that she had woke up and spoke.

DOCTOR. Well, like I said, if Mrs. Martin is strong enough to pull through this, then the baby has a chance. And she did speak, but then she passed back out.

JAKE. Thanks, Doc.

(*As the doctor was leaving the room, Dennis looked over at Jake. Jake had that look in his eyes. He looked like he wanted to kill, rip open, and chew that skinny pimp up and spit him out.*)

JAKE. That punk-ass coward!

FAYE. Jake, what are you saying?

JAKE. Excuse me, but that skinny punk. If he was half a man, he would have come at me, not at my wife.

FAYE. Jake, what about controlling yourself?

JAKE. I am under control. I'm not out looking for him. Lord knows I want to. It is taking everything I believe to not look for the sorry piece of—

FAYE. Jake! You should try to get some rest.

JAKE. Faye, you're right. Maybe I should just try to get some rest. I'll just go call Mr. Johnson to check on Jacob.

DENNIS. Jake, here's a phone right here. You don't even have to leave the room to look for one.

JAKE. Maybe I just want to get some fresh air.

FAYE. Jake, come on. I will go with you.

FAYE. Dennis, do you mind if Jake and I go get some fresh air?

DENNIS. Well.

FAYE. Dennis, you don't mind if I go with my brother to get some fresh air!

DENNIS. Oh, I don't mind at all.

(*Jake and Faye walked out of the family waiting room down two halls and out the side door. Jake turned and looked at Faye, and then it happened again. Tears started to flow from Jake's eyes. Tears flowed like Niagara Falls. They continued to flow for about what seemed to be two minutes. Faye simply put her arms around him and whispered in his ear. After she whispered in his ear, he held his head up and dried his eyes and said thank you. They both looked at each other, smiled, and walked back into the hospital.)*

JAKE. I want to thank you again. Sometime we can know a thing, but we still need to hear it to be reminded. Faye, thanks.

FAYE. Jake, this is what baby sisters are for.

(They both smiled again, walked back into the family waiting room, only to find Dennis sleeping. He wasn't only sleeping, he had his head back and mouth wide open. They both looked and started to laugh.)

FAYE. Jake, what are we going to do?

JAKE. Faye, I really don't know. I want to go after this punk, but I know in my spirit that would be so wrong, but me doing nothing makes me feel like a punk also. Yes, I know what the Word says about vengeance, but how much can a man take?

FAYE. Jake, you must remember that we do not fight against flesh and blood.

JAKE. Yeah, yeah, yeah, I know, but I have to do something!

FAYE. Well, why don't you start by calling the police and giving them the information that you have on this skinny punk. Oops, I mean pimp.

JAKE. You're right. At least they can be looking for him, and besides, they just might save me the trouble.

(Faye bucked her eyes.)

JAKE. Hey, I'm only joking.

(A few days passed. Jake had returned to working during the day, but he still stayed at the hospital at night. One evening, as he was entering the hospital, he had a funny feeling. He went to the floor where Cleo was housed, and as he got off the elevator, he saw a new orderly going into Cleo's room, so he started to walk faster, but as he started to walk faster, hospital security noticed, so they started to walk up behind him. They didn't catch him. Before he made it to Cleo's room, he flung the door open, and the orderly had a pillow that he was about to put over Cleo's face. Jake went to grab him, but the security, not seeing

what was going on, grabbed Jake. Jake struggled, and the orderly ran out and away. The nurse ran down there and told security to let him go as this was Mr. Martin, and this was his wife. Once they turned him loose, he ran after the skinny orderly. But it was too late; he had disappeared. But Jake got a good look at him, and he knew exactly who it was. The orderly ran until he knew he was no longer being chased. He slowed down to a normal walk in order not to draw any attention to himself. While he was walking, he started reflecting back on his own life. "Yeah, I'm a pimp. I'm the best damn pimp. If I'm so good, how did I get myself in this situation?" Then he went all the way back. He started thinking back when his momma often spoke to him with slurred speech.)

PIMP'S MOTHER. Yeah, look at my little pimp. You gonna have all the whores you gonna be, just like your sorry-ass daddy. Then she would tell all of the rest of the ladies, "Here's your next pimp. Y'all better be careful, or he gonna wimp all of y'all sorry asses." Yeah, this is my pimp, just look at him. Don't he look good?

(*He also thought back to the nights where he used to lie in bed and hear his momma and one of his many uncles screaming and grunting all during the night, but he never woke up to see any of the so-called uncles.)*

PIMP. Now look at the predicament I've gotten myself into. My wife left me and took my kids, and I've lost my main whore. She was the only one actually making money, but worst of all, the big son of a gun knows that it was me who put his wife in the hospital. There are only two things I can do—I can run, or I can kill him!

(*While back at the hospital.*)

SECURITY. Mr. Martin, we are extremely sorry.

JAKE. Sorry! How in the hell can you say that you are sorry? You all let this sorry piece of … never mind. Nurse, did you check on my wife?

NURSE. Yes, I did, and it looks like you walked in right on time. He didn't have time to do anything.

SECURITY. Mr. Martin, this will not happen again. We are going to post security at her door 24/7.

JAKE. Yeah, that should help, but in the meantime, I'm going to do what I should have done in the beginning.

(*Jake stormed out of Cleo's room with fire in his eyes. The security officers tried to say something else to him, but he just blew by them. Jake walked like a man on a mission. Dennis and Faye were trying to settle in.*)

FAYE. Dennis, I'm worried.

DENNIS. Worried? Worried about what? I know you're not worrying about us getting married.

FAYE. No, Dennis, I'm worried for the guy who did that to Cleo.

DENNIS. What? You mean to tell me that you care about what happens to that sorry sucker!

FAYE. Dennis, now don't take this the wrong way. I kind of feel sorry for him.

DENNIS. You feel sorry for him?

FAYE. Yeah, you see, he has nowhere to go. And if you knew his background, you might understand. You see, when he was young, his mother was a whore, so he never knew his father. She didn't know how, nor did she have time to bring him up. All he has ever known is the streets; he never had a chance, seeing man after man with his mom and all of them being called uncle. He once told me that he would be in his bed at night just listening to his mom screaming and grunting. You see what I'm talking about? He never had a chance.

DENNIS. You sound like you love him or something.

FAYE. Dennis, will you ever learn? I do love him, but it's not the type of love you're thinking of. You see, true love … well, let me put it like this. This word for *love* doesn't refer to warm feelings but to a deliberate attitude of good will and devotion to others. Love gives freely without looking at whether the other person deserves it, and it gives without expecting anything back.

DENNIS. Yeah, I see what you mean, but what you better hope is that your brother doesn't catch up with him or change his mind about letting the law handle this.

(*Just as soon as they finished talking, the phone rang.*)

FAYE. Hello, yes, this is Faye Martin.

DETECTIVE WILLIAMS. Ms. Martin, I need to know, is your brother with you, or have you recently seen him?

FAYE. No, is there something wrong?

DETECTIVE WILLIAMS. No, Ms. Martin. We just had an incident here at the hospital.

FAYE. An incident, what do you mean an incident?

DENNIS. What is it, honey?

FAYE. Hold on, Dennis. What type of incident?

DETECTIVE WILLIAMS. Well, it appears that someone was masquerading as one of the orderlies, and he had entered into Cleo's room.

FAYE. What?

DETECTIVE WILLIAMS. Well, Mr. Martin came in before anything happened.

FAYE. We are on our way!

DETECTIVE WILLIAMS. Ms. Martin, what we really need is for you to find your brother. I was told that he left out of here with death in his eyes.

FAYE. Why, did he see who this person was?

DETECTIVE WILLIAMS. Yes, he did.

FAYE. Oh no, he can't. He promised Cleo.

DETECTIVE WILLIAMS. Ms. Martin, are you okay?

FAYE. I'm okay. Did anyone else see this person, and can you describe him?

DETECTIVE WILLIAMS. Yes, they say he was a kind of tall, skinny fellow.

FAYE. Oh no, we are on our way! Did anyone see which way Jake went?

DETECTIVE WILLIAMS. He left going south.

FAYE. Dennis, you have to go to Jake's house!

DENNIS. Jake's house, for what?

FAYE. You have got to stop him!

DENNIS. Stop him from doing what?

FAYE. He is going to kill him!

DENNIS. Kill who?

FAYE. Stop asking so many damn questions and get over to Jake's! I'm sorry, honey. I didn't mean to curse or yell at you, but we must stop Jake from doing something that he will later regret! But now, I'm really worried. He tried to kill Cleo again, and Jake saw him!

DENNIS. My god, now you do have a reason to worry!

(But what they didn't know was when Jake walked out of the hospital, he started to pray, and as he prayed in the spirit, he lost his wanting to kill that low-down skinny excuse of a male. He wanted to rip his head off his body. He wanted to tear open his chest and pull his heart out. Jake had all of those killing thoughts and more, but once he started to pray, those thoughts started to fade. He started to think about Jacob. He started to thank God that he showed up at Cleo's room before that low-down dog could do anything to her. While they were thinking that Jake was going home to get his gun, he was actually going to the police station to give them the information. In a moment of panic, Faye called Mr. Johnson.)

FAYE. Mr. Johnson?
MR. JOHNSON. Yes, who is this calling this late?
FAYE. Mr. Johnson, this is Faye, Faye Martin.
MR. JOHNSON. What's the matter, Faye?
FAYE. Mr. Johnson, it's Jake!
MR. JOHNSON. Jake, what about him?
FAYE. He's about to kill Simon!
MR. JOHNSON. Simon, who in the world is Simon?
FAYE. You know, the pimp!
MR. JOHNSON. Simon, that's his name? My god, okay, slow down and start from the beginning.
FAYE. Well, Jake went back to the hospital, and when he was about to go into Cleo's room, he saw Simon in there.
MR. JOHNSON. He saw Simon! Did he do anything to him?
FAYE. He tried, but I think the security grabbed Jake, and Simon got away!
MR. JOHNSON. So where is Jake now?
FAYE. I don't know, but I'm worried. I'm worried that Jake is going to find him and do something to him. He is going to kill him!
MR. JOHNSON. Sister, we must have faith. We must know that the God in Jake will speak to him and intervene. There is little more we can do. Has anyone tried to find Jake?
FAYE. Yes, Dennis has gone to his house.
MR. JOHNSON. Well, let's just pray that Dennis can find him, and if he finds him, he can talk him down.

(Dennis made it to Jake's house and knocked on the door.)

DENNIS. Jake, Jake, it's me, Dennis. Please don't shoot. It's me, Dennis!

(Dennis continued knocking, but there was no answer. Soon the neighbor across the street yelled out.)

KAREN. There is no one there.
DENNIS. Are you sure?
KAREN. Yeah, I'm sure. I've been watching over there all night, and I haven't seen anyone.
DENNIS. Okay, thanks, nosy heifer.

(Dennis started to feel some relief, yet he didn't. He started to think, "Where can he be? Where has Jake gone?" Dennis thought, "I will check back later." Jake made it to the police department.)

DESK OFFICER. How can I help you?
JAKE. Yes, I need to speak to Detective Williams.
DESK OFFICER. Just wait here for a minute. Hey, Detective, some big—oh, I thought I asked you to wait in there. I really need to speak with Detective Williams.
DETECTIVE WILLIAMS. I have been looking all over for you. Hello, sir. How might I help you?
JAKE. Look, Detective Williams, I'm Jake, Jake Martin, and my wife was severely beaten within inches of her life, and then a few minutes ago, the guy tried to finish the job.
DETECTIVE WILLIAMS. Hold on, you have to fill me in from the beginning.

(Jake sat down and started to tell the detective the story from the beginning.)

JAKE. Look, you just said that you've been looking all over for me. So why don't you stop your bull… Well, since you want to pretend, my wife was raped and beaten and just a few minutes ago this same guy tried to kill her while she is still in the hospital! So you see, this is why I came here.

DETECTIVE WILLIAMS. Are you sure that this is the guy who raped and beat your wife at your home?

JAKE. Look, why would he be at the hospital, trying to kill her, if he wasn't the guy?

(By this time, Jake was getting frustrated.)

JAKE. Wait a minute. I remember you now. You are that same officer when that sorry excuse for a human being and I got into it before you stood on his side. What, are you still on his payroll?

(Jake stood up; the officer got scared.)

DETECTIVE WILLIAMS. Look, you just need to sit down and stay calm. I promise that we are going to look into…

JAKE. Look into what? If you weren't a cop!

DETECTIVE WILLIAMS. Watch what you say. I can get you for threatening an officer.

JAKE. So you can try and lock me up but that sorry punk pimp can do what he did to my wife, and all you can do is continue to question me? Look, I'm about to get up and get out of here before I do something to get locked for!

(Jake got up, and the detective placed his hand on his .45 revolver as if he wanted Jake to do something so he could use it. Jake got up and walked out of that so-called police department. He didn't have any idea what his next move would be. So for now, he just walked. He thought about going to his house to get his gun. He thought about hunting him down and do to him the same that he had done to Cleo. He could not think of anything but evil thoughts. They were racing through his mind. They were coming one after another. It felt as if he was going to lose his mind. All of this continued until he uttered one name, and that name was Jesus.)

Finding Help

JAKE. Jesus! I need you right now. I don't know what to do. I can't handle this all alone. I need you. You said that you would never leave me nor forsake me, and well, I truly need you right now. What am I to do?

(As Jake was walking, he found himself in front of his supervisor's house, Mr. Johnson. Jake thought to himself, "How did I get over here? I wasn't even heading in this direction." But he was glad to be there because he knew that if anyone could help him, it would be Mr. Johnson. He walked up and knocked on the door. Mr. Johnson answered the door.)

MR. JOHNSON. Who is it? *(He said it with a forceful tone.)*

JAKE. Mr. Johnson, it's me, Jake. I know that it is late, but I was walking, and somehow I looked up, and I just happened to be in front of your house.

MR. JOHNSON. Come on in, son!

JAKE. Mr. Johnson, I just don't know what to do. I went to the hospital, and there he was trying to kill CLEO. Then I went to the police, like I was supposed to, but they tried to arrest me. What am I to do?

MR. JOHNSON. Jake, you just remember, when you are lost and don't know what to do, you can always turn to the Lord for guidance. Proverbs 3:5–6 says, "Trust in the Lord with all your heart, lean not until your own understandings acknowledge Him in all your ways and he shall direct your paths."

MR. JOHNSON. Jake, my boy, I can't tell you what to do, because in my flesh I want to do the same as you. I want to go out, hunt that low-down dog down, and severely punish him, but in my spirit, I know that wouldn't be the right thing to do, so all I can tell you to do is to get on your face before God and trust that he will lead you in the right direction.

(Just a few blocks away, Simon sat thinking of ways that he could trap and kill Jake. Then all of a sudden, he heard a voice.)

THE VOICE. What are we doing?
SIMON. Who are you, where are you?
THE VOICE. Just look at us here. We're sitting in an abandoned building, trying to think of ways to kill someone.

(There was another voice.)

SECOND VOICE. Yeah, so what? We need to kill him before that big on of a … finds us and kills us.
THE VOICE. How can you say that? For all we know, he might not be looking for us.
SECOND VOICE. Look, are we going to take that chance that he might not be looking for us? Look, we know where to get guns, and we know that the cops are on our side. We can kill him and just disappear, and no one will ever have to know. The Voice. We will know, and you will always have to remember another murder.
SECOND VOICE. Another murder, now we know that was an accident. How could we have known that his mother was going to jump in front of that pimp?
THE VOICE. Yet we still pulled the trigger. We pulled the trigger that took our mother's life.
SIMON. No, get out of my head! I don't need you or you. I can do this on my own! If I decide to kill that punk-ass dude, I'll do it on my own. I don't need you telling me to do it, nor do I need you telling me not to do it, because I am a pimp, a *P-I-M-P*, and I am the man. I am the shit. *(Simon balled up as if he was a babe in his mother's womb and went to sleep. He started to toss and turn.)* No, I don't want to. No, I don't want to.

(He was dreaming of when he was a child, when he was at one of his mother's many parties. Everyone was getting either drunk, high, or both, and the pimp grabbed him away from under his mother and took him into another room.)

MR. BIG. So you're Gwen's big man, so you gonna be the next big pimp, huh? I gonna show you that you ain't nothing but a punk. You ain't no pimp.

(The pimp took out his penis and made Simon open his mouth.)

MR. BIG. Look, if you don't open your mouth, I gonna put it somewhere else.

(Simon tried to scream, and it was then the pimp put his oversized penis in his mouth.)

MR. BIG. Suck it, boy, 'cause if you don't or if you bite it, I's gonna kill you and your momma!

(Simon did as he was told. But when the pimp exploded in Simon's mouth, he slapped him.)

MR. BIG. You will never be a pimp, because if a nigga had put his dick in my mouth, I would have bitten it off. You ain't no pimp. You ain't nothing but a little sissy that will always be under your momma's skirt.

(He laughed and walked back into the room, leaving Simon in that room. Simon sat there wanting to cry, but for so strange reason, he couldn't. He just sat there getting angrier. The more he thought about it, the angrier he became. He started thinking of ways that he could get him back. He started looking around; he looked in a dresser drawer and saw a .45-caliber pistol. He wondered if it was loaded. He looked, and it was. He picked it up and thought, "He had no right to do that to me. I will show him I will show him that I ain't no punk. I am a pimp. I will show him." While in the other room, Simon's mother and Mr. Big were engaged in some pleasurable moments. Simon burst in the room, yelling.)

SIMON. I ain't no punk!

(He pointed the .45 at Mr. Big.)

SIMON. I ain't no punk!

(But just as soon as he was about to pull the trigger, his mother jumped up in front of the pimp to try to stop Simon, but it was too late, for he had closed his eyes and begun to pull the trigger. He fired four times, hitting his mother twice in the chest and once in the head. The fourth round was the only one that struck where it was meant to hit. It hit the pimp in his mouth. By the time Simon opened his eyes, he was surrounded by all the other ladies, and he saw what he had done. Simon let out a loud scream and woke up to find himself in that abandoned building. He laughed and settled back down into a deep sleep. While he was sleeping, he started to dream again. He was all of a sudden being chased by a vicious dog; he shot at the dog. The dog ran away only to return with several more. Simon ran into a house only to be followed by the dogs and some men. They were all trying to kill him. Simon was shooting each one of them, but none were dying. All of a sudden, a man-like creature looked up and made a comment.)

THE MAN. I've been here before.

(Simon was pouring with sweat and, with fear in his eyes and with fear in his heart, woke up.)

SIMON. I was dreaming!

(While sitting there with tears in his eyes, he was still trying to figure out what to do about Jake, Cleo, Dennis, but most of all, Faye. Back at Mr. Johnson's house.)

MR. JOHNSON. Jake, are you going to stay here for the rest of the night?

JAKE. No, I think I will go back to my house so that I can think. And besides, I don't want Jacob to wake up and see me, because I'm not ready to take him home yet.

MR. JOHNSON. I fully understand. Jake, I wish I could have been more help to you.

JAKE. Mr. Johnson, you have been more help than you ever could imagine.

(Jake left with some peace of mind. He decided to go to his house to try and rest a little, for he knew that he was going to go back to the hospital to see his wife. After Dennis woke, he decided to go back to Jake's to see if he was there. Just as Jake was getting home, Dennis pulled up.)

DENNIS. Jake, I'm so happy to see you.

JAKE. Happy, for what?

DENNIS. Well, you know, I was just wondering.

JAKE. Wondering about what? Wondering if I found that pimp?

DENNIS. Uh, Jake, his name is Simon.

JAKE. Simon? I really don't care what his name is, but you were wondering if I went to find him? I should slap you. Well, come on in.

(Jake and Dennis went inside.)

JAKE. Dennis, after I saw what he was trying to do to Cleo, I could have cut his head off his body. But on my way here, I started thinking, thinking about the promise I made Cleo. So I decided to go to the police instead, but after I got there, they acted like I was a criminal. I looked and remembered that detective. He was a beat cop before, and he was the one that had come when me and Simon had gotten into it once before, and he just let him go. So you see, it appears that the deck is stacked against me. Dennis. Jake, what are we going to do?

(With tears in his eyes, Jake looked around as if he was looking for someone or something to tell him what to do.)

JAKE. Dennis, I really don't know. I really don't know. Dennis, I remember, when some of the women were talking, they were talking about my dad. They were saying that my dad was out cheating on my mom. They weren't talking to her, but they were saying it loud enough for us to hear. I looked up at my mom. She looked at me, and all she did was smile. She smiled at me. She smiled as if everything was okay. But later on that night, before my father got home, I heard my mother talking. At first, I didn't know who she was talking to, not until I heard her call his name, Lord. I knew then that she was praying. But she wasn't praying for herself. She wasn't even praying for my dad. She was praying, thanking God for his son, Jesus, thanking for giving her a son, thanking him for the life she has lived. All she did was give thanks. No wishing for my dad to die, no wishing for whomever he was supposed to be cheating with to die. She didn't even mention those women who wanted to start up some mess. All she did was to give thanks. Now I find myself in a situation where I know that all I need to do is to be thankful, not to have strife or hatred in my heart.

DENNIS. But Jake, this scum had just raped and tried to kill your wife, and there is no telling what else he might try to do!

JAKE. Dennis let me ask you this. My wife, is she still alive? My son, is he still alive? My sister, is she still alive? My baby, is she still alive? I'm I still alive. And is Jesus still alive? So you tell me who should I be focused on?

(*All Dennis could do was to drop his head.*)

JAKE. No, Dennis, this is no put-down. I really want you to answer this, because you are going to be marrying my sister and I need to know that when—not *if* but *when*—times get hard, you will know what to do and know who to turn to.

DENNIS. Jake, I guess you need to be focused on the positive and not the negative.

JAKE. Dennis, you're right, but I don't want you guessing. Matthew 6:27 says, "Which of you by worrying can add one cubit to his stature?"

JAKE. So you see, the question even suggest that worrying will not add anything, and if you look at it, worrying can actually shorten your life.

DENNIS. Jake, since you put it like that, I know who you should be focusing on. But what are you he pushes the issue and try something else?

JAKE. Dennis, you don't get it yet. If I focus on what-ifs, I might as well be worrying. I can and will tell you this. If Simon wants to act foolishly and do something else stupid, he had better hope that the grace of God in poured heavily on me and I cannot reach him. You know, being humble does not mean that you are a push-over. Now I take it that Faye is at the hospital, Jacob is over Mr. Johnson's, and we are right here, so let us get some sleep, because I plan on staying at the hospital for the rest of her time.

(Although Jake had made peace with the situation, he was no fool. Before he would lie down, he went into his closet and got his .45 and placed it next to his side. Daylight quickly came.)

JAKE. Dennis, it's time to get up. Oh, Mr. Johnson has given me off, but he said that you need to cover for me.

DENNIS. What?

JAKE. You know how Mr. Johnson is. He wants to be able to go check on Cleo, and with him knowing that I'm out, he thinks enough of you that he figures you can run the place.

DENNIS. He said that?

JAKE. Well, yeah, most of it. Now I'm going to shower, shave, and get something to eat. Then I'm going to the hospital to support my beautiful wife.

DENNIS. All right, Jake, as soon as you come out, I will.

JAKE. What? You better take your butt home and get ready for work. Get out. Hey, Dennis. Thanks, man. I really appreciate you.

DENNIS. Hey, just keep me informed while I'm holding down your job.

(Jake went on and got ready to go. As he was taking a shower, his mind started to wonder. Was Dennis stalling to leave, and was he afraid? Jake shook off the thought and continued to get ready. It wasn't long before he made it to the hospital.)

FAYE. Jake, I'm so happy to see you. The police have been in and out of here all night. I thought you had done something. You didn't do anything, did you?

JAKE. Faye, if you are asking if I found and crushed that sorry excuse for a pimp, the answer is no. Oh, I thought about it. I thought about it a lot, but once I made it home and started to talk to Dennis, I realized that I have so much to be thankful for and that I should focus on those things and not on finding and destroying lives.

FAYE. Wait a minute, you discovered this while talking to Dennis? My man, Dennis?

JAKE. Yes, but I must say that it was the Holy Spirit that revealed this to me. Hey, you must be tired. I'm here to relieve you.

FAYE. You will do no such thing. I'm here for the long haul.

JAKE. What about your job? What about your rest?

FAYE. First of all, I called Mr. Johnson, and he told me to stay as long as I needed to and for me to keep both of my eyes on you, and as far as my rest go, I slept very well.

JAKE. I guess we can sit here and talk. You know, get to really know each other.

FAYE. Oh no, Jake, here comes that Detective Williams.

JAKE. Yeah, I know him.

DETECTIVE WILLIAMS. Well, hello, Mr. Martin. Hello again, Faye.

MR. MARTIN, I need to talk to you.

JAKE. What you need to say to me you can say it right here.

DETECTIVE WILLIAMS. Well, I know you think you know who did this to your wife. Well, I have spoken with Simon, and he said that he doesn't know what you are talking about.

FAYE. How can you stand here and tell us that? Jake saw him in here. How about that?

DETECTIVE WILLIAMS. He had an alibi. He said that he was here to visit a sick friend but got the wrong room.

FAYE. What's his friend's name?

DETECTIVE WILLIAMS. I don't have to give that to you.

FAYE. You sorry piece of sh—

JAKE. Faye!

JAKE. Don't worry about it. Before it's over, all that's involved will have to pay for what has happened.

DETECTIVE WILLIAMS. Uh, Mr. Martin, if I was you, I would be careful of my words. I could take those words as a threat.

JAKE. No, Detective Williams, they weren't threats. They were promises.

DETECTIVE WILLIAMS. Watch it, Mr. Martin. Watch it.

JAKE. You have a great day, Detective. You have a great day.

(*The detective turned and walked out.*)

FAYE. Jake, I can't believe what just happened!

JAKE. Calm down, Faye. There is no need to get yourself all worked up. Right now it seems like they have the upper hand, but before it's all over, we will have victory. They will do something stupid, and it will catch up with them.

FAYE. Jake, look how long they have been doing things.

JAKE. Yeah, I know. Their time is running out.

FAYE. What has happened to you? I'm so used to being the one trying to talk you out of things, but now, I don't know which one I like the most.

JAKE. Faye, you remember when I went in to see Cleo and she whispered to me? I should have known then that she was not the one speaking to me. He was speaking to me, and he was trying to tell me to let him handle the situation.

FAYE. Jake, I'm speechless.

JAKE. Faye, now that is a miracle!

(*Jake and Faye had a good laugh, sat down, and started to tell childhood stories.*)

JAKE. Faye, you want to know something?

FAYE. Sure, why not?

JAKE. Well, I knew you before I knew you.

FAYE. What?

JAKE. Well, let me tell you about it. It all started in a dream, and in my dream, I met you, and we started talking. You told me that your name was Faydra but your friends called you Faye. But seeing that we were not friends, you told me to call you Faydra!

JAKE. Faye, I knew then that you were special.

FAYE. Is that it? Is that all?

JAKE. No, let me finish telling you the dream.

* * *

JAKE. I would like to become your friend. You look so good to me, and I ain't never saw no woman made up like you. How 'bout it? Can I be your friend?

* * *

FAYE. I was fine, huh?

JAKE. Now look who's interrupting my story.

* * *

FAYE. That depends on what you got in that bag.

JAKE. What you mean? What in the bag? What do that gots to do with anythang?

FAYE. You knows, you is cute, and those muscles, I could do a lot with all that.

JAKE. I gots to be leavin'. If Mr. Eli…

FAYE. Mr. Eli, is you workin' for that no-good some of a…

JAKE. Don't you badmouth Mr. Eli! I's gots to be goin'. Can I sees you later?

FAYE (*under her breath*). Oh, he is working for that snake in the grass. This is gonna be mo' fun than I ever dreamed. Sure you can see me later.

* * *

JAKE. You followed me. I delivered a package to Lenny. He was one of Mr. Eli's goons. He was upset because I was late.

* * *

JAKE. Here is the package, Lenny.

LENNY. Boy, what da hell takes you so long?

JAKE. I knows that I's a little late but…

LENNY. But nothin'. Just waits till Mr. Eli gets wind of this.

JAKE. Lenny, you's just gots to help me!

LENNY. Help you with what, fool? Is you in trouble?

JAKE. Naw, I ain't in no trouble, but this girl…

LENNY. Gal, I thought yo says that you ain't in no type of trouble. Well, tells me about her.

JAKE. She is the most beautifulest creature I done ever saw.

LENNY. Yeah, yeah, tells me 'bout the body.

JAKE. Huh body is like a picture-book girl. She gots mo' curves than that old Coon Creek Road.

* * *

JAKE. I didn't know any better then.

FAYE. I bet you didn't.
LENNY. Damn, boy. Do this gal gots a name?
JAKE. She sho do. Her name is Faydra.
LENNY. Faydra, I's don't thank I's knows ta at tall.
JAKE. Well, she saids that all huh friends call huh Faye.
LENNY. Holy Moses, booy, you's talkin' 'bout ha ha ha ha whoa ... you's talking 'bout nas, nice Faye. Yeah, she sho is a fine one all right.

★ ★ ★

JAKE. I was so confused. I didn't know what to think. I knew it was getting late, and I had to finish my business and get home to my momma before it got too late. But Mr. Eli stopped me.

★ ★ ★

MR. ELI. Boy, what done took you so long, and where is my money? You gots to go! Boy, you is forgettin' two thangs—one is my money, and two, I tells you when you gots to go!
JAKE. Mr. Eli, here is yo money. I's thought that I's was finish for the day. My momma will worry if I's.
MR. ELI. Looks here boy, I's 'bout to let you's go.
JAKE. Yeah, you were around the corner, peeping in on Mr. Eli and me.

★ ★ ★

JAKE. Mr. Eli told me that I could go. I started home, but you had other plans for me. I was about halfway home when I ran into
FAYE. I asked you what you were doing there.

★ ★ ★

FAYE. Well, I's was thankin 'bout you, and I's wants to know some mo' 'bout you.
JAKE. Well, I's on my ways home now.
FAYE. Do you gots to be there now, or do you gots a little time?
JAKE. Well, I's guess I's gots some time yet.

★ ★ ★

FAYE. Boy, you were having some dream!
JAKE. There you go interrupting again.

* * *

JAKE. What fur?
FAYE. I thank that the woods is so romantic this time of evening!
JAKE. Yeah, romantic, what you mean?
FAYE. Ha ha ha, you means to tells me that you is that—well, let's just says green. Well, I's guess I's just gonna have to teach you.

* * *

JAKE. You began doing things to me that I never dreamed of. My eyes were crossing, my toes were popping, I felt lightheaded, and I felt as if my heart had moved down into my pants. I let out a scream so loud that it could have awakened the dead. You didn't know what to think. Then you realized what had just happened. Now you must remember that this was just a dream.
FAYE. This was your first one!
JAKE. Several minutes had passed. In the back of my mind, I knew that I had to get home.

* * *

JAKE. Cans I sees you later?

(*Faye didn't answer.*)

MOMMA. Jake, where is you been? Look at your britches, they is so dirty! You knows what time it is? Did you has to works late? Well, yo supper is kept. Boy, you knows you better not sat at my table with those dirty britches!
JAKE. Momma, you don't knows how hungry I is!
MOMMA. You must have had a hard day of work.
JAKE. If you only knew how hard!

* * *

JAKE. All night I tossed and turned. I could not sleep, thinking about you. The next morning, I could not wait to go tell Lenny what had happened. Before I could reach Lenny, I ran into you. Like a schoolboy after his first kiss, I smiled and kicked the ground, but to my surprise, you acted as if you didn't see me at all. I ran and stopped in front of you, making sure that you saw me. But you told me to get out of you face. You acted like you didn't even know me.

FAYE. Boy, I was cold, huh?

JAKE. Yeah, you were cold.

JAKE. You told me that until I was done messing with that low-down snake in the grass Mr. Eli, I didn't have anything to say to you. I was torn up on the inside. I had not felt that bad, not since I had to kill my pet pig for food. I still felt as if I had to find Lenny. I wanted to tell him about the day before and ask him how he could keep you and continue to keep working for Mr. Eli.

★ ★ ★

JAKE. Lenny, guess what done happen to me on my way home, yesterday.

LENNY. Let me guess. You gots wet.

JAKE. Naw, it don't rain yesteda, but I was on da way home when all da sudden, Faye was right…

LENNY. Hold on, boy, you says Faye was there? You mean she was waiting for ya? She was where?

JAKE. I was 'bout half da way home, when there she was in da front of me.

LENNY. You aims to tell that gal just happen to be in da same neck of the woods as you?

JAKE. What is you trying to say? Anyhow, on my way here today, I runs into her, and she tolds me that if I wanted to see her some mo', I's gots to quit my job.

LENNY. Boy, I is trying to tells you that no-good stankin' B ain't up to no good! I is gonna tells Mr. Eli as soons as I sees him. He gonna be one mad boss!

JAKE. Lenny, you cain't tells him. You just cain't!

LENNY. Listen, boy, I is just trying to help you

★ ★ ★

JAKE. Fearing what Mr. Eli might do to me or even to you, I knew that I had to do something to get Lenny's mind off what we had just spoken of. I panicked. I picked up an old tire iron off the ground and started hitting Lenny in the head. I must have hit him nine or ten times before I came back to my senses. Blood was gushing out. It was all over me. It was everywhere. There Lenny lay in the cold, dark, bloodstained alley, with a stonecold killer standing over him, thinking about how good it felt to have such power, the power to take another's life. I knew he had to get cleaned up before I saw Mr. Eli, but there was one problem. I didn't know where to go. You were the only person that came to mind, but how was I to find you? I was covered with blood, so I couldn't just began asking people. I spotted you, but you were on the other side of the street. I ducked and dodged and made my way over to you, but seeing the blood on me, you were afraid to approach me. The funny thing is that I was just as afraid to approach you, not knowing how you would react.

★ ★ ★

FAYE. Jake! What in the name of?

JAKE. Faye! Just hush up and listen. You 'member Lenny…

FAYE. That stooge?

JAKE. Yeah, you know he be Mr. Eli's number-one man. Well, I done, done away with him. You see, he was talking sumin' bad 'bout cha!

FAYE. Jake, you fool! Boy, you ain't got the sense. God gives a mule. We is gots to get cleaned up.

★ ★ ★

JAKE. We made our way to your one bedroom apartment, which I thought was the best thing ever. You began cleaning me up. I could not help that I still had feelings for you. After all, I had just killed for you. I began touching, rubbing, and kissing you as you finished cleaning me. At first, you were fighting your feelings. You were trying not to get caught up in the heat of the moment, but you knew you wanted me as much as I wanted you, if not more. Yeah, in that dream, you broke my heart. I even killed poor ole Lenny for you. But what were revealed to me was that you needed my help then, but instead of me helping you, I perverted the dream and wanted to get with you.

FAYE. Is that the reason why you didn't let me give you a lap dance at your bachelor party?

JAKE. Yeah, I was sort of in awe. I didn't know what to think.

FAYE. And what about at the pub?

JAKE. Well, when I saw you, I knew that I had to get your name. I just knew that you needed me.

(*Across town, Detective Williams and Simon, the pimp, met up.*)

DETECTIVE WILLIAMS. Simon, let me give you a bit of advice. If I were you, I would forget all about that guy Jake Martin and his family.

SIMON. Forget about him? All I can do is think about him. I think about how I'm going to make him suffer. He thinks that he's suffering now? Wait until I'm finished with him!

DETECTIVE WILLIAMS. Simon, you might need to rethink that. There's something about that guy.

SIMON. What? You think he has a guardian angel or something? What, you afraid of him?

DETECTIVE WILLIAMS. There's something about him.

SIMON. Look here, if you shakin' in your boots, I suggest you go and hide, but when it comes to giving me advice, I don't need it. As a matter of fact, I suggest that you get lost, and don't let me see your fat ass around here for a few weeks. Take a vacation or something.

DETECTIVE WILLIAMS. Look here, you poor excuse for a pimp, I've covered for your sorry ass for long enough, but no more, and besides if anything else happens to Mr. Martin's wife or family, I will come looking for you. Got that?

SIMON. Yeah, I got it. By the way, say hello to the missus for me.

(They both turned and walked away. Meanwhile, back at the hospital.)

NURSE. Mr. Martin, the doctor will be in to talk to you all in a few minutes.
JAKE. How is she doing? How is my baby?
NURSE. Mr. Martin, the doctor will be in to talk to you all in a few minutes. I have to let him tell you what he has to tell you.

(Minutes seemed to be more like hours before the doctor would enter.)

DOCTOR. Mr. Martin, by your wife being so early in her pregnancy just might have been a positive, but you still have a decision to make. Mr. Martin, your wife has suffered some very serious injuries, and we cannot guarantee that you child won't have any deformities.
JAKE. So what are you are telling me? Is my child still alive?
DOCTOR. Yes, the fetus is still alive.
JAKE. Thank God, that's all I need to know.
DOCTOR. Mr. Martin, did you not hear me?
JAKE. Look, I heard you, but I would rather know if my child is alive, and by my child being alive, I know that all is well. Now, what about Cleo, my wife?
DOCTOR. Your wife seems to be recovering at a rapid rate. I have never seen someone that was in her condition heal so quickly. Well, Dr. Ingram will be in to discuss the issues with your baby.

(The doctor turned and walked out of the room.)

FAYE. Jake, I have never seen you like this.
JAKE. While we wait for this Dr. Ingram, let us truly get to know each other. You see, I've told you about my dream, and I've told you about seeing you for the first time. Now I want to hear about you.
FAYE. About me, huh? Or do you want to hear about me and my former profession? Well, as you know, as I was growing up, there was only me and my mom. Oh, I used to see our dad. I used to see how he was spending time with you. I used to see all of the fun you had with him.

JAKE. Fun with him?

FAYE. Well, when you don't have a dad, anytime spent with one seems like fun. Just having his attention would have been nice. So as I was growing up, I made myself a promise that my children would not be without their father, but when I went off to college, I discovered that I could have all the attention I wanted. First, my professors would come on to me, telling me how sexy I was. Then I started looking at myself as being sexy, and I started to enjoy the attention I was getting from them. I know that I told you that I became a call girl and a stripper to help me pay for my education. Well, that wasn't all true. The truth is I went looking for Simon to be my pimp. Well, he was already a pimp. One of my girlfriends had stripped for one of his parties, and she got paid, well paid. So I decided that if I could get paid and get the attention I wanted, hell, why not? I was getting paid. Oh, don't take me wrong. Most of my clients were high class. The professors, some of the coaches, and I even had a dean and chancellor. Heck, I even had female professors trying to get with me, but it was something in my spirit that just wouldn't let me do it. They paid well, and the female professors even offered to double my normal price, yet again, I just couldn't do it. They paid well because they had husbands, wives, and a reputation. If it had ever gotten out that they were messing around with a call girl who just happens to be a student at their university, their careers and marriages would have been ruined. So you see it was a win-win situation for me. I got paid, I got my grades, and I got all the male attention I ever wanted. Jake, but there was one thing that I discovered. The attention that I was getting was false, and it took you coming into my life for me to discover that. I guess I kind of knew it all along, and I guess that's why I continued to see Dennis. You see, Dennis showed me true love. He showed me that he cared for me as a person and not just someone that he could live out his fantasy with. A lot of time, Dennis would pay me just to sit and talk. We would talk about his job, and he even talked about you. He would tell me how great of a guy you were and that he looked up to you because you had it all together. That's why I agreed to do your bachelor party for only tips. I wanted to see this great guy that he so often talked about, and you know what, Jake, you are a great guy, and you do have it all together. So here we are, brother and sister, together.

JAKE. Yes, we are together, but I must tell you that having a dad was nice but I think you've done great by yourself. No, I don't agree with your past occupation, but that is behind you now, and we move forward.

(*Another doctor entered the room.*)

DR. INGRAM. Mr. Martin and ... ?

JAKE. Oh, this is Faye, my sister.

DR. INGRAM. I'm Dr. Ingram. I'm a neonatologist, a big name for a specialist on babies. Mr. Martin, the only news I have concerning your child is that she's still alive. As far as if there will be any deformities, it is simply too early to tell.

JAKE. Did you say *she*?

DR. INGRAM: Yes, although it's still early, looks like your wife is pregnant with a girl.

JAKE. Thanks, Doc. That's all I need to know.

DR. INGRAM. Mr. Martin, don't you want to hear your options?

JAKE. All I need to know is that if we continue with this pregnancy, will it jeopardize my wife's health?

DR. INGRAM. Not that I can see.

JAKE. Okay, once again, thanks, Doc.

(*Dr. Ingram turned and walked out of the room.*)

JAKE. Faye, did you hear that? A girl. We are having a little girl.

FAYE. Jake, I heard that, but I also heard the doctor say something about deformities.

JAKE. Faye, I know my God, and I know that his will is for all of us to be healthy and to walk in love. I am not concern about deformities, nor do I want to hear anything else about them. You know why? Proverbs 18:21 says, "The tongue has the power of life and death, and those who love it will eat its fruit." So, Faye, I refuse to let anything but positive words come out of my mouth. Positive thoughts enter into my head and positive feelings in my heart. Now I strongly suggest you to do the same.

(Faye suddenly looked up.)

JAKE. What are you looking at?

FAYE. I thought I saw one of my old coworkers walk by the window, but I guess not, because what would she be doing in a nurse's uniform in the hospital?

(Jake and Faye looked at each other.)

JAKE. Faye, which way was she going?

FAYE. She was heading in the same direction as Cleo's room.

(Jake burst out of the door and ran toward Cleo's room. He ran past the cop who was supposed to have been watching Cleo's room. He ran into Cleo's room. The officer came in behind him.)

OFFICER. Mr. Martin, what's the matter?

JAKE. Did you see a nurse come into this room?

OFFICER. Yeah, they have been checking on her every two hours.

JAKE. No, did you see one just come in here?

OFFICER. No, Mr. Martin, I did not, and as a matter fact, we have about five minutes before the next one comes in to check on her.

JAKE. Five minutes, huh? Well, I suggest that we just sit in here for five more minutes to see that nurse.

(By that time, Faye made it into Cleo's room.)

JAKE. Faye, we are going to sit in here and wait for the nurse to come in.

(The nurse entered.)

FAYE. Jake, that's not her. That is not who I saw walk by the waiting room.

NURSE. Hello, I'm Catherine. I'm the head evening nurse for the evening, and how may I help you all?

JAKE. Nurse Catherine, is there any other nurse that comes in to check on my wife?

NURSE Catherine. No, Mr. Martin, we have strict orders that only the head nurse on each shift is to see about our Cleo.

JAKE. Thank you.

(Jake, Faye, and the officer walked out of the room.)

JAKE. Officer, how are you all pulling shifts?

OFFICER. Well, this is my assigned duty for my shift, which is a tenhour shift. I get relieved for an hour, and then I finish up here. Jake. Have you all been given a list of the head nurses on each shift?

OFFICER. Mr. Martin, what is going on here?

JAKE. My sister saw one of her former coworkers dressed in a nurse's uniform walk by the waiting room, and she was heading in this direction.

OFFICER. Maybe she was just trying to come and visit.

JAKE. Look, you don't understand. Her former boss has tried to kill my wife, and I strongly believe that he was the one that did this to her! Now are you getting the picture?

OFFICER. Yes, sir, I see where you are coming from.

(Jake called Faye over toward him.)

JAKE. Faye, I have taken all that I can take. I know that I promised Cleo that I would let the law handle this, but my God do not want us to live in fear, so I have to do something. What is worse, to be the hunted or the hunter? It's time for Mr. Simon to see how it feels to be the hunted. Faye. Jake, are you sure?

JAKE. I'm as sure as I'm going to get. I didn't say that I was going to do anything to him. He just need to feel what's like to be hunted. Faye, I'm going to need you to stay here close to this officer and any other one that comes.

FAYE. I understand. I will keep my eye out for anyone that might look suspicious.

JAKE. Thanks.

(Jake thought how he could get the word out that he was looking for Simon. Then he thought, and he knew exactly how. He went to a phone booth outside of the police and called Detective Williams.)

JAKE. Detective Williams, this is Mr. Martin. Jake Martin, I know you told me not to take things into my own hands, but I just want you to know that if I happen to see Simon, I will not go the other way.

DETECTIVE WILLIAMS. Now, Mr. Martin, I will not sit here and listen to you make threats toward another citizen.

JAKE. Hold on, Detective, not one time did I make a threat. I simply said that if I see Simon I will not turn and go the other way. Now what part of that sounds like a threat? Detective Williams. Mr. Martin, I'm warning you!

JAKE. Now, Detective, there is no need to get upset, and I must say that it's not me that you need to be warning. You have a wonderful day, Detective.

(Jake had put the first part of his plan into action, and that was to let Simon know that he was not afraid of him and that he was also looking for him. All he had to do was to wait for Detective Williams to leave to go warn his buddy Simon. It was taking a few minutes, but Jake thought that he would call his friend so that they could meet up. He knew that the good detective wouldn't chance saying too much while he was at work. And sure enough, just like a rat taking the cheese, the good detective ran out of the station and got into his car and drove off at a fast speed. Jake carefully followed behind. Oh, the detective would have seen him if he wasn't so concerned with warning Simon. They drove to this old rundown neighborhood where most of the houses were empty and the rest were stayed in by squatters. The detective drove to this one house that actually looked like someone lived there. It actually was a nice house. It had two armed guards on both sides of the door. Jake stayed his distance; he didn't want the detective or the guards to see him. The detective stopped in front and got out of his car. The two guards walked up to him and patted him down. There he was, Simon, looking like the coward rat he is. Jake wanted to pull his gun and do away with both of them, the detective and that sorry excuse for a human.)

SIMON. So, Detective, with what do I owe this visit?

DETECTIVE WILLIAMS. Simon, what have you done? I told you not to go fooling with this Jake fella. I told you that guy is bad news. I told you that he has something that I can't explain!

(All of a sudden, Simon slammed the detective, and the two guards grabbed him and forced him to his knees.)

SIMON. First, Detective, you are not worthy to look me eye to eye. When you talk to me, you need to be looking up at me. Second of all, I run this. This is mine. All of this is mine! And you are worried about one puny man? What can he do with all of this? I tell you what, Detective. I want you to crawl back into that car and drive the hell away from here, never to let me see your cowardly face again, because the day that I see your face again, I will kill you! Get away from me.

Waking Up

(The detective indeed crawled back into his car and drove off, thinking to himself, "I hope that Jake Martin cut his dick off and stuff it down his throat." After witnessing that, Jake knew that Simon was already afraid and that it wouldn't take much, only if he could get close to him. Jake waited for his time. He waited all day, watching the guards and their habits. All of a sudden, Simon came out. He said something to them, they left, and Simon went back in. While Jake was sitting, a voice from deep within told him to leave. At first, Jake didn't pay any attention until he thought back to when his ole long-headed pastor was preaching on the Holy Spirit. He remember him saying that the Holy Spirit will speak to you but it's up to you to listen and act. John 10:27 says, "My sheep hear My voice, and I know them, and they follow Me." So Jake started his vehicle and slowly drove. But as he drove off, he looked in his rear-view mirror and saw the two guards circling around where he had been parked. Jake could do nothing but praise and thank the Lord. As he was driving off, he once again started to wonder if he was doing the right thing. He started to pray and ask the Lord what to do, and as he prayed, a scripture came to mind, Luke 6:27–36. "But to you who are listening I say: Love your enemies, do good to those who hate you, bless those who curse you, pray for those who mistreat you. If someone slaps you on one cheek, turn to them the other also. If someone takes your coat, do not withhold your shirt from them. Give to everyone who asks you, and if anyone takes what belongs to you, do not demand it back. Do to others as you would have them do to you.")

JAKE. Lord, have I been going about this all wrong? But if I show him love and be kind, he will take me as a punk. He will think that I'm soft. He will try to destroy me and my family. You have to help me here Lord. You have to help me. Proverbs

3:5–6 says, "Trust in the Lord with all your heart and lean not on your own understanding; in all your ways submit to him, and he will make your paths straight." Lord, I'm going to trust you. I'm going to give it to you, and I'm going to walk in love and not hate. Now you do know that I'm going to need your help, a whole lot of your help, because every time I think about my wife lying in that hospital, every time I think of my son Jacob having to stay with Mr. Johnson, and every time I think about my little baby girl, I want to rip that sorry son of a ——.Proverbs 23:7 says, "For as he thinketh in his heart, so is he: Eat and drink, saith he to thee; but his heart is not with thee." Okay, Lord, I get it. I need to watch what I say as well, but like I said, I'm going to need your help, a whole lot of your help! (*Back at the hospital, Dennis visited Faye.*)

DENNIS. Faye, I understand you want to support your brother, but, honey, I am missing you so much.

FAYE. Dennis, I understand, but you must understand also. I never had my dad. I knew him, but I never had a real family, and now I have a chance to be a part of a real family, and besides, we're kind of responsible for this.

DENNIS. I was afraid you would say something like that. I was hoping that you didn't blame me.

FAYE. Oh, Dennis, how can I blame you? I love you, and besides, we are in this together.

DENNIS. I do understand that you want to be part of a family, and, baby, that's what you and I are going to be, a family. We will have our own, plus we will have Jake and his family also.

SIMON. Did you two see anything? I could have sworn that we were being watched.

GUARD. Look, boss, if you want us to, we can finish that Jake sucker off for you

SIMON. No! Don't you touch him. His big ass is mine. I will show our detective friend that Jake ain't nothing but a man. He ain't got no special powers or no angel on his side. I will punish him.

(*Jake drove to his job to speak to Mr. Johnson.*)

RECEPTIONIST. Mr. Johnson, Jake Martin is here to speak to you.

MR. JOHNSON. Tell him to come on in. Jake, my boy, how's everything going?

JAKE. Mr. Johnson, I have a confession. I was going to try to make that sorry Simon know that I was behind every corner. I followed Detective Williams and found out where he was staying. I sat and watched. I saw and heard the detective talking. I sat there a while longer until the Holy Spirit told me to leave, and as I was driving off, I looked in my rear-view mirror. I saw his two bodyguards moving around in the same area where I had been parked. Mr. Johnson, it is so hard. I want to kill him, but I know that I should love him. I want to cut his sorry balls off and cram them down his throat.

MR. JOHNSON. Jake, my son, all that is saying is that you are human, but you are being led by the Holy SPIRIT. Jake, I too am having a hard time dealing with this.

JAKE. You, Mr. Johnson?

MR. JOHNSON. Jake, my boy, I have not always walked in the Lord. I used to be a stone-cold killer, a real gangster. How do you think I got this business? Sit down, boy. Jake, it was about forty-five years ago. I was working the streets. If anyone wanted to stay in business, they had to pay me for protection. Yeah, protection, mainly from me and my crew. Women, let me tell you, I had more women than I care to try and count. Yeah, you see, I have not always been the person that you see before you today. You see, we all were someone else before we became who we are. What made me change? Well, one day I was making rounds, and I ran across this beautiful young sexy lady. I mean, she was so fine. She would put toad hair to shame. So I stopped her and started to shoot my Mac, only to get shot down by her. I chased in behind her, and I started to use mine and my dad's lines, but she wouldn't budge. I went on to introduce myself to her. "Excuse me, I'm William Johnson, but my friends call me Willie and the women call me Slick Willie on account that I'm so smooth." "Well, Mr. Johnson, you and Willie—Slick Willie, that is—if you would be so polite to let me pass, I would be much obliged. In other words, get thee behind me, Satan." That was the first time that I had been referred to as Satan. Well, at least to my face. All of a sudden, I snapped. I didn't like it, nor did it feel good. That evening, when I made it home, I took a long look at myself, and then I looked at my life. What was I doing? I knew that my mom would be turning over in her grave if she knew what and how I was living, and I had to change. But I didn't know how. I went for a long walk, and as I was walking, I passed by this church. I wanted to go in, but who was I to just walk into someone's church, so I passed by again and again. There were two guys working in the parking lot, I guess. One of them approached me.

★ ★ ★

GUY: Hello, how are you? Are you all right? I saw you walking by several times. Would you like to come in and join us for our Wednesday night service?

MR. JOHNSON. Uh, I was just walking. I didn't mean to cause any alarm.

GUY: No, sir. I was just wondering if you would like to join us.

MR. JOHNSON. I guess I could come in for a minute or two.

(As William walked in, there was this beautiful young lady with a heavenly smile and pearl eyes, greeting. Right then, he knew he had walked into the right place.)

GREETER: Hello. Welcome to Canaan, where I know you will be blessed. As a matter of fact, you are blessed. Is this your first time visiting?

MR. JOHNSON. Uh, yes, it is.

★ ★ ★

MR. JOHNSON. Jake, I knew right then and there that I had to get what she had, her spirit. There was just something about her spirit. Her spirit touched me in a way that I haven't felt since my mother was alive. I mean, it was like life had just come back into me. And yes, I did look at her finger. She was already married.

(Jake and Mr. Johnson started to laugh.)

MR. JOHNSON. Jake, it's good to hear you laugh. I know that times may seem to be dark, but light defeats darkness all of the time. So just look toward the light.

JAKE. Mr. Johnson, I hope Jacob is not too much trouble.

MR. JOHNSON. Trouble? How could a great little boy like Jacob be trouble? Besides, he keeps Mrs. Johnson on her toes. Shoot, she's even acting younger during the day and even at night, if you know what I mean.

JAKE. Mr. Johnson!

MR. JOHNSON. Hey, just because there's snow on the mountain doesn't mean that there's not any fire in the pit, and besides, they didn't call me slick Willie for nothing.

JAKE. Oh yeah, what about that young lady that you met on the streets?

MR. JOHNSON. Who you think Mrs. Johnson is? Come to find out she belonged to that same church. We started talking, and we got married within a year, and we've been together now for thirty years.

(Jake left, feeling pretty good. But as he drove toward the hospital, a voice started to speak to him.)

VOICE: So here you are, big bad Jake, the mountain of a man, the provider of your family. So you are just going to let that sorry sucker get away with raping your wife, putting her in the hospital? Come on, man. Oh, should I say man? How can you just turn the other cheek? How can you say I will let the Lord handle it? If he was on your side in the first place, how would he let this happen? You need to take care of this sucker for yourself. You need to take a baseball bat and stick it up him just like he did your wife, an eye for an eye. Make him hurt, make him bleed!

(Sweat started pouring off Jake's forehead. He knew where the voice was coming from, but it sounded so true. It sounded like he needed to do just that. In his mind, it sounded like it was the right thing to do. But in his heart, he knew that if he was to do something on his own. His family could be without him as well. There was no more thought of what he should do. James 4:7 says, "Submit yourselves, then, to God. Resist the devil, and he will flee from you."

As Jake was driving back to the hospital, he passed by several fire trucks, police cars, and ambulances. He didn't know what was going on, but he decided to go on to the hospital. When he arrived, he was met by Dennis and Faye.)

JAKE. What's wrong? What's the matter?

FAYE. Jake, have you heard?

JAKE. Heard what?

FAYE. There was an explosion in the old neighborhood where Simon and his family used to live. They say that someone was still living there. They found three bodies.

JAKE. How do you know all of this?

FAYE. We were listening on this policeman's radio. Jake, do you think it could be him?

JAKE. I don't know. All we can do is to just wait. How's Cleo? Has the doctor said anything?

FAYE. No, they haven't been out. I guess all we can do is to continue to wait. Let's go back into the waiting and wait.

(Just as they got into the waiting room, the nurse burst in.)

NURSE. Mr. Martin, it's a miracle, it's a miracle!

FAYE. What's a miracle?

JAKE. Faye, do you have to ask? It's Cleo. She's awake, isn't she?

NURSE. Yes, she's awake, and her body is as if nothing has ever happened!

FAYE. Jake, you knew, didn't you?

JAKE. I prayed, and I believed.

(On their way to see Cleo, the EMS, police, and emergency personal passed them with a burned victim. Faye and Jake could not help but look, and when they looked, they saw, yes, they saw that it was indeed Simon. Faye and Jake looked at each other. Jake grabbed Faye's hand, and before they made it to Cleo's room, Jake stopped just outside the door and said Faye.)

JAKE. Let us pray for Simon.

(She looked at Jake as if she was in shock.)

JAKE. Yes, Faye, we need to pray for our enemy. Matthew 5:43–44 is about love for enemies. You have heard that it was said, "Love your neighbor and hate your enemy. But I tell you, love your enemies and pray for those who persecute you."

FAYE. Yeah, I see what you're talking about.

JAKE. We have and our Lord will take care of the rest.

(Jake and Faye walked into Cleo's room. She was sitting up.)

CLEO. I thought no one was here. It is so good to see you two. With tears in his eyes, Jake walked to her bedside.

CLEO. Aw, come on, my big baby. Why the tears? You're about to make me tear up.

JAKE. Cleo, we have reason to rejoice.

CLEO. I know, but I don't want to dwell over the past. Let us live now in the present. Oh, I'm ready to get out of here and go get my other little man. By the way, where is he?

JAKE. Oh, he has been over Mr. and Mrs. Johnson's. They have been so helpful.

CLEO. Good. I thought you were going to leave him over Karen's.

JAKE. Oh, do I detect a bit of jealously?

CLEO. No, not jealously, but just call it a woman's discern.

(They all had a good laugh, then the doctor walked in.)

DOCTOR. Mrs. Martin, how are we doing today?

CLEO. Well, Doc, I can't speak for you, but for me, I am fine.

JAKE. She sure is.

CLEO. Jake, I think he was talking to me. Doc, I am ready to go home.

DOCTOR. Well, we have a few more tests to run, and it looks like you will be ready to go. Now if Mr. Martin and the charming young lady…

JAKE. Watch it, Doc, that's my sister.

DOCTOR. Well, if you three would be so kindly…

JAKE. We got you, Doc. See you in a minute, baby. Love you.

Cleo. I love you too, honey.

(Just as Faye, Jake, and Dennis walked out of the room, they ran into Detective Williams.)

DETECTIVE WILLIAMS. Jake, you are just who I need to talk to. I guess by now you've heard about Simon.

JAKE. Yes, I've heard about him, but I also heard that it was more than him in there.

DETECTIVE WILLIAMS. Yes, it was. He had two bodyguards with him. I guess those bodyguards couldn't stop this.

JAKE. Hey, Detective, what did happen?

DETECTIVE WILLIAMS. Well, it was a gas leak in that old building, and I guess it was just his time. It just was time.

JAKE. Well, we saw them bring Simon in. He didn't look too good.

DETECTIVE WILLIAMS. Well, he just died, but before he died, he said that he wished his life could have been different. He said that he wished it could have been more like yours.

JAKE. Wow, like mine? Wow.

(After all of the tests were run. Jake was able to take his beautiful wife home.)

JAKE. Dennis, Faye, I want to thank you two so much. I could not have made it through this without you two. And Dennis, my brother, I want to be the very first one to say you will be a welcome addition to our family.

DENNIS. He called me his brother! Did you hear that he called me his brother?

FAYE. Come on, Dennis. Jake, we will see you all later. I know that we all need to get some much-needed rest.

CLEO. I am so ready to get my family back together. Jake, I have to ask what has happened since I've been out.

JAKE. It has been an adventure, but we all have been made stronger.

CLEO. Who is this talking? This can't be my Jake. Wow, Jake, the Lord has really been busy.

JAKE. What are you talking about?

CLEO. Jake, my Jake, I love you, my big mountain of a man.

JAKE I love you too, Cleo. I love you.

About The Author

Paul Jones was born in Pine Bluff, Arkansas. Although born in the South, his experiences have taken him as far away as California, Germany, and Honduras. He has over fourteen years of experience in the United States Armed Forces, as well as twenty-one years in law enforcement. As a law enforcement officer, he has served as a member of the SWAT team and bicycle patrol, and he has been a school resource officer. He also received many awards. Today he resides in Pine Bluff, Arkansas, and is an active member of his church and community. He is a sports car enthusiast, as well as a husband, father, and mentor to youth. He is available for interviews, book signings, and public speaking.

Printed in the United States
by Baker & Taylor Publisher Services